THE UNITED FEDERATION MARINE CORPS

BOOK 4: CAPTAIN

Colonel Jonathan P. Brazee
USMCR (Ret)

Semper Fi Press

A Semper Fi Press Book

March 2014

ISBN-13: 978-0692438497 (Semper Fi Press)

ISBN-10: 0692438491

Printed in the United States of America

Acknowledgements:

I want to thank all those who took the time to pre-read this book, catching my mistakes in both content and typing. I would like to thank my good friend, Lizzette Contreras for helping me with my Spanish, and I want to thank John Baker, my editor, for catching my many typos and mistakes. Any remaining typos and inaccuracies are solely my fault.

Original Cover Art by Panicha Kasemsukkaphat

SUNSHINE

Chapter 1

"Come on, give me something!" Captain Ryck Lysander, United Federation Marine Corps pleaded with his AI.

Somewhere, ahead of him, the remaining opposing forces were holed up, and Ryck needed to know just where they were if he was going to succeed. The OF, on the other hand, were doing everything they could to jam and spoof Charlie Company's sensors, and they were doing a pretty good job at it. A ghost contact flared briefly on his PICS' face shield readout before fading. Had his AI penetrated the opposing countermeasures, or was that a clever misdirection?

Charlie Company had entered the built-up area at full strength: 212 PICS-mounted Marines and sailors. At the moment, there were exactly 31 bright blue icons on his display, 31 Marines left to carry on the fight. This was his first operation as a company commander, and within hours, he'd lost 85% of his men. He knew that his every move was being watched and analyzed, but he tried to suppress that thought and focus on the task at hand. He couldn't worry about what the evaluators or the CO thought about his actions.

"Sams!" he passed on the P2P. "Can you see anything?"

Gunnery Sergeant Bobbi Samuelson was his only staff NCO left. He and Sams went way back, and he'd brought Sams along with him when he took over the company, along with First Sergeant Phantawisangtong and a few others of his trusted crew.

"A lot of nothing," Sams answered. "Their shielding is too good."

"I'm thinking—no, I'm pretty sure—that the main body has to be in M344," Ryck said, indicating a three-story office building some 200 meters and two roads ahead of them.

Every building, intersection, and landmark had been assigned an alpha-numeric designator which made identification simple and quick.

"That's where I would be," he continued.

"And maybe that's where they want you to think they are," Sams countered.

"You're an evil bastard, Sams," Ryck told him. "Well, we can't sit here. We've got 58 minutes until the main landing force arrives, and this town needs to be clear before then."

The new face shields had an improved eye interface, and with a little practice, using the interface was almost as easy as using a pen and plastisheet. Through a series of ocular gymnastics, he passed an overlay to what was left of Sergeant Kashmala's squad. The sergeant was the third senior surviving man of the company, and Ryck needed him to clear the left flank and provide security for a final assault by the rest of the company.

Kashmala acknowledged the order and within moments, the seven blue icons on Ryck's display started to move. Ryck then whipped up another frag[1] to get the remainder of the company ready. The original ops order had been trashed almost at first contact, and the remainder of the fight had been through a series of frags. With his lieutenants and most of his staff SNCOs lost, Ryck had been effectively reduced to being a platoon commander again—which might have been appropriate given the fact that he had less than a platoon-sized force left.

Sams and Sergeant Mercure acknowledged the frag while Ryck motioned in the three Marines and Doc Pure Soul, who he had gathered into a small headquarters, to gather around. Frag overlays were fine, but a face-to-face was better.

"Look, time's running out," he said over his externals. "We've got Sergeant Kashmala and his team moving up on our left flank, and the rest of the company needs to cross Route Tiblisi so we can be in position to assault their last stronghold. But if you look here," he said, highlighting M213, "the underground passes below it. If I was trying to keep out a company of PICS Marines, and I knew they had to cross Tiblisi, I think M213 would be a good spot to refuse the

---

[1] Frag: Fragmentation Order, an ad hoc order adjusting the original operations order.

crossing, and if it got too hot, I'm thinking there's an entrance to the underground here. So the five of us are going to take care of that.

"Only, what did I say about breaching buildings?"

"No doors," LCpl Jersey Hollington quickly offered.

"Right, no doors. No, we're going through the wall right here," he indicated on their displays.

"Through the wall, sir?" Doc asked.

"Yeah, I don't care what the grubbing ROE says, I'm in it to win it, and I'm tired of this shit. We're in PICS, and we're going to use them," he said.

"Ooh-rah!" the others chimed in.

"Sams," he passed on the P2P. "Give me two minutes, then I want you to move it. Tiblisi's going to be covered, but we don't have much choice. I'll be securing M213, so get your ass across as fast as you can."

"Roger that."

Ryck wished he would have been leading the crossing instead of Sams, but the vagaries of the battle meant that Second Platoon, with which Ryck had been moving, had been decimated, while Third, with Sams, had been the least hit. Ryck didn't want to think of First Platoon, and with it, the first sergeant. The entire platoon had been wiped out to the last man.

There was a flash of an explosion up ahead to the left, and immediately, the seven blue icons of Kashmala's team turned to gray.

"Mother grubbing shit!" Ryck yelled.

Just like that, his left flank security was gone. It had to have been a pretty big booby trap to take out seven Marines in PICS.

He had to move. He couldn't give the enemy the initiative. Charlie Company had been pushing, and he knew he was hurting the OF, keeping him on his heels. But the enemy was on the defense, and that gave him the advantage of shaping the battle space to suit his needs, not those of Ryck and Charlie Company.

"OK, let's move it!" he shouted at the others. With a servo-powered jump, he cleared the almost three-meter-high wall, easily landing on the other side. He immediately moved into a run, building up momentum. A PICS could get up to 40 KPH, and at 900 kg, that should generate more than enough force to destroy the wall of his target. He had just picked his spot when Hollington sprinted past him, leaned forward and slammed into the wall, or more accurately, *through* it, in a cloud of dust and rubble.

Ryck's instincts had been right on. There were four of the OF in the room, weapons trained to cover Tiblisi. With clear fields of fire, they would have had a Turkey shoot with Sam's force.

Ryck immediately took the one with the big autocannon under fire. His M222 was made for close quarters like this, and it poured kilojoules of energy into the other guy's armor. Within seconds, his opponent was dead, and he slumped to the ground, back against the wall. Ryck could swear he saw the enemy give him the finger as he went down.

Energy weapons sizzled while Hollington's M77 put out a steady stream of 8mm fire, each round a flash of red light. Ryck's shields started to degrade to the danger point when one of Hollington's rounds penetrated and took Ryck's attacker out.

It had taken only moments, but the room was secure. He'd lost PFC Gnish, though. He was down to four here and 23 with Sams. He should feel sick to his stomach, but that would come later. Now, he had to keep his head and lead his men.

"Sams, move it!" he passed on the P2P, only to cringe as a horrible caterwauling filled his interior speakers. He tried to lower the volume when the sound stopped. With his ears ringing, he tried to call Sams again.

"Sams, do you read me?"

Nothing.

He switched back to the command circuit. "Any listener, do you read me?"

Still nothing.

Those mother-grubbing sons of bitches! They've taken out the comms! he realized.

He pulled open the window to motion Sams across, but as he looked, big PICS were dashing across the road some 150 meters away. Sams had already started to move.

One Marine stopped as he was hit and went to the ground. The rest, at least from Ryck's vantage point, made it. They would be 100, maybe 120 meters from the objective. A PICS could cover that over open ground in seconds. With another building between them and someone trying to stop them, it seemed like forever.

"Hey, Skipper!" Hollington shouted out over his externals. "You were right about the underground. Looks like there's an entrance here."

Ryck went over and took a look at the hatch where his lance corporal was standing. There were no lights below, so Ryck switched on his infrared torches and went to night vision. The stairs went down one flight to a landing, and he could see another flight of stairs leading farther down. He pulled up the city schematics again, but he knew he wouldn't see anything. The schematics became notoriously inaccurate when combat loomed. It made sense, however, given the layout to the city, that the underground would run close to this location.

The stairs leading down, though, looked pretty shaky. He glanced back at the dead enemy. They were in armor as well, and if they had arrived via the underground, then the stairs should hold his men and him. If they had come using the surface streets, then the stairs could just be a trap waiting to collapse under their weight. Still, the thought of possibly making it behind his objective had some real tactical appeal.

"Sir, we've got someone coming in," LCpl Jaanson called out.

Ryck immediately checked his display, but the company disposition was frozen to the moment when they'd lost comms. Things like the city schematics could be pulled because they had been downloaded into his PICS, but no new data was available.

Jaanson reached through the window and motioned the two runners around in back of the small building to come in through the breached wall.

"Sir, Gunny Samuelson sent us to let you know he's going to go through with the assault. He's going to go through M315 if you want to link up with him there."

Ryck didn't know who was inside the PICS facing him, and with the system out, he couldn't pull it up. It didn't matter.

He looked back at the stairwell leading down. This could be one of the shifting winds of opportunity that could bring success, or it could be a deathtrap.

Make up your grubbing mind, Ryck! he told himself. *You're the commander, so command!*

Any action was better than inaction, and that settled it. As the old earth wet-water navy hero, John Paul Jones, said, "He who will not risk, cannot win." He was going all in on this.

"You, get back to the gunny. Tell him to move around and be seen. But I don't want him to assault before . . ." he paused to look at his display timer, ". . . 10:43 local. Then I want him to hit them with everything he's got! But watch long for friendlies.

"You," he said, pointing to the second runner, "what's your name?"

"PFC Müller, sir, Third Platoon."

"Well, Müller, you're now with my headquarters element. You're staying with me.

"And you, go! What are you waiting for?" he told the first runner.

As the unnamed runner took off, Ryck gathered his four fighters. "Hollington, I want you to go down the stairs. We'll be watching. If you get to the bottom, and it's part of the underground, shot back up. Doc, you and Müller stay her and provide security. Jaanson, you and I are going to watch Hollington. Let's do it!"

Ryck kept watching his readout. Even if the underground gave him a straight shot, he was cutting it close. But he was running out of time. He just hoped he wasn't sending Sams and the rest on a suicide mission.

He watched Hollington slowly make his way down the metal stairs. They creaked, and Ryck could see them stress under Hollington's weight, but they held.

"I'm in the tunnel," Hollington blasted over his externals from below.

Ryck winced. He should have told him to signal them with a light or something. If anyone was there in the underground, he would have heard the lance corporal, too.

"Jaanson, go," he told the lance corporal.

"I'm next, then Doc, then Müller, you come in after Doc. Wait until each of us clears the stairs until the next one gets on."

It took almost three long minutes, three minutes Ryck wasn't sure he had, before all five were in the underground. It was pitch dark, but the infrared torches on a PICS were pretty powerful, and with their night vision turned on, they could see the entire passage tunnel. Using hand-and-arm signals, they moved in the direction of their objective. It was the correct choice. Within 30 meters, the tunnel joined the station.

The turnstile almost stymied them. This was an industrial strength turnstile, and none of them had any credits, even if the power had been on. They tried bending the gate, but it was way over-engineered and didn't even flex under the combined power of two PICS. They were wasting time when Müller, who was providing security, pointed at an attendant's booth. This wasn't nearly as strong, and while it was a tight fit, each of them was able to pass through and onto the maglev tracks.

If the power had been on, the maglev tracks would have proved tricky for a Marine in a PICS. With the power off, though, the tracks were just a nice path for them to follow.

Underground, Ryck was blind as to where they were. He could pull up the schematics, and he knew where they had entered the underground, but that was about it. He pulled a grid over the schematics and counted out the distance to their objective. It was 175 meters. But that objective would be somewhere above them. This underground had to have an exit or at least an access tunnel, and Ryck was guessing that would be at the I28 intersection 200 meters beyond the objective.

He checked the timer.

Grubbing hell!

He wanted to break into a run, but he held back, instead falling into the slow trot that conserved the PICS power packs and kept overheating to a minimum. Ryck also knew that at a trot, each stride was exactly 1.6 meters long. That was just over 234 strides. That was going to take them three minutes, 54 seconds.

It took a discipline of will to keep at the trot. He could get to where he hoped was an exit quicker, but if he wasted time searching for it, any time-savings would be lost.

An excruciating four minutes later, he brought his small team to a halt. There wasn't a station, nor even the access tunnel. There was no way out.

Ryck was positive that they were at the intersection, and so there had to be a way out. Modern cities were not simply laid out on top of the dirt. Power conduits, sewage, robotic rails, inspection trails, building foundations—all of these crisscrossed the subterranean levels of a city. He just had to break into them.

If he were on any of his previous combat operations, he would simply blast enough holes into the underground walls until he found one of those spaces. However, with the weapons he had, that would be impossible. They would have to rely on the PICS' brute force.

"Hollington, you and Müller, make a hole there," he said, pointing to a spot on the wall he chose at random. "Doc, you and Jaanson, you make a hole there."

The three Marines and the Navy corpsman attacked the wall with vigor. With only a few massive swings of Doc's fist, the first wall collapsed into a control room of some sort. Vampire lights showed that whatever equipment that was in there was turned off, but power was available.

Better than the control room was the utility tunnel leading away, right in the direction of M344. Ryck gathered his troops, and with his display timer steadily ticking down the time, he took off in a shuffling trot. The tunnel was only ten centimeters or so higher than the top of their heads, and it was less than a meter wider than their PICS, so the odd gait was the best they could do.

Unbelievably, their objective was marked. The door leading into the building was marked with the actual name of the building along with a recipe of sorts of what power cables and who knows what else went into it. Ryck stopped his team as the sound of fighting barely reached out to them through the door. He pointed to Hollington, giving the signal for him to break through.

Ryck followed right on his heels and immediately took the lone enemy in the room under fire. When Jaanson joined in, the combined power of three weapons overwhelmed their opponent, and he was down before any of their own PICS became too degraded. Ryck thought it odd that there hadn't been more securing the entrance, as opposite from their entry hatch was what looked to be a large parking garage. Either the enemy forces had been seriously attrited, or the sound of fighting had lured one or more of them up to join the fight.

A heavy gun could be heard spitting out fire above them. Ryck knew that his surviving Marines were bearing the brunt of the fire. It was now or never.

Ryck led the charge up the stairwell, knowing full well that leading a charge was not his job. Sometimes, however, a leader had to lead from the front—at least that was what he kept telling himself. He's been most comfortable as a Marine while a sergeant, and as others had told him ad infinitum, he had to let that inner sergeant go. But that was not going to happen today. It was crunch time, and his Marines needed him.

The next floor up was empty, but the sound of the big gun above them was a beacon. Five PICS slammed up the wide stairs, pieces of tile chipping off and flying in all directions. They reached the wide hallway and turned as one to the left, barely slowing down as they pelted to whatever was at the end.

His display timer read 3:22 as Ryck and his Marines burst through the big wooden doors. There were six of them in the room, two on the cannon, four firing their M77s. Ryck let loose his shoulder rockets as he took the enemy on the far left under fire. The two on the cannon would have to wait. They couldn't get that thing around to engage his team, but the other four could.

His felt a thrill as his target went down, but not before Ryck's PICS came close to redlining. Two more of the enemy went down, and he saw one of his men go down, too. Two of his team focused on the last gunfighter while Ryck charged the two men on the cannon. They were well aware of what was happening, but they stuck to their guns, firing at what was left of Charlie Company.

It took only a few moments for the last of them to fall.

And the power came back on.

"Cease fire, cease fire," came over the circuits. "The exercise is over."

The "dead" enemy and Charlie Marines stirred and sat up.

Ryck hurriedly checked his display. There were eight blue icons: Doc, Müller, Jaanson, and his along with four outside the building. Sams wasn't one of them.

"Is that you, Lysander?" a voice asked from behind him. "Leave it to you to be the fucking hero!"

"Hell, if I'd known that was you, I would have gone hand-to-hand," he said to Captain Donte Ward, the Bravo Company commander.

"How did you get in here?" Donte asked.

"You'll get it in the debrief," Ryck told him. "Come on, let's get out of here."

The eleven Marines went down the stairs where the dead rear security caught up with them. If it was possible to look sheepish in a PICS, then that Marine somehow managed it.

They walked out of the front of the building and into a wide courtyard where the living and dead were gathering. A low murmur began to get picked up by Ryck's mics. It took a moment for him to make it out.

"Charlie, Charlie, Charlie!" reverberated from the adjoining buildings.

As the battlefield contracted, the exercise referees had brought in the boundaries, and all the dead, Bravo and Charlie alike, had climbed to the tops of the combat-town buildings to watch the final battle. Ryck knew the feeds would have been available to them, so they had watched the entire assault unfold. Their reaction hit him in the heart.

He knew he was famous, but that came with baggage. This was his first exercise with the company and one in which the attacking force almost always lost. Yet they had pulled it off. They probably wondered about him, how he would be as a commander. And now, he had proven himself.

"Charlie, Charlie, Charlie. . ." the chant sounded.

Ryck stopped and looked.

Behind him, Doc, Jaanson, Hollington, and Müller started chanting, too.

This was what it meant to be a commander, he realized: to earn the respect of his men. That was all that mattered.

He lifted a fist, and with his externals on max, shouted "Charlie!"

Chapter 2

Ryck and Donte, along with their XOs and first sergeants, sat outside the conference room, waiting for their exercise debrief. The two had been platoon commanders together back with K 3/6 for the first part of the Trinocular War, and by chance, they were now company commanders together with 1/11.

Ryck looked up at First Sergeant Hector Phantawisangtong, who was deep in conversation with his Bravo counterpart. He and Hecs went back even further, to where "King Tong" had been his recruit training heavy hat. But Hecs and he being together was no coincidence. Ryck had pulled strings to get Hecs assigned to him, just as he had pulled strings to get Sams, Jaob Ling and a few others. A captain normally did not have that kind of pull, but what good did it do to be a certified "hero" if he couldn't get some favors done, right?

"You ready for this?" Donte asked.

"Heck yeah. I won, didn't I?"

"*Charlie* won, but yeah. And winning is breathing, as they say. But I heard the FCDC[2] is pretty pissed at you, breaking down their walls."

"Oh, screw them. There's no rules against that."

"Maybe not, but we don't get real projectile weapons for a reason. They've got to repair Combat Town now, especially as you destroyed the control room down in the underground," Donte said.

Ryck took a moment to glance up at his fellow captain. Donte looked fine, but Ryck thought he detected just a hint of annoyance in his voice, as if he thought Ryck had cheated to win the battle.

Screw you, too, he thought.

Donte was a friend, but it was not his fault that Donte hadn't foreseen Ryck's assault. No matter, what was done was done.

The Federation Civil Development Corps could be another matter, though. Sunshine was the FCDC's primary training world in this sector, and the combat town was one of its pride and joys. It was heavily used by them for crowd control training. As it was far better than anything the Marines had, it was often rented for UO—Urban Operations—training. It was a given that the FCDC resented

---

[2] Federation Civil Development Corps: The FCDC is the federation's answer to a land Army. Heavily armed and outfitted, it is not technically a military which gives the Federation more leeway in its deployment.

the Marines using their facility, and the restrictions they placed on the Marines were pretty heavy. Projectile weapons were only simulated, and no explosive ordnance could be used.

Ryck had essentially simulated breaching charges by using his team's PICS as battering rams. This would have raised an issue on the small building along Route Tiblisi, but when he broke through the walls in the underground, he'd damaged a small training control room, something not part of their exercise but vital for the Combat Town exercise staff for other scenarios.

Ryck wasn't worried about any fallout, however. He hadn't broken any explicit rules, even if he had skirted the intent of those rules. The FCDC assholes could bitch, but there was not much they could do about it. Ryck knew for a fact that the Corps was not about to throw him to the wolves over a battlefield success.

He glanced down at the readout Top Forrest, the battalion operations chief, had handed him before they arrived. On it was the raw battle data, which included each "casualty." This had only been an exercise, but as he read over the names, it hit him hard. Hecs, Sams, Ling: all dead. Each of his lieutenants: dead. Corporal K'Nata, his new admin clerk who had reported in just the day before: dead. Out of 212 Marines and sailors, 204 had "died."

It was just an exercise, Ryck knew, and he'd been more liberal with lives because of that. And with Marines in PICS, all combat casualties were listed as KIA, ignoring the fact that some would have been WIA and would recover. But still, that was a lot of dead.

Ryck was finally beginning to feel comfortable with the "hero" label slapped on him, but in order to earn that designation, he had seen too many die. He'd sent his own brother-in-law to his death, for grubbing sakes! Those deaths ate at him and left a black hole that he could never completely cover up.

This had been an exercise, but seeing the names on the list of KIA brought it home to him. You fight as you train. Was this an omen of the future? He closed the folder and leaned back in his chair.

"What, done gloating over your numbers?" Donte asked.

"It's all grubbing bullshit, Donte. You know that. If this had been real, none of it would have gone down like that. The numbers don't mean squat. We'll go in, have the training staff tell us how great we were, then we're gone. Until it's real, none of this matters."

"Whoa! I didn't mean to get you going all Socrates on me. You OK?"

"Yeah, sure. Don't mind me," he said, his mind already wandering.

He'd been pumped up at the win, pumped up at the chants of "Charlie!" But seeing the names on the list had snapped him back. This wasn't some huge video game developed just for him. When they did go out on an actual mission, and he was sure that time would come, losing men would be for real. He hoped he would be able to handle that.

FS INCHON

Chapter 3

"And when I say no liberty incidents, I mean *no* liberty incidents. Zero!" LtCol Fearless uKhiwa told his gathered staff and commanders.

Even after four months with the battalion, Ryck was still slightly in awe of his battalion commander. He'd actually been born with the name "Fearless," and whether his parents had seen something in him or if the colonel had simply grown into it, the name fit.

He certainly did not "grow" tall, though. At 165 cm, he was at the bare minimum height to fit in a PICS. The ongoing joke was that he didn't need a PICS. He had a huge chest and shoulders and could bench 300 kgs. For such a muscle-bound man, however, he could run forever. Ryck thought he was in pretty good shape, but the CO had run him into the dirt, leaving him gasping and almost throwing up, on more than one occasion.

There was one more thing about him, at least as it pertained to Ryck. The CO was not a combat vet. During the "disagreement" with Greater France, the French had bypassed much of the Federation forces, including the CO's unit at the time, and he'd been stuck at Headquarters during the Trinocular War. Despite this, he didn't seem impressed with Ryck at all. Ryck wasn't used to this. Marines all seemed to have an opinion of him: most Marines gravitated to him, and some seemed to resent him. But at least they had an opinion. It wasn't as if the CO didn't seem to like Ryck. He just didn't seem to have much of an opinion of him one way or the other.

Ryck wanted to change that. He wanted the CO's approval and respect. He knew his past was the past, as far as the CO was concerned, and all that mattered was how he performed as the Charlie Company commander.

"Any saved rounds?" the CO asked. When no one said anything, he turned off his PA and said, "OK, then. Let's get the men off the boat and on their way. This might be their only chance for a decent libo for the entire cruise. Dismissed!"

The staff came to their feet as the colonel left the wardroom.

"Staff NCOs, I want to see you in the Chief's mess in five," the sergeant major called out as the staff started to file out.

Ryck clapped Hecs' shoulder. "It sucks to be you. I'll be a six-pack down by the time you get off the ship."

"Don't worry. I'll make it up tomorrow when your wife gets here," Hecs told him as they left the wardroom, the Navy stewards standing along the bulkhead, patiently waiting for the Marines to clear out so they could begin the evening meal prep.

The *FS Inchon* was a *Falklands* Class Integrated Assault Transport. The IATs were designed to bridge the gap between putting Marines on Navy battleships and cruisers or putting them on simple, unarmed transports. During the conflict with Greater France, thousands of Marines had been killed who were nothing more than spectators. The idea was to have a ship that could carry battalion-sized Marine Expeditionary Assault Force with enough firepower to protect itself and even carry the fight to smaller naval vessels. Not everyone at the top levels was convinced that this was the way to go, but Ryck rather liked being in space with his entire battalion.

Ryck hurried down to officer's country where he had his own, if small, stateroom. It was tiny, with barely enough room to turn around if his rack was lowered, but he was glad it was his. The colonel's stateroom had a small office in the front, and the three majors—the XO, the Ops O, and the Flight Commander—all had slightly larger staterooms than Ryck's, but of the captains, only the four company commanders rated their own staterooms. Drayton Miller, the S4, shared a room with two of the pilots, and Frank Lim, the chaplain, Shabah Mouldin, the surgeon, and the last pilot shared another.

Ryck threw off his skins[3] and pulled on his skivvies. He was glad that Hannah would arrive tomorrow, but that meant that this evening would be his only boys night out. Coulder 45, or "Colt 45," was not one of the wildest military liberty planets around. There wasn't much of the more prurient night life that many young Marines and sailors sought, but the draft beer was rumored to be the best in Federation space, and its well-stocked mountain lakes had produced more than a few UGFA[4] records. Food, fishing, and beer was on the agenda of most of the ship's crew and Marines, and while Ryck was not going to do any fishing, he intended to sample the food and beer before his wife arrived and he'd have other things on his mind.

---

[3] Skins: the nickname for the working uniform of a Marine. When inserted with the "bones," it became an effective fighting uniform.

[4] UGFA: Universal Game Fishing Association

"I have permission to go ashore," Ryck told the quarterdeck watch officer, as he saluted aft to where the Federation Shield was engraved on the stern of the ship. He'd never actually seen the shield, but tradition was tradition, and salutes were required. He rushed into the waiting shuttle, sure he was the first captain to make it. To his disappointment, Donte, Drayton, and Frank were already there, taking up a row of seats. At least he was on the first shuttle.

Within a few minutes, the shuttle was full, and the hatch closed. With an almost imperceptible lurch, the shuttle detached and started the 3-minute descent to the planet's surface.

The mood was festive as the shuttle descended. Colt 45 might not be Vegas, where Ryck had his first liberty call, but they had at least nine months ahead of them, and this might be their last chance to relax until they returned.

Once down, the four of them grabbed an autocab to Saja. While on liberty, there wasn't any segregation by rank, at least formally. But with some sort of herd instinct, ranks somehow congregated together. Saja was a well-regarded beerhall, its micro-brewed pilsner having won more than a few awards, and this became the defacto headquarters of the O3s.[5]

The entrance was impressive, with two huge stylized Asian lions guarding the door. Inside was Korean kitsch, but it was the smell of hops in the air that grabbed their attention. Two Navy lieutenants had already claimed a table, and from the look of it, had already made a good dent on the beer stocks. They lifted their steins in a toast as the three Marines and Frank came in.

Frank went right to their table and poured himself a stein out of their pitcher. The ship was smaller than most, and most of the men already knew each other, and if the chaplain wanted some of their beer, then who were they to object?

The drinking started, and the next six hours went by in a blur. Ryck remembered the CO and the ship's captain stopping by for a round. He remembered seeing three young privates, probably just out of recruit training wander in and then look at them in panic as they realized who had laid claim to the place before they took off at a run, much to all of their amusement. He vaguely remembered standing on the table with Felipe Something-or-other, one of the Navy lieutenants, and singing "That's Why I Love You," while getting doused with beer from the unappreciative gallery. But that was about it.

---

[5] O3: A Marine captain or Navy lieutenant. "O" designated officer, and "3" designates the third officer rank.

Somehow, probably with help, he made it back to the ship where he collapsed in his rack. Tomorrow, he would be the good husband and spend time with his wife, but tonight, that had been righteous!

Chapter 4

Thanks to modern medicine, Ryck felt surprisingly human the next morning as he went back down to the planet's surface. Shabah hadn't made it back to the ship the night before, but the duty corpsman didn't even ask when Ryck showed up at sickbay and simply gave him the injection. Within minutes, his head shrank to half its size, and his brain actually started to work again. His mouth still tasted like a sewer, but a quick shower and brush, and he was ready to go meet Hannah.

He was looking forward to the four days with her. During workups and getting ready for deployment, they hadn't had much time together. Ryck's schedule, Hannah's schedule, and most of all, the demands of the twins had them parenting instead of being husband and wife. Now, with Hannah's cousin watching the twins, they could focus only on each other, and Ryck could use the loving. It was going to be a long stretch of sleeping alone, and he planned on making good use of their time together.

There was a flower vendor at the commercial terminal, so he scooped up a dozen roses. He buried his nose in them, inhaling. These were some new strain, and their scent was heady. It reminded him of Hannah—not so much that Hannah liked roses, but that Ryck did, and he continually bought her rose bubble bath and toilet spray. The more he smelled them, the more excited he was to see her and the harder the wait.

There were no immigration formalities for Federation citizens on Colt 45, but still, it took quite a bit of time for a passenger liner to unload close to 6,000 passengers. Ryck looked up anxiously each time a shuttle unloaded, but it wasn't until the seventh load that he spotted his Hannah.

She looked a little bedraggled as she followed the throng through the glass entryway, pulling her small suitcase. Hannah was a Torritite, and so she was never much into make-up. She had gained a little weight over their years together, especially after having the twins. But to Ryck, she was as beautiful as ever. He still wondered how he had ever gotten her to fall in love with him, and he prayed she would never realize she was too good for him.

They'd had a rocky patch after Joshua, her brother, had been killed by the trinoculars, but since then, Ryck thought their relationship had become stronger than ever. And now with the twins, his personal life was about as good as it had ever been.

She didn't see him as she came through the exit. He snuck up behind her and thrust the roses around and in front of her face.

She took a sniff, then without looking behind her, said, "Thanks for the roses, but you should know, I be married to a Marine, and he'd not be taking kindly to you hitting on me."

"He can't be that tough," Ryck said, sliding an arm around her belly.

"Yes he is, but if we get out of here quick, he won't be knowing where we've gone."

Ryck turned her around and gave her a kiss. "Missed you," he said.

"I missed you, too, but I'm here now. I want to see this resort hotel you've picked out. Care to escort me there, Marine?"

"Your wish is my command, my lady," he said, taking her suitcase.

Outside was something of a madhouse with people breaking the line to grab autocabs. Each autocab was programmed to wait its turn despite the admonitions of those who'd jumped the line to get going on their way. This was a tourist destination with heavy influxes of arrivals, so Ryck would've thought they'd have it more organized. It took them a good twenty minutes before they got their own cab and were on their way.

Hannah snuggled up against Ryck on the ride, hands roaming a bit in a promise of what was to come. If the windows on the cab could be darkened, Ryck thought they might not have waited until they got to the Spruce Look Resort.

It took almost an hour, but at last, the "We will be arriving at your destination in approximately two minutes. Fergusson's Autocab wishes you a pleasant stay, and we want to remind you to press Star 5558 for your future travel needs," came over the autocab's speakers.

Hannah leaned forward to look out the window as the resort came into view. Ryck had to admit that it was pretty impressive. Huge conifers—which had to be genmodded, they were so big— surrounded a white two-story building with extensive brown wood molding and trim. Behind the resort, a picture-postcard lake could be seen through the trees. It looked quiet, inviting, and just like the type of place where the two could lose themselves in each other.

There was a human receptionist to check them in, which was a nice touch. "Byron" was a young man, but his manner was impeccable. He reminded Ryck of some of the characters in any of the recent flicks taking place in 19th Century Britain. Ryck knew that the resort was a meticulously planned product from the Brilliant

Travel Experiences Corporation. In many ways, it was a facade of sorts. The fanciful Hollywood version of English life at the time may not be accurate, but it fit the company's vision of what its customers wanted. Ryck tended to be a bit cynical about Corporate Federation, but when an actual bellhop came to take their bags, he couldn't help but feel impressed. It may have been a show, but it was working.

The room was beautiful, and Hannah actually made an audible intake of air as she saw it.

Score one for Ryck!

Kreicher—the bellhop—went around the room, explaining the features. Hannah was listening with rapt attention, but Ryck wanted Kreicher to wrap it up and get out. When he finished, Ryck wasn't sure how to tip the bellhop as he didn't have a PA on his uniform. Kreicher had out his own PA, and the bellhop had obviously been through this before.

"Captain Lysander, assisting you is our pleasure. We do not need a gratuity, but if you insist, there is a recpad over here," he said, pointing to a small screen by the door that Ryck had missed. "So with that, I will leave you alone now. We at the Spruce Lodge hope you have a very enjoyable stay."

Kreicher left, and Ryck tapped in 20 credits on his PA.

"Oh, more than that," Hannah said as she watched. "He was so helpful."

Ryck had thought that 20 was more than generous, but he dutifully increased it to 25, then tapped the recpad. Done and done, and now for more important things.

He grabbed Hannah and pulled her in for a kiss. She returned the kiss, but only briefly before pulling away.

"Not like this, Ryck. I'm a mess. Let me get prettied up, OK?"

Ryck wouldn't have minded if Hannah had just come out of the gym, but as dense as he could be, he'd learned a few things about being married. He gave her a kiss on the forehead and let her go. She took her suitcase and disappeared into the bathroom. When he heard the shower turn on, he contemplated joining her but decided she would rather he wait. It was OK—they had four days together.

He took a seat on the foot of the bed, thought about turning on the holo, and once again, with his married self the voice of caution, figured that wouldn't be the most romantic thing to do. He cupped his hand over his mouth and took a whiff. His breath seemed OK, but he threw down a breath bud anyway, feeling the explosion of mint as the little nanos cleaned his tongue and throat.

He was wondering what was taking her so long when his tether sounded. The "tether" was the nickname given the Personnel

Communications Receiver given to each Marine and sailor while deployed. It looked like a small, old-fashioned watch, but its purpose was to enable anyone to be reached within a planetary system. With a sinking feeling, he flipped open the cover.

His heart sank. It was a Class 1 recall. Something was up, something big.

He stood up, went to the closed bathroom door, and opened it.

"Hey!" Hannah protested, a toothbrush in her mouth, her hair in clips sticking in all sorts of directions. "Keep your pants on . . ." she started until something in Ryck's expression registered with her.

"Recall?" she asked with a resigned tone, but one in which she was hoping she was wrong.

Ryck just nodded.

"What class?"

"Class 1."

Her expression fell, as she put the toothbrush down. Toothpaste foam still bubbled around her lips as the nanos went about their mission, oblivious to the drama.

"Do you think it be a drill?" she asked without too much hope.

"The sergeant major promised us no drills. No, I think it's real," Ryck said, not knowing if he was more disappointed for himself or for seeing his wife's expression.

Being married to a Marine was tough. The separations and demands put on a Marine had destroyed more than a fair share of Marine marriages. Hannah actually worked for the military in her civilian capacity, so she might have a better feel for the Corps than some other wives, but that didn't make it any easier. They'd been married now for almost ten years, and they had spent exactly two anniversaries together. Ryck had missed countless birthdays and other holidays. He had missed the twins' birth.

"Well, that be life, I guess," she said. "I'll wait here until we know for sure. If I don't hear from you by evening, I'll be getting on the next ship out."

Ryck slowly walked over and leaned in to kiss her. The toothpaste foam filled his mouth. She returned his fierce hug.

Ryck loved the Corps, but sometimes, he resented its demands on him.

He tugged at the towel Hannah had wrapped around her, dropping it to the floor. He pulled Hannah in tight, forcing the air from her lungs. She eagerly sought his mouth with hers before breaking off.

"Ryck, I want you, but the recall. . ."

"Screw the recall. I've got two hours to report back to the shuttle, and I'm going to use every single minute allotted to me so I can spend time with my wife. I assume that's OK with you?" he asked facetiously.

She didn't verbally respond, but her physical response was more than enough.

This wasn't as he had imagined it. Her hair was a mess. She had foam all over her mouth. She didn't have on the sexy negligee he could see hanging on a hook by the sink. But she was his wife, and he loved her.

He took her by the hand and almost dragged her out into the bedroom. He'd have to be quick, but he figured he was more than up to the task.

Chapter 5

"At 22:15 MST, the *FS Julianna's Dream*, a registered Federation yacht was seized by the Confederation System Guard while in neutral space. It was taken under traction and towed to the CF-32 system where we have learned through the Brotherhood embassy on Neuvo Bogata that a Confederation Navy cargo vessel, probably the CS *Prince of Celeste*, will bring it back to the Firenze Station," LT Brisco Telemark, the ship's intel officer, briefed the gathered staff.

"We have lodged a complaint with the Confederation of Free States and demanded the ship's immediate release, but the Confederation has accused the *Julianna's Dream* of being on a spy mission in their space. Since that response, the President of the Confederation has recalled his ambassador and pulled our ambassador's credentials.

"Here is the CF-32 system," he said, pointing to an image over the portable holo base that had been put on the wardroom table.

The *Inchon* was extremely advanced in most ways, but for a troop transport, there was no central briefing room. Each stateroom was connected for conference briefs, but the sailors and Marines quickly abandoned the system except for entertainment. A briefing needed to be face-to-face for the best conveyance of information, so the wardroom was quickly chosen as a defacto briefing room. It was crowded with all the required staff, but it was better than the alternative.

"The system has no habitable planets, but it has two research stations, one which is experimenting with methods to mine the atmosphere of its gas giant, CF-32-5."

The holo centered on a ringed planet.

Ryck wasn't up-to-date on all mining research, but he was basically aware of the drive to develop an economically viable method to pull substances such as hydrogen deuteride, which increased efficiencies in modern fabrication, out of gas giants. Most of the gas giants' atmospheres were simple hydrogen, but with such huge volumes of gasses, even trace amounts of hydrogen deuteride resulted in tremendous amounts of the gas.

If the *Julianna's Dream* strayed too close to the system, then Ryck wasn't surprised that the ship was detained. Why the Confederation wouldn't release the ship now was another story, though.

"The *Prince of Celeste* is a *Tonder* class heavy hauler, and we don't think it can arrive on station before 05:15 on June 8, MST. It could be preceded by a warship, of course, but we've had no indication of sudden unplanned departures of capital ships in the region.

"That leaves the System Guard ship. We do not have a firm identification of the ship yet, but it is probably a *Wrym* class packet, which would put it at 50,000 tons, armed with a second generation 50 KJ plasma cannon, four torpedo tubes, and a 50mm railgun."

Ryck could almost see the slight easing of the tension among the Navy staff. While that ship might be more than enough to be a deterrent of pirates and tax runners, it was hardly a match for the *Inchon*.

"The *Julianna's Dream* is a Cessna 900," he went on perking up the ears of all the ship groupies. Ryck was not up on all the newest and greatest in the yacht fleets, but even he knew the Cessna was top-of-the-line.

"The owner-pilot is Mr. Terrance Gilbreath, a businessman. Onboard are his wife, three children, and four personal staff.

"That's all for my initial assessment. I will feed more out as I receive it. Let me turn it over to Commander Marsov."

"So are we going to show the flag, you think?" Donte asked Ryck as they sat in the second row of seats.

"You've got me," Ryck said as he looked at the other staff crowded around.

Over half of the men were in civvies. At least everyone had gotten back on the ship before it left orbit, which was a minor miracle. Ryck had made it back to the shuttle port with minutes to spare, but both the battalion and the ship's CO, along with several key staff had been out on some alpine lake, and the LCDR Wyzusky, the senior watch officer, had sent one of the ship's Storks to pick them up. That was sure to result in an official complaint from the planter officials, but they couldn't very well leave without the senior officers on board.

Luckily for those who had been enjoying themselves a bit too much, Doc Shabah had met them at the hatch to the wardroom with Soberups. They would pay the price later, but the pills were considered mission essential for a good portion of them.

Ryck hadn't really met the commander yet. Along with most of the junior officers, Ryck was on the wardroom's second seating. The ship's XO presided over the seating, but all the other senior officers were on the first seating. According to the other navy officers in his seating, the commander was competent, but a flaming asshole. Ryck looked on interestedly as the Ops Officer took the small portable podium.

"Captain, colonel, gentlemen," he began. Technically, he was the same rank as LtCol uKhiwa, but as the colonel was the commander of troops, military etiquette stipulated that the Ops O address him separately.

"We left orbit 25 minutes ago, and we will enter bubble space in 12 minutes."

That brought a low murmur from the wardroom. That was no time at all, and the ship would still be in close proximity of Colt 45. To enter bubble space that close would have required clearance at the highest authority.

"According to our calculations, we will emerge from bubble space within the CF-32 system at least five hours before the Confederation heavy hauler. Our mission upon arrival is to rescue the ship's company, retrieve the ship, if possible, destroy it if it is not."

The murmur rose again, and the commander raised a hand to quiet them down.

"If the Confederation releases the ship before our arrival, we will attempt to re-enter bubble space undetected. We'll be the first ship to use the new cloaking systems in an actual operation, so even then, our mission is vital."

Since the human cloaking systems had proven to be inferior to those of the trinoculars, there had been a mad rush to improve the human systems. Both the *Falklands* and the *Han* Class destroyers were the first two classes of ships to get the upgrades.

"By the Grace of God, we are one of the closest ships to CF-32, and we are the most capable of performing the mission. Our Marines will make the crossing and take down the ship. If we need it, the *Inchon* herself will try out her new meson canon that Lieutenant Commander Jewel has been so anxious to break in. And if anyone tries to stop us, we are authorized to use maximum force to complete the mission.

"But time is short. I'd like everyone except for my staff and Major Snæbjörnsson's staff to clear out. We need some elbow room to hash this plan out. The rest of you, you've got lots to do, so I suggest you get at it. Captain?"

"I've got nothing for all of you now. But you heard the Ops O. Better get going."

He stood up, immediately followed by the rest of the wardroom.

"Holy shit!" Donte whispered beside Ryck as everyone started filing out the hatch.

Going into Confederation space? "Maximum force" is authorized? Holy shit indeed!

Chapter 6

Ryck rushed down B deck to get to Hanger Bay 2. He'd just received the final brief, and L-hour was less than 15 minutes away. He forwarded the updated operations order to his own staff which should be waiting in the rekis[6] for the crossover.

The mission was pretty straight forward despite the time crunch and the close entry and exit from bubble space to planetary bodies. With the new cloaking system, the *Inchon* would pull to within 100 km from the *Julianna's Dream*, which was spitting distance for ships in space. The Marines would use the rekis to close the distance before debarking and flying their EVA vacsuits the last kilometer to their objectives.

Charlie Company was to secure the *Julianna's Dream*, Alpha would disable or isolate the System Guard ship, while Bravo was the task force reserve. If the System Guard ship offered any resistance to Alpha Company, they were to back off and let the *Inchon* herself disable or take it out.

Ryck was disappointed that he wasn't taking on the opposing ship. Frankly, he had wanted and expected that mission, and he wondered if the CO was sending him some sort of message by not giving him the mission.

He dashed into the locker room where his vacsuit and a Navy suit tech were waiting for him.

"You need to hurry, sir," the tech said as Ryck stripped to his cotton longjohns. He's spent most of his time in the Marines either in PICS or in recon, but sliding into the vacsuit was almost second nature to him. Within a minute, the tech had sealed him in, ran the check, then gave the thumbs up. He stepped into the lock, cycled it, and entered the hangar where Sandy Petlier-Aswad, his XO, and the first sergeant were waiting for him.

"We've got you in B-6," the XO said, pointing the way.

Ryck knew what reki he had, but the XO was earnest and trying hard, so he said nothing as he was led to the reki and clambered aboard. The reki was nothing more than an open sled with a propulsion system. Marines in their vacsuits stood like sardines in old fashioned-cans while the sleds transported them up to 50,000 klicks. There was no life-support. Men were kept alive by

---

[6] Reki: open four to eight-man open sleds that can quickly transport suited Marines through space.

their suits. There was nothing around each Marine but the vastness of space.

During basic training, several recruits had freaked out, mentally unable to take the sensation. Ryck rather liked it. Once his sole plates were locked in, he glanced up at the open hangar doors. In this section of space, the interstellar gases put on quite a show, and even from within the lighted hangar, they were sensational.

His timer display slowly ticked off the seconds until launch. Ryck did a quick check of his own systems. It wasn't as if he didn't trust the sailor's word, but it was going to be his ass out there, and he wanted to make doubly sure he was good to go.

All suit specs were at 100%. He was ready.

Now, he pulled up the company specs. Without going into the weeds with specific Marines, he noted the overall numbers. Overall readiness was at over 99%, with only a few Marines dipping below 97% in any category. Ryck felt the urge to remind his leaders to monitor those few Marines, but with an effort, he bit that back. Gunny Sams and the platoon sergeants would be on that.

The tendency to micro-manage and be an NCO again was something he'd had to fight ever since getting commissioned. It had almost been his undoing at NOTC,[7] but while the urge was still there, he had it under control—mostly.

He set his comms on monitor and listened in as the timer clicked down. He could hear all the chatter over the company nets, and with his AI assisting, could pull specific conversations. If Ryck had known this was possible as a corporal or sergeant, he might have been a bit more circumspect in his own conversations, and he still felt a little guilty for listening in to others' conversations now. However, the mission came first, and if knowing what was happening could help, it was a valid course of action.

One conversation caught his attention, and he toggled to isolate it. SSgt Grimes was in earnest conversation with Private Hans Çağlar. Çağlar was a big, powerful-looking Marine, Ryck remembered from his last inspection, a new join from Gaziantep. This was his first operation, and his nerves might be on edge. Ryck toggled over to pull up Çağlar's readouts. Pulse was 105, breathing was 35. Yes, the young man was nervous.

"Nothing to it, Hans," his platoon sergeant was telling him over their P2P. "Just like training. Besides, if I was some

---

[7] NOTC: Naval Officer Training Course

Confederation jimmylegs and I saw your big ugly ass coming at me, I would give up right there on the spot."

"But Staff Sergeant, what if I screw up?" Çağlar asked.

"You won't. You're a Federation Marine."

"But what if I do? I could get someone killed," he persisted.

"If you do screw up, then just double down and do what's right. Corporal Sands will be watching out for you, so you just follow him and do like he says, OK?" SSgt Grimes said in an even, calm voice.

Ryck toggled back out of the conversation. Grimes had things in hand. Ryck made a note to look at both Grimes' and Çağlar's mission record after the company got back. Grimes, in particular, might have potential for bigger and better things in the Corps.

Then he had no more time for idle contemplation. The display countdown reached zero, and the first three rekis lifted up and passed through the plasma gate and into open space. Ryck's coxswain, a Navy bosun's mate, lifted his reki up a few moments later, and along with B-4 and B-5, they passed through the gate. Ryck couldn't hold back a slight start as the bow of the reki made contact with the gate. If there was any breach in a vacsuit, the touch of the gate could cause an instant death. It was for this reason that after a combat mission, the gates were turned off, but before the mission, with the suits checked, there was no reason to diminish the ship's integrity even in the slightest amount.

Ryck looked over to his left where the first six A-flight rekis were already outside the ship. In a moment, they would all be accelerating, and most of the rekis would be out of visuals from each other until they converged on the *Julianna's Dream*. He could pick out A-3, the one with 1st Lieutenant Jefferson de Madre in it. Jeff was Ryck's First Platoon commander, and more pertinently, the assault element leader for their mission.

Until a month ago, the XO was the First Platoon commander, but Jeff had transferred to Charlie, and he was a month junior to Sandy. Sandy was bumped up to XO, and Jeff took over the platoon, much to Ryck's relief. Jeff was a picture-perfect Marine: fit and good-looking, but more importantly, he had the ingrained manner of a natural-born leader. Ryck felt much better with Jeff as a platoon commander than if he'd still had the more cerebral, quieter XO.

Normally, rekis were dispatched immediately after debarking their ship, but this time, due to the short distance, the rekis gathered while the rest exited the hangar gates. The rekis' approach would deviate in random paths to avoid mines and other unwanted welcoming presents, but if the *Inchon's* AI was on top of it, the rekis would all converge on their debark points at the planned times. With such a small distance to cover, they had to start on their crossover almost simultaneously in order to reach their debark points as planned.

Finally, on some unheard signal, the rekis started accelerating. All Ryck could do now was to sit and enjoy the ride. He took a moment to look up at the brilliant display that gave color and light to the dark reaches of space, then settled in to go over the plan one more time.

He needn't have bothered. There wasn't time for much before the rekis started converging on the *Julianna's Dream*. The reki came to a stop, and the green light flashed for the Marines to debark. Ryck released his sole plates, and with a kick, rose several meters "above" the reki before he hit his controls to stop his motion.

"Above" the reki was all relative. In space there was no above and below, and Marines were taught to ignore the spatial terms that had worked for mankind for millennia. For the Marines, "above" and "up" meant towards their target, "down" and "below" away from it.

And their target was clearly visible less than a klick away. The *Julianna's Dream* was a sleek ship, clearly visible in the reflected light of CF-32-5. Ryck had no idea how it was outfitted inside, but from his vantage point, the Cessna 900 reeked of money. With all the top-of-the-line navigational gear it had to have onboard, Ryck wasn't sure how it could have strayed so far off the beaten path just to be close to Confederation space. It wasn't as if there were any tourist destinations in the region.

"Taco-Six, this is Taco-Three-Alpha,[8]" Ryck's headphones picked up as the S-3A came up on the battalion circuit.

First Battalion, Eleventh Marines, had the Mexican *Fuerza de Infantería de Marina* as its patron unit. For longer than anyone could remember, the battalion staff had adopted "Taco" as its call-sign. There had been some talk about changing that before Ryck had even enlisted after the call sign had become common knowledge. The battalion had earned the Chairman's Battle Streamer on Garret's Hold, and a book about their fight had been written. However, traditions are a mainstay of the Corps, and the

---

[8] Taco-Six, Taco-Three-Alpha: call-signs designating the battalion commanding officer and assistant operations officer. "Taco" is for battalion, "Six" is for Commander, "Three" is for Operations, and "Alpha" is for assistant.

Jonathan P. Brazee

dispersed people who could claim Mexican descent took "ownership" of the battalion, proud of its accomplishments. The callsign stayed.

Captain Virag Ganesh was the assistant three, or assistant operations officer, and his place for the mission was back on the *Inchon* within CIC. He was the conduit between the ship and the Marines.

"We have two incoming signatures centered at 47884-63789. We think one is a Federation destroyer, the other a packet. There is no indication that they are aware of our presence yet. The two ships could reach your pos in fewer than 90 mikes under impulse drive, and the *Inchon* Six requests that we move up the timeline accordingly, over."

"Three-Alpha, this is Taco-Six. I understand. I will push up the operation," the CO passed back to the ship.

Technically, once the Marines had left the ship, the entire operation was under LtCol uKhiwa's command, hence the "request" from the senior Navy captain. However, the *Inchon* was their ride back, and if the captain thought his ship was in danger, he would have every right, even duty, to abandon the Marines to save the ship. The *Inchon* technically more than matched up with any destroyer, but with a Confederation packet there as well, and with possibly more ships arriving, the captain would not want to get into a fight here in Confederation space.

"You heard the Three," the CO passed on his command circuit. "Alpha, I want you to isolate the System Guard ship now. We don't want them firing up."

That's an understatement, Ryck thought.

If the System Guard ship decided to move, there wasn't much Marines in vacsuits could do about it. The *Inchon* could easily take it out, but not only would that alert the Confederation ships that had just arrived, but it could wipe out any Marines near the vessel. Alpha company had to close in with the System Guard ship and either board or disable it.

"Charlie, don't wait for Alpha. I want you to move now."

Ryck toggled the acknowledgement. He didn't like it, though. Originally, he wasn't to start the breach until the System Guard ship was neutralized. Now, he not only had to worry about booby traps or hostiles on board, he could be having a ship crawl up his ass.

"Platoon commanders, listen up," he passed on his command circuit. "We've got company, and not the heavy transport we expected. We need to move up the operation. But that doesn't mean we're going to forget caution. I'm not getting any Marines

30

killed on this, so Ephraim, I want the ship scoured for any boobytraps before Jeff breaches."

First Lieutenant Ephraim Davidson was Ryck's Weapons Platoon commander, and for this operation, the security element commander. With an attached Navy EOD team, he was to sweep the ship to identify and disable any booby traps. Ryck didn't want any Marine entering a space until it had been cleared.

"Jeff, as soon as Ephraim's cleared what he can, you need to get your team inside and find our hostages. We don't have time to waste, so let's move it now!"

There was a flurry of activity as the security element started to move to the *Julianna's Dream*. Ryck hesitated for only a moment. They seemed too exposed. But if the ship was rigged to blow, he did not want his entire force to be compromised.

"Sams, keep your eyes open. If you see anything, I want you to stop Davidson," he passed on a three-way P2P with the gunny, the first sergeant, and him.

Having a gunny "watch over" a lieutenant, especially a well-regarded first lieutenant, was not standard practice. But Ryck had never seen his lieutenants in real action before, while he was intimately familiar with both Sams and First Sergeant Hecs. He trusted both of them, and if Sams "overruled" Ephraim, Ryck would take care of wounded egos after the fact.

"Roger that," Sams said.

"And Hecs, I think de Madre is the real deal, but you're my eyes and ears. If you see anything about to blow up, I want you to take action."

"He'll be fine, sir, but I'll keep my eyes open," the first sergeant responded.

Ryck had really wanted to position himself with the assault element. Two things stopped him, though. One was that he remembered how he'd have felt if he had his first company commander looking over his shoulder when he was a new lieutenant. He'd have felt betrayed at the lack of trust. The second reason was that by doing that, he would be broadcasting to the rest of the battalion that he'd been unable to adequately train his lieutenants to do their job.

Still, Ryck had turned into somewhat of a control freak, he had to admit to himself, and he had to make sure that no mistakes were made. So he used the first sergeant as his stand in.

Ryck trusted First Sergeant Hector Phantawisangtong more than maybe anyone other than Major Nidischii'. Hecs' calm demeanor and rational view of life made him an anchor for Ryck, a sounding board. So he trusted Hecs to make sure Jeff didn't screw up, and as the lieutenant was senior to the first sergeant, it wasn't a blatant case of micro-managing.

"Move it out, Captain," the CO's voice came over the P2P.

"Aye-aye, sir," Ryck said, toggling his display to take in the entire battalion.

Preston already had his company on the move towards the System Guard ship, some 20 klicks sunward from the *Julianna's Dream*. The CO, with Donte and Bravo, was ten klicks back and acting as the reserve. Ryck could see the specks that made them up. If anyone in the System Guard ship was on optics, or the two newly arrived ships were on optics, for that matter, they would all be easily spotted. The System Guard ship probably didn't have anything onboard sophisticated enough that could see the Marines or rekis, but a Confederation destroyer most likely had the instruments to pierce their countermeasures, at least those of the Marines in vacsuits. A simple kiss of the destroyer's plasma gun would wipe out every Marine, and that destroyer was well within range of them.

Ryck hoped that the *Inchon* was monitoring the two Confederation ships, and if their plasma guns started to power up, the captain would give the order to intercede.

Lieutenant Davidson quickly closed the distance to the *Julianna's Dream*. If the ship took off, there was nothing much the Marines could do about that. It was difficult to lasso a spaceship, after all. But the ship remained quiet with only life support power registering.

A flash lit up the edges of Ryck's face shield.

"Ion tubes are disabled," Preston's voice passed over the battalion command circuit.

That was one headache gone for Ryck. Preston's EOD team had been able to attach a flash limpet to the System Guard ship's tubes, and with them breached, that ship was going nowhere.

"Roger that," the CO passed. "Move your company back to your rally point."

An entire Marine company had just made a crossover in hostile space only to have an EOD team complete the mission. The EOD team, or possibly just a recon team, could have done that without a company-sized escort.

Charlie Company, though, had to actually breach the *Julianna's Dream* and find the Federation citizens. That could not be done by a small team.

"Security element is at the objective. We are commencing our sweep."

The assault element had halted about 500 meters from the ship. If the *Julianna's Dream* blew, her parts would act as shrapnel, travelling hundreds of kilometers outwards. Five hundred meters of vacuum would not diminish the force of any shrapnel, but it would lessen the chance than anyone would be hit. Every 100 meters away decreased the chance of shrapnel hitting someone by better than 99%. The security element would be wiped out, but most of the assault element and support elements would have a good chance to survive.

"What's holding you up, Captain?" the CO asked on the P2P.

Ryck looked at his display. Only six minutes had passed, and he wondered what the CO's problem was.

"We're sweeping the ship now, sir. We should be ready to breach momentarily."

"Time's of the essence. The Confederation ships know we are here now. Let's get this done."

"Roger, sir. I'm on it," Ryck said.

If the Confederation ships hadn't picked up the blast that took out the System Guard ship, the crew inside would have reported it. But the AIs had determined that the probability was high, over 85%, that any Confederation ship would hesitate before taking action. Ryck agreed with that assessment. The destroyer would not open up with an allied ship in the area, and it would have to consider that there was an opposing capital ship in the system. It would be more concerned with finding that threat than anything else.

"Don't miss anything, Ephraim, but pick it up. Battalion's on my ass," he passed on the P2P.

"Roger that, sir."

Ryck started to edge his small headquarters element forward, falling just behind the assault element. It really made no difference if he was floating 450 meters out rather than 550, but he was getting antsy. He watched the progress of his Marines on the ship through his face shield rather than on his display. He kept expecting to see the *Julianna's Dream* power up and pull away, but the ship remained quiet.

"Captain, do I have to repeat myself?" the CO passed.

"No, sir. We've almost completed the sweep," Ryck said.

You can get off my ass and let me do my job, he thought.

"We've got two capital ships approaching, and we need to get the hostages now," the CO insisted.

"I'm on it, sir," Ryck said.

"Ephraim, where're we at?" he said, switching channels.

Ryck could see the progress on his display as each section of the ship was cleared, but he wanted his lieutenant's input.

"We've cleared 32%. I'd say we are about 12 minutes out."

Twelve minutes? There's no way the CO's going to accept that, he thought, wondering what to do.

He had to breach the ship, but he was not going to get one of his men killed from something as stupid as a simple booby trap.

"Ephraim, move the breaching tube up. I want it secured and ready to go. Try and scan what's inside the best you can," he ordered.

He watched as the four Marines on the breaching team began to move forward, like pallbearers carrying a coffin. The breaching tube was a very primitive, but effective method of getting into a ship. It was essentially an airlock with a plasma gate on one end, a cutting blade on the other. The tube was placed against the skin of a ship and locked into place. An ion vibration blade would then begin to cut into the skin. Only the most hardened ships could withstand the blade for more than a few moments. For most ships, and the *Julianna's Dream* would fit in this class, the breach could be cut in less than ten seconds. For sturdier warships, the blade could be exchanged for a molecular dissolution projector or even shape charges.

The other end was initially closed off, but once the air pressure between the tube and the breached ship stabilized, the cover would be removed so the plasma gate would allow passage while keeping atmospheric integrity.

"Lieutenant, the ship's hatch is not secure," someone passed to Lieutenant Davidson on the element circuit.

Ryck had to toggle his display. It was Sergeant Bondi, one of the heavy gun section leaders.

Leaving the ship's hatch unsecured could be a big break. But it could also be a trap. Like burglars finding the bank vault open, it sent every nerve in his body tingling. They could use the hatch to enter, probably six Marines at a time. But that could put those six Marines in grave danger.

"What are you scanning inside the hatch?" he asked Davidson.

"Uh, wait one, sir."

Ryck waited impatiently until finally, "It looks clean, best we can tell," came over the net.

Looking clean and being clean were not always the same thing, Ryck knew. He hesitated.

"Captain Ward, I want you to move your company to the *Julianna's Dream* and take over the rescue," the CO ordered over the command circuit.

"No, sir!" Ryck blurted out. "We're moving in now!"

He figured the CO had his AIs scanning all the transmissions just as Ryck could within the company, so he would know that Ryck hadn't given any such order.

Ship's hatch or breaching tube? Make a decision, Ryck!

"Steer clear of the hatch. Commence breach now!" he ordered.

"Jeff, move your men up. You've got 15 seconds to have your first team inside the ship."

Fifteen seconds was probably not feasible. The breach would just be reaching completion, but Jeff's men were still floating 400-500 meters off. A vacsuit could manage that distance in 15 seconds, but not when the Marine had to come to a stop and steer into the gate of the breaching tube.

"Target breached," Sergeant Jordan passed.

Ryck was leading his headquarters forward, trying not to get in the way of anyone in the assault element. Jeff had his element well-drilled, and it was only after 32 seconds that the first Marine flew headfirst into the tube.

"Breach clear!" was reported as the first four Marines entered the ship and formed a mini-security.

Jeff was working like clockwork, getting his men into the ship. It took less than a minute before the entire element of 35 men was inside and moving throughout the ship.

Ryck followed the last man in. He burst through the tube into a well-lit interior. What looked to be real wood panels covered the walls of a master bedroom. It was one of the larger rooms on the ship, which was the reason the breach location had been chosen.

Behind Ryck, the first of the support element was following him, so Ryck moved into the ship's main corridor. The ship was not that large, and this was a lot of Marines to be on board, but the Ops O had directed a maximum and quick buildup to overwhelm whoever was on the ship.

"Hold your fire! Hold your fire!" filled the net.

"Give me a feed of that Marine," Ryck subvocalized, telling his AI to give him a view of what was going on.

Immediately, in the lower right side of his face shield, Lance Corporal Thomas' feed appeared. Four men in what had to be Confederation System Guard uniforms were standing in front of Thomas, hands in the air. They didn't seem concerned or worried, and that raised yet one more warning flag with Ryck. Another

Jonathan P. Brazee

Marine moved forward and started to check the four men for weapons.

Beyond the four guardsmen, Ryck could see three adult males, an adult female, and two children. The children were obviously frightened, but the adults seem to be taking things in stride.

"Jeff, do not stop clearing this ship. Something's not right, and we don't need any surprises."

At least the CO was quiet. He would be monitoring everything, so there was no reason for Ryck to take time to report up.

Marines were lining the corridor as Ryck passed between them and got up to the bridge. The four guardsmen had been isolated on one side, their hands press-tied together, and with two Marines watching them. The four were in grey vac suits, their helmets off.

Doc Adams was kneeling in front of the two children, giving the little girl a quick exam. As with the rest, he was still in his vacsuit, but the caduceus on the sleeve identified him. Jeff, on the other hand, had cracked open his helmet and was talking to one of the civilians. Ryck would have to talk to him later about that.

Ryck moved up as Hecs joined him. The man saw Ryck approach turned to face him hand out.

"Colby Stein," the man said as Ryck took the proffered hand. With vacsuit gauntlets on, macho tests of hand strength were moot, but Ryck thought he felt a little hand judo going on as he shook.

"Captain Ryck Lysander, Federation Marine Corps," he said in return. "Is this your entire party?"

"Why didn't you just come in the shop's hatch?" the man asked, ignoring Ryck's question. "We made sure it was unsecured. Do you know how much damage you've done?"

Ryck was taken aback. He hadn't expected to be questioned like that, and certainly not about damage to the ship. The man had been arrested, for Pete's sake, along with his family and personal staff.

"We didn't know if the quarterdeck had been boobytrapped," Ryck said, despite the fact that he knew he owed the man no explanation.

"Well, it wasn't, was it?" the man said, obviously peeved. "It's done, but I'm not responsible for that."

What the grubbing hell? Why is he worried about being responsible? Isn't it his grubbing ship? Ryck wondered.

"If you are done with your chitchat, Captain, may I remind you that we've got incoming ships, and we need to get out of here?" the CO's voice came over his P2P. "I want the hostages suited up and

36

taken to the rekis. For the System Guardsmen, release them and give them a reki. I've got a Navy team inbound now, and they are going to rig the ship to blow. You've got 15 minutes to be out of range."

"Charlie Company, begin to extract now," Ryck passed on the net, but activating his external speakers as well. "This ship will be destroyed in 15 minutes and we need to be well off by then."

The guardsmen were startled at that, and the children began to cry.

"That's not going to happen," Mr. Stein started before Ryck held out a hand to stop him.

"You're going to be released and given a reki to get out of here. I'm sure you know that you have Confederation ships inbound. If you have anyone else onboard, you'd better tell us now so they can get off, too," he told the senior Guardsman.

"There's no one else—" Stein started, but the look on the four guardsmen's eyes told Ryck differently.

"Uh, yeah, they'se maybe twos more, sorts of. Likes be hidin' in the aft head," the Guardsman said in some sort of local accent.

"First Sergeant, take this man to the aft head so he can get his two companions off the ship," he ordered before turning to face the excited Stein.

"You can't destroy this ship," Stein said. "Do you know how much it cost?"

"Doesn't matter. I've got my orders, and it is not in my hands."

Stein looked back at one of his servants. To Ryck's surprise, the manservant nodded, as if giving Stein permission or something.

"Then we need to get our luggage. It'll take us 15 minutes just to get it," Stein said.

"I don't think you understand, sir. The ship is going to be blown, and everything on it. Look at your kids. They're terrified. Don't you think you need to be concerned with them rather than luggage?"

"Captain, I don't think you understand," the manservant said, stepping up. "A certain piece of luggage will be taken," he said with a degree of certainty.

"I would suggest that these three gentlemen be escorted off the bridge," he said, indicating the three remaining Guardsmen.

Something about the man's tone gave him pause, so Ryck told the two Marines to take the men to the ship's hatch.

"Now, I suggest you call back to your commanding officer and give him these numbers: 55983221."

"I've got them," the CO spoke over the P2P, confirming that the man had been monitoring everything.

That got Ryck slightly angry, but he had to admit that he'd been doing much the same thing within the company.

The children's sobs turned to snuffles as the adults stood staring at each other as time ticked away.

It seemed longer, but less than a minute had passed when the CO came back with, "They'll be taking a piece of gear. We will wait until you have it to blow the ship."

Ryck looked up at the servant, not that Ryck now thought the man was subordinate to anyone on the ship. "You've got it."

The man nodded and then started giving orders. Stein and the other servant snapped to, one clearing an ornate carpet from where it was tacked to the bridge deck, the other reaching under a cabinet to bring out a torch. Without a word, Stein started cutting into the featureless deck.

"Lieutenant de Madre, leave two Marines here, but then get everyone else off the ship. With Mr. Stein's permission, that includes his wife and two kids," Ryck said, not looking at Stein but at the servant, who nodded his assent.

"You might want to tell your commander that he doesn't need to worry about blowing the ship. I'll take care of that," the man said.

"Noted. I'm recalling the Navy team," the CO passed, once again before Ryck relayed anything.

Whatever the bridge deck was made of, it was extremely tough. The torch flared and sputtered as it slowly cut. The three men had to put their vacsuit helmets on as the bridge filled with black smoke.

It took close to 15 minutes before the second servant was able to remove and set aside the cut deck piece and then reach in and pull on something, an action Ryck thought was foolish given that they would soon be doing a spacewalk, and a hot, jagged piece of deckplate could easily puncture a vacsuit.

Servant #1 reached down, and together with servant #2, they pulled out a meter-long black cylinder and dropped it on the deck. Number one punched in a code, then flipped open an access panel. He pulled out a disc of some sort, put it in his shoulder pocket, then latched the pocket shut.

"Mr. Stein?" the servant asked, still role-playing.

Stein pulled out a key, and both he and the servant went to the nav panel. The servant inserted one key, Stein another. The servant entered something on a touch pad, then both men turned their keys simultaneously.

"Well, Captain, I suggest we get off this ship. We've got six minutes and forty seconds."

Six minutes and forty seconds? Why not six minutes thirty, or seven minutes? Ryck wondered.

With the two Marines leading the way, Ryck followed the three civilians out of the bridge, down the hall, and to the ship's hatch. Sams, Hecs, and four Marines were waiting for them there.

"The XO's got the rest standing by a klick off," the first sergeant said.

"I'd make that ten kilometers, Sergeant," the servant said.

Ryck knew the man had no military experience when he called Hecs "Sergeant." That was a big military faux pas.

"Go ahead and tell them to start back. It will take some time for each reki to load, and we're going to want to get the ship moving quickly," he told Hecs.

"Now you're beginning to get it," the CO passed.

Ryck was really beginning to resent having the CO hovering over him like that.

The ten men cycled out and flew the 40 meters to the lone reki waiting for them. With the Navy coxswain, that was three more than normal, but that wouldn't matter until they arrived at the *Inchon* when the extra mass could affect handling.

The three civilians (not military, but Ryck was pretty sure by now that they were not simple tourists) had to use the auxiliary straps to secure themselves. The soles of their vacsuits did not have the lock-down feature. They had barely snapped in the straps when the coxswain took off. Ryck looked back as the *Julianna's Dream* quickly receded out of sight. He was watching his display timer which was counting down the time. The *Inchon* was already in view, and the coxswain was maneuvering for an approach when the display timer hit 6:40. Immediately, a small sun seem to come to life, the brightness of the light penetrating through the back of Ryck's vacsuit helmet and blinding him for a moment.

Grubbing hell!

He looked at the civilians in front of him as his vision came back. It had been obvious that this had not been an innocent error in navigation, nor a Confederation grab of a ship in neutral space. Any remaining doubts about that had disappeared when the *Julianna's Dream* was reduced to its component atoms so spectacularly.

Chapter 7

"Enter!" the CO shouted out.

Ryck took a deep breath, squared his shoulders, and stepped into the CO's stateroom. He'd been in it before, of course, but this was the first time it was just the colonel and him. This couldn't be good.

The debrief with all the officers had been strange. The ship's CO had congratulated everyone, the Ops O had gone over a very basic timeline, but it was almost as if the people who were rescued were forgotten. No mention was made other than the "cargo" was recovered. That "cargo" was somewhere on the ship where, if scuttlebutt was true, they would be transferred to a Navy sloop for parts unknown.

After only 15 minutes, they had been dismissed, and the CO had told Ryck to see him in his stateroom. Ryck waited five minutes, his mind racing, then reported.

"Sit down, Captain," the CO said from behind his small desk.

Ryck sat, ass on the edge of the chair just likes when he was a recruit. The CO leaned back, hands behind his head, elbows splayed out as he looked at Ryck for a few moments. Ryck began to feel more nervous as the CO kept quiet.

Just say something!

Finally, the CO leaned forward, and with his gravelly voice asked, "How do you think the mission went?"

That surprised Ryck.

How did the mission go? We recovered the passengers, and that was the objective, right?

But the CO had been on his ass the entire time, continually on the P2P, and he'd threatened to send in Bravo. That had pissed Ryck off. He wondered if he should say something about that, but decided to answer with the obvious and then see where the colonel was going with it.

"We accomplished the mission without loss of life, sir. I would say that was a success."

A look of, what, disgust? fleetingly flashed across the CO's face. Ryck knew the colonel had expected another response.

"You do know that I came that close . . ." he said, holding his thumb and forefinger four or five centimeters apart, ". . . to relieving you on the spot?"

"Yes, sir, I do."

"Well, that's one good thing, I guess. And do you know why I came to that decision?"

"Because you were not happy with the tempo," Ryck said.

"Exactly! And if I was not happy, then why the hell didn't you do anything about it?" the CO asked.

"Sir, the safety of my men came first. I was not going to risk them with irrational actions."

The CO stared and Ryck, his thoughts obviously warring on what to say next. He came to a decision.

"Captain, the elephant in the room is that you are one of the Corp's heroes. You are well-known, and you have friends in high places. But I am the commanding officer of this battalion, and I will not let anyone, even a Federation Nova holder, endanger my men."

Endanger? What grubbing bullshit are you saying? I was keeping my men safe! he thought, even if he was smart enough to say nothing.

"I've gone over your operations, from where you won your silver star as a PFC to your operation on GenAg13. All your successes were because you acted and acted decisively. Your performance reports all noted this tendency.

"I've also gone over your psych reports. After losing most of your men on G.K. Nutrition 6, including your brother-in-law, you retreated within yourself and almost resigned your commission."

Ryck wanted to protest, but he knew it was true.

After you were awarded the Nova, the powers that be hoped you had gotten past that, and your assignment here is your proving ground. The Corps wants their heroes, and you fit the bill. They want you to succeed."

"Uh, sir, how do you know all of this?" Ryck asked.

"Please, Captain. Do you think I wasn't briefed about the great Captain Ryck Lysander? That I wasn't briefed to make sure you succeed and get past any remaining demons?"

Ryck said nothing and simply digested what the CO had just told him. So the top brass had their eyes on him?

"But let me make one thing perfectly clear. I don't give a rat's ass for what the general staff wants with you. You are one of my company commanders, and I expect you to perform. And if you don't, I will run you out of the battalion."

At that, Ryck started to protest, but the CO held up his hand.

"And yes, I know that could cause me to be relieved, too. But if you screw up in a fight, I need to do what is best for the Marines.

"I was trying to do what was best for the Marines," Ryck said sullenly.

"You were dawdling, Captain, afraid to take decisive action. You knew that two Confederation capital ships were inbound, but you delayed, giving a potential enemy time to prepare and putting the entire task force at risk, all because you were trying to protect a few Marines. There might be times that you will have to send a man to his death, Captain, all for the greater good."

Ryck winced, thinking of Joshua, his own brother-in-law, whom he had ordered to his death, along with three other Marines.

"And frankly, I don't know if you have it in you," the CO went on.

"I called you here for two reasons, and no, I don't have a hard-on for you. I want you to succeed. I want you to be the very best Marine you can be. The first is to give you fair warning. You need to step up your game, Captain. You need to find the Ryck Lysander who went fearlessly into battle and made immediate, effective decisions. You have not shown that to me yet, so consider yourself on probation. The second thing is that I want you to know your medals won't help you. I don't care about them, and I don't care if you have godfathers looking out for you. I will do what I think is best."

You grubbing pogue, Ryck thought, keeping his face expressionless. *Of course you care about my medals because you've never seen combat, and you're jealous. You don't ride Preston like you ride me, right? Because Preston doesn't have a Nova and a Navy Cross.*

"Do we have an understanding?" the CO asked.

"Yes, sir," he said, his voice calm and even.

"OK, Captain. I know you have it in you, and I expect to see it. Go see to your men, now. Dismissed."

And that was that. Ryck had been dismissed like a recruit who'd just screwed up. In the back of his mind, a tendril of thought kept trying to surface, that the CO had been right, that Ryck had been endangering the entire battalion and the *Inchon* by playing it too cautiously. But Ryck successfully pushed that tendril back into the recesses of his mind.

The CO was out to get him, pure and simple. And Ryck was not going to give him any excuse to relieve him and take away his company—both by his performance and, if he had to, by calling in one of his purported godfathers. What was the use of having a godfather if he didn't use one of them?

SIERRA DORADO

Chapter 8

"Come on, Ryck. We're going to miss the command shuttle, and I don't want to hang around at the quarterdeck," Preston implored from Ryck's open hatch.

"We'll just leave his ass," Frank said sourly from the passage beyond Preston.

For a man of God, the chaplain had somewhat of a gutter mouth, Ryck thought. He was a great guy, but not many chaplains used the word "ass," at least not in Ryck's experience.

"OK, OK, I'm coming," Ryck said, trying one more time to get his medal bar straight. "Or you could help me with this thing."

Ryck thought that after hundreds of years, someone would have figured out an easy and quick way to put a ribbon or medal bar on a uniform. But here he was, trying the same methods that Napoleonic soldiers had used. If his blues blouse was off, he could see to align the bar, but as soon as he put the blues on, the curve of his chest threw the alignment off.

"Geez, Lysander," Donte said, shouldering his way into the stateroom. "If there was ever a man more in need of a wife, it's you."

"Just don't assume all the wifely duties, Donte," Frank said.

Donte rolled his eyes, but he removed Ryck's ribbon bar, gave a good look, then pressed it home.

"Hey, watch it!" Ryck said as one of the bar's prongs poked his chest.

"Oh come on you big baby. If you don't want to deal with it, then quit being such a fucking hero," Donte said.

Ryck reached under his blouse and slipped on the backings to the prongs. He took a quick look in the mirror. The medals were straight and parallel to the deck, exactly as per regulations.

"OK, let's vamoose," he said.

"Uh, you forgetting something?" Donte asked.

Ryck checked his gloves and cover, then his ID and PA. Donte pointed behind him, to Ryck's small desk.

Ryck looked, and his Federation Nova case was sitting on a stack of papers.

"Oh, shit," he said. "Thanks. The CO would have been all over my ass for that."

The battalion was on Sierra Dorado to celebrate the June 1st Mexican Marine Day, but Ryck knew that as one of two living Marine Nova holders, he was on display at all times. Not wearing his medal could be taken as an affront to the government and people of the planet.

The medal itself was somewhat understated, and Ryck appreciated that. The Brotherhood did not issue medals, but Ryck had seen some of the most gaudy pieces of ego on a ribbon among the military of other governments, all probably awarded for making sure the coffee was hot at the weekly staff meetings.

Ryck put the ribbon around his neck, then centered the medal itself right below his throat. *Now* he was ready.

"Come on, move it," Ryck shouted to Preston, Frank, and Donte. "Don't make me miss the shuttle!"

Franks said something entirely un-chaplain-like as the four O-3s hurried out two decks and aft to Hangar 3. This was the smallest of the hangars, large enough for one shuttle and the Captain's skiff. The skiff was gone, so the CO, XO, and LtCol uKhiwa were undoubtedly already on the surface. A petty officer stood by the hatch of the shuttle, and as the four climbed aboard, he checked them off his PA.

The shuttle was only half full. Evidently, others were even later than the four of them. Ryck elbowed Preston in the ribs. It wasn't for another ten minutes that the shuttle was loaded and it was able to depart for the planet's surface.

The mood was high in the shuttle. This should be a great time. The battalion's patron unit was the Mexican *Fuerza de Infantería de Marina*. Each battalion in the Marines had adopted a patron from the extant Marine Corps at the time the Federation Marines were formed. All Marines celebrated November 10th as the birthday of the Marines and February 27 as the founding of the first modern Marine Corps, the Spanish *Infantería de Marina*. Each battalion, though, had another holiday, that of its patron unit's anniversary date. The Mexican *Fuerza de Infantería de Marina* was founded on June 1, 1822, Old Reckoning, so that was First Battalion, Eleventh Marines' battalion holiday.

What made the battalion lucky when compared with some of the other battalions was that both in old Mexico and on Sierra Dorado, the largest Mexican-settled world, the people had embraced their history and had adopted the battalion as its own. Whenever possible, the battalion was sent by the government to help celebrate the festivities. No one doubted that this was a political move by the

Federation government, but no one cared. The Doradons put on one heck of a good party. *

"I hope there are *mucho senoritas* who love the uniform," Donte told the others, keeping his voice low so the majors and lieutenant commanders would not overhear him.

"Doesn't matter much for you. Even with your blues, your face looks like the north end of a south-facing hog," Preston put in.

"Oh, you wound me," Donte protested. "But when they see my magic feet, they will all want to flamenco with me."

"You're getting your ethnicities mixed up, there, Donte-my-lad," Ryck put in. "Didn't you download the brief?"

"*Si, señor*. How do you think I became so fluent in Spanish?"

"I think you missed something. Flamenco is from old Spain, not Mexico," Ryck told him.

Donte looked confused. "But they're the same thing, right?"

"Grubbing hell, Donte. Who's our patron?"

"The *Fuerza de Infantería de Marina*," he answered automatically.

"From Mexico. And what do we celebrate on February 27?" Ryck asked.

"That's our birthday, for the oldest Marine Corps."

"And who was the first Marine Corps?" Ryck asked.

"The *Infantería de Marina*, the Spanish Marines."

"Exactly, the *Spanish* Marines, not the Mexican Marines. This is June 1, not February 27."

"Ugly *and* dumb," Preston said. "And you're leading Marines into battle?"

Donte seemed to think for a moment, and Ryck could see comprehension dawning over his face.

"Well, sweat-balls. Of course they're different. But it's an easy mistake. Spanish language, both have *Infantería de Marina* in them. You can see that, right?" Donte asked.

"No one over the age of five would see that," Preston said.

"So I guess all those flamenco lessons were wasted," Donte declared, lifting one hand over his head and snapping his fingers a few time. "I guess I'll have to rely on my sparkling personality instead."

"God help the women of Sierra Dorado," Frank interjected.

Ryck had never been on the planet, and while Donte, Frank, and Preston went back and forth with their smack talk, Ryck watched the screen which displayed the view from the shuttle's cockpit. The planet, with the blues of the ocean, then browns and greens of the land and the white of clouds, did not look much different from most of the inhabited planets of human space. But watching the images helped screen out his friends' banter. He shifted the Nova around his neck to keep it from digging in. Because of the Nova, he'd be on display, sitting with the VIPs, but keeping his mouth shut. The ship's PAO[9] had briefed Ryck on his duties, but this was getting old hat to him. Smile, say how proud he was to be there, and praise the heck out of the Federation.

He looked back to his friends. Once the official ceremony was over, they could exfiltrate the throngs of local officials and find a small pub where they could enjoy the best this planet could brew. Ryck almost wished he could chuck the Nova and just be one of the guys tonight.

As the shuttle neared the surface, the view on the forward display became more detailed, and talk died down as Los Lobos, the capital city, came into view. Once again, there was nothing much to make it stand out. That didn't quell the good spirits, though. Several of the Marines and crew had been on Sierra Dorado before on Marine Day, and their stories had worked to amp them all up.

The shuttle came in for a smooth landing, and they quickly debarked. A local official was waiting right outside with an electric tram of some sort, and he ushered them on board as the shuttle took off to return to the ship and pick up its next load.

"Welcome to Sierra Dorado," the young man said with way too much cheerfulness. "I'm Greg Sanduski with the mayor's office. I'll be escorting you to Polk Hall where the ceremony will be taking place. There will be a small buffet set up for you, and as we still have almost two hours, please feel free to help yourselves. If you need anything, I'm your man, so don't hesitate to ask."

Sierra Dorado was an Admin 1 planet where other Federation citizens merely got scanned upon entry, but with Greg as their guardian, they even bypassed this minor formality, with the tram operator driving around the terminal.

As they pulled in front of the terminal, the enlisted men from a previous shuttle were coming out the main entrance. Among the rest of the people, there were two lines of locals. In front of one line was an LED sign with a red "Married" being displayed. In front of the other line, the sign was a green "Single."

"Saint Pete's nose!" Donte exclaimed. "Look at them!"

They'd all been briefed on the tradition, of course, but seeing it in action had far more impact.

---

[9] PAO: Public Affairs Officer

In the married line, men, women, and family groups waited to be paired up with married sailors and Marines. After the ceremony, they would adopt the servicemen, be their tour guides, and offer them a bed at their homes.

Every man on the shuttle had his eyes locked on the single line. The women standing in the line to be paired with their sailor or Marine were dressed to kill. Some had on traditional Mexican costumes, some had on more modern clothes. But from the tram's vantage point, all looked amazing. What might happen after the "hostess" showed the men around was up to them, but those who had been there before claimed that for quite a few of the newly formed couples, the pairing would last beyond the afternoon's celebration and evening. Gunny Heija in Alpha claimed that when he was here four years prior, seven marriages resulted.

"That's Brubaker! He's one of mine!" Donte said in awe as the next Marine, a young PFC, was ushered up to meet his hostesses, a stunning brunette in high heels and a rather short skirt. "He's as shy as they come!"

"Doesn't look too shy now," Preston observed. "Look at that shit-eating grin."

"Man, this isn't fair. Why do the men get all the fun?" Donte said.

"That's because we're officers, far above the primal need for carnal pleasures," Frank said.

"Speak for yourself, Frank. I need me my carnal pleasures," Donte replied.

Then the tram eased out on the main road and the welcome lines were lost to view. Ryck didn't mind their bypassing the pairing up. He wouldn't mind meeting a local family, but he figured he would be kept pretty busy for the next three days.

One lane of the road seemed to be kept clear of traffic. The tram glided along, barely making a sound. Other vehicles were in the remaining lanes, but their lane remained clear of other traffic. Within five minutes, they were pulling into the concert hall where the ceremony would take place.

Polk Hall was pretty impressive. The Aztec influence was evident, but it was only influence. This was not Chichen Itza transported to Sierra Dorado. As they walked through the main entry, they left the stone exterior for a shining expanse of marble and metal. Two winding staircases led to the upper seating section of the concert hall itself. The lobby was as impressive as anything Ryck had seen.

Jonathan P. Brazee

As they stood and gawked, their guide shooed them to the left to an auxiliary hall—one that could easily hold a Marine division, much less a battalion. Quite a few Marines and sailors were milling about. Liberty would not start until after the end of the ceremony. A good half of the single men had their hostesses with them. Ryck guessed the one who were paired with families would meet them after the ceremony ended.

"This way, gentlemen," Greg said, still in sheepdog mode as he tried to herd the officers to the far right side of the hall. A long table covered in food dishes and surrounded by a gold rope was his destination. Ryck joined the rest as they converged on the food. Some of the food was traditional Mexican dishes: Fish and carne asada tacos, chips and guacamole, rice and bean burritos (Ryck remembered reading that burritos were actually more of an American dish than Mexican), carnitas tostadas, puerco caldara, and the like. But shrimp tempura? Cocktail wieners? Chocolate-dipped panderfruit? Either the lines had been blurred over the years, or the people of Sierra Dorado just liked to party with whatever food tasted good.

There was one cake, *tres leche*, that was new to him. The name sounded Spanish, and it didn't strike him as a traditional Mexican food—but he loved it, and made a note in his PA to get the recipe. He knew Hannah and the twins would go crazy over it.

"This is good stuff, better than what the enlisted guys are getting," Drayton Miller said, four big shrimp tempura on his plate.

Ryck glanced over at the nearest table, one surrounded by sailors and Marines. He couldn't see the whole table, but it did look rather less-filled. That struck Ryck as odd. This was a battalion and planetary celebration, and he would have thought everyone would be treated equally. He felt a little guilty as he looked down at his cake.

At least the beer looked to be the same. No one was drinking it yet, however. The ship's CO had ordered that no alcoholic beverages be served until after the ceremony, and the cases stacked behind the tables were watched over by sailors in duty belts.

"Welcome, Captain Lysander," a middle-aged woman said, hand out to be shaken. "I'm Gloria Perez, the governor's press secretary."

Ryck took the proffered hand as Drayton quietly backed away, a wry grin on his face.

"I hope you are being well taken care of. I know Greg Sanduski from the mayor's office is here at your beck and call."

"Yes, ma'am, everything's fine." He held up the cake to show her.

"Yes, the *tres leche*. 'Three milk,' it means. One of our traditional favorites. I hope you like it."

"It's delicious. I was hoping to get a recipe to take home."

"Really? Well I'll make sure you get it. I've got to run—as you can imagine, I've got a lot to do. But I was wondering if you could spare a few minutes after the ceremony to meet with the governor. Nothing formal, of course, just for a little chat."

Yes, a little chat that comes with photographers to capture the moment, Ryck thought cynically.

"Of course, ma'am. I would be happy to," he said instead.

"Great. I'll track you down. Until then, enjoy yourself." She shook his hand again and then rushed off.

"Yep, the hero strikes again," Donte said as Ryck rejoined them.

"Eat me," Ryck muttered.

The room didn't exactly fill up, as large as it was, but more and more Marines and sailors as well as civilians came in a steady stream. At five minutes before the ceremony, the bigwigs arrived. The ship's CO, LtCol uKhiwa, and the senior staff arrived with who Ryck knew were the mayor, the governor, the Federation administrator, and other noted luminaries. Ryck didn't recognize any of the civilians, but he knew who was going to attend. Most of them stepped up to a raised dais that had been erected in the back of the room, and people started to drift away from the food table to stand in front if the VIPs.

Exactly at 5:00 PM, one of the battalion drummers marched into the room, pounding away on his side drum. People parted for him as he marched through the crowd to the dais. As always, Ryck felt a tingle of both pride and anticipation when he saw a drummer. Each man in the corps of drums was a volunteer, and being accepted into the corps could be difficult. Rank was not considered. This drummer was Sergeant Horatio from Bravo Company, a squad leader by billet. In his dressed blues, draped by a leopard skin and armed with a short sword, he presented an imposing figure.

He marched to the front of the VIPs, and in very precise, almost mechanical movements, he performed an elaborate about face, his arm steadily pounding a slow beat. His face like stone, he stood there, one arm in motion, the rest of him completely still. The crowd quieted.

The sergeant drew out the moment, and Ryck could almost see people lean forward in anticipation. With a suddenly flurry, both of Sgt Horatio's arms flew into a blur, beating out *Present the Colors!*

"Color Guard, forward, march!" a voice rang out with authority from near the entrance as soon as the drummer fell back into a measured cadence.

The crowd turned around, and with a little help from the duty sailors, a corridor was cleared leading up to the dais. With the Federation flag in the middle and the Sierra Dorado flag to its left, the Marine Corps and Navy flags on the ends completed the color guard.

Ryck joined all the military in coming to attention as the color guard made its way to the dais and did their reverse marching move to finish up facing the crowd. The three subordinate flags were lowered to the Federation flag, and a small local band, accompanied by a young lady, broke out into the anthem. The crowd broke into applause as the last strains died away and the color guard split to go around the dais and put their flags in holders on a raised platform in back of the VIPs.

The first person to address the crowd was the Federation administrator. Mercifully, he kept it short, and within a couple of minutes, relinquished the podium to the governor.

"*Buenos tardes*," the governor began, in an atrocious accent that even Ryck knew was so far removed from old Mexico as to beggar belief.

Evidently, Spanish was only a historical footnote on the planet. Luckily, he switched right into Standard, welcomed the Marines and sailors, and recited a scripted list of how well the planet had been doing since he took office. Ryck wondered if elections were coming up soon.

The governor gave way to the mayor who gave way to the *Inchon's* CO. Finally, it was LtCol uKhiwa's turn. The crowd perked up. This was Marine Day, after all, and the CO was the senior Marine present.

"On September 13, 1847, Old Reckoning, forces from the United States of America, to include US Marines, stormed Chapultepec Castle in Mexico City. Six young cadets: Juan de la Barrera, Juan Escuita, Francisco Márquez, Agustín Melgar, Fernando Montes de Oca , and Vicente Suárez refused to surrender. Juan Escutia, determined to keep the Mexican flag out of the hands of the Americans, wrapped himself in it and plunged off the walls and to his death. Thus began the celebration of the Niños Héroes, which has been celebrated on every September 13th since.

"On February 18, 2029, Old Reckoning, the Mexican Coast Guard seized a Chinese long-line boat that had been shark fishing in Mexican waters. Shark-finning had been banned by an international treaty, and the Mexican Coast Guard was within its rights to seize the boat, which was towed to Isla Clarión where a small garrison of the *Fuerza de Infantería de Marina* were stationed. The 14 Marines, commanded by Lieutenant (Junior Grade) Michael Suarez, were given the task of holding the Chinese ship until its disposition could be decided," the CO continued in his deep, stentorious voice.

"The Chinese Navy had been flexing its muscle in the Pacific Ocean, and the decision was made to free the fishing boat. The *Heifei*, a destroyer, was dispatched to Isla Clarión, arriving on February 20, where the ships commanding officer demanded that Lt(jg) Suarez turn over the shark fishing boat. Lt(jg) Suarez refused. His orders were to hold the boat, and that is what he was going to do.

"The Marines were armed with M2 carbines and one Dodge Ram with a mounted M2 Browing .50 cal machine gun. The Chinese had 250 sailors and all the weaponry available to a destroyer.

"When the Marines refused to release the fishing boat, the Chinese captain sent over two boarding parties. Four Marines— Oscar Fuentes, Rodrigio Alicante, Diana Sandoval, and Maria Pérez— were onboard the boat, and they beat back the attempt, losing both Sandoval and Alicante in the fight. Lt(jg) Suarez, realizing that the Chinese would try again, quickly took off the fishing crew and locked them in the Marine barracks.

"The Chinese captain did try again, twice more, and both times the assaults were forced back, thanks to Petty Officer Nakumura on the Browning. Then the *Heifei's* 5 incher opened up, and Nakumura was killed and the Browning destroyed.

"The nearest reinforcements were on Isla Socorro, 314 kilometers to the east, and the Marines knew they could not hold out long enough. Yet they still refused to surrender. With the *Heifei* shelling their positions, the Chinese sailors boarded the fishing boat and steamed it out of the harbor.

"Lt(jg) Suarez reported the developments one last time as the *Heifei* moved to within 500 meters of the shore and commenced shelling the station. There is no record after that of who fell in what order. The last transmission from the Marines was a single "*¿Mi bandera? ¡jamás!*" made by Lt(jg) Suarez. As we know, this means "My flag? Never!" in Standard.

"What we do know was that all 14 Marines died defending their homeland. The Chinese casualties were not known, although there is evidence that some of the fishermen were killed in the *Heifei's* shelling.

"Thirteen of the Marines were found where they had fallen. It took two days, but the body of Lt(jg) Suarez was found by divers in the harbor, the Mexican flag stuffed inside his uniform blouse. He had been wounded several times, but just as Juan Escuita had done 182 years prior, he had leapt to his death rather than let the enemy capture the flag.

"His last words became the new motto of the *de Infantería de Marina,* and upon the formation of the United Federation Marine Corps, First Battalion, Eleventh Marines, the *"Tiburónes,"* inherited their proud tradition.

So, please, honored guests, ladies and gentlemen, give three cheers, in the Marine Corps style of "Oorah!" for the 14 Mexican Marines of the Isla Clarión garrison and all subsequent Marines and sailors who have served in the battalion."

As he raised his fist into the air, every voice was lifted in "Ooh-rah, ooh-rah, ooh-rah!"

Immediately the crowd broke out into applause. Ryck was sure they all knew the story, but hearing it like this gave it a deeper sense of history. Ryck had served in four battalions, many with a more storied history than 1/11, but he was choked up as he applauded. There was no direct connection, of course, between the Mexican Marine Corps and the battalion, but there absolutely was an emotional connection, and it would be the battalion's job, for however long it was in existence, to keep the memory of Marines such as Lt(jg) Suarez and his men and women alive.

"Thank you, Lieutenant Colonel uKhiwa for that moving speech. You gave me a tough act to follow," a portly man said as he stepped up to the podium. "My name is Justin Morales, and I'm the governor's cultural assistant. Please, we've got more food coming out, and the bar is now open."

Ryck could see the Staff NCO's move to position themselves among the men. The bar may be open for the civilians, but the sailors and Marines had to wait until the ceremony was over.

"I take great pleasure in presenting our first entertainment, the Chavez Community College Flamenco Dancers!"

"Hey, did you hear that?" Donte asked, punching Ryck in the shoulder.

"Doesn't matter. It's still a Spanish dance," Ryck said as he watched four musicians in costume position themselves in front of the dais.

Six young women in heavy make-up, bright black and red dresses, and slicked back hair strode forward. The musicians started playing, and the ladies started dancing. Despite himself, Ryck was captivated. He didn't know if this really was a flamenco dance or not, but the ladies were doing a very credible job with the intricate steps.

When the dancers stopped to the applause, Ryck thought they were done, but they formed a corridor, and a single dancer in a stunning white dress came to take her position between the two lines. She had very dark, almost obsidian-colored skin and looked very exotic in the white dress and framed by the other, lighter-skinned dancers. After only a few steps, it was obvious why she was the lead dancer, moving gracefully, but with a sense of power as she simply destroyed the dance. As the final strums of the guitars faded away and she slowly bent into a bow, Ryck enthusiastically joined in the applause.

After the dancers came a string of others: a chorale group made up of Federation staffers, an old-fashioned ventriloquist, two ballet dancers, and a small boy doing what was described as a "Mexican hat dance." A children's choir was cute, but not very good, but they were noteworthy because a little girl went to present flowers to the battalion CO and had to be intercepted to give them to the *Inchon's* CO. Ryck could understand the mistake. This was Marine Day, after all, and the captain was in the Navy.

Ryck edged back to the table where a big warming tray of meatballs had been brought out. He was supposed to eat with the VIPs after the ceremony, but the meatballs were delicious. He stabbed two more with a toothpick when the lights went out. Even though he knew what was coming, he felt the goosebumps on his arm.

After ten or fifteen seconds, a spotlight snapped on Sgt Horatio, who was standing perfectly still, one raised hand holding a drumstick. He waited another 20 seconds before he started slowly bringing the arm down, like a mechanical man in a giant Swiss cuckoo clock. At the last second, he flicked his wrist, sending out a single drumbeat reverberating through the hall. After a moment, that drumbeat was answered by another from somewhere back in the darkness.

Sgt Horatio raised his hand, a little quicker this time, and brought it down for another beat. The answering beat followed almost immediately. Sgt Horatio repeated, and this became a 30-second case of dueling drums. With a shift that was hard to catch, suddenly, the two drums were pounding out an intricate beat together. More spotlights snapped on, illuminating 21 Marines standing in a V at the back of the hall.

The beating had begun.

When the Federation Marine Corps was formed from the 48 extant Marine Corps at the time, there had been a competition to see who would form the basis of the new Marine band. Not surprisingly, the US Marine Corps band, made up of who were essentially professional musicians, won the competition—as judged by senior Marine and Navy officers—and became the bulk of the new band. The members would no longer be professional musicians and would come from the ranks, but they would serve alternate tours with the band. "The Chairman's Own" couldn't be complete amateurs, was probably the thinking.

However, the Royal Marine Band, especially the Corps of Drums, caught the attention—and hearts—of the rank and file. Almost immediately, separate Corps of Drums sprang up in almost every unit. They followed Royal Marine traditions, including the leopard skin worn by the members. All corps members were Marines first, drummers second. They were infantry, armor, artillery, support, or whatever and practiced when they could. Rank had no bearing, and they kept up a degree of mystery about themselves. Practices were almost always hidden from public view, and their performance plans might as well have been Corps-wide operation orders stamped TOP SECRET.

Ryck had no idea what the corps had planned, only that it would be stirring.

The 21 Marines in the back started a slow, almost straight-legged march to close the distance with Sgt Horatio. As they beat their drums, each man paused in turn for two beats, drumsticks raised and frozen, before joining back in. Ryck couldn't hear a difference in the sound, but it sure looked good.

The second to last man, just in front of the bass drummer, was Major Tschen, the battalion XO. He was the second senior Marine in the battalion, but in the Corps of Drums, he was just another drummer.

The Marines married up, and Sgt Horatio slipped into his position within the group. For the next ten minutes, the 22 Marines moved through a series of intricate maneuvers, never stopping their drums. When the two bass drummers came to the front and somehow performed a duet that would put a side drummer to shame, the crowd erupted into cheers.

Ryck was caught up, and he thought he could feel his heart beat in time with the corps. He'd been at many beatings over the years, but they never failed to move him.

Too soon, the Corps of Drums went into their finale, the crescendo rising as they moved like Dervishes, sure to crash into each other, but never doing so. The crowd was calling out and cheering, but the drums' pounding beat drowned the crowd out.

Just when Ryck thought their drumsticks surely had to burst apart, they stopped dead, one stick raised, the other on their drum. Ryck shouted himself hoarse as he cheered. He had the rhythm of a drunk with one leg, so there was never a hope that he could be in a corps, but even listening, he felt that he was part of them, that they had somehow invaded his body and taken him over.

The drummers stood like statues, not moving. The applause started to die out, and Ryck took a look back. The Navy shore patrol was motioning to the civilian stewards to start uncovering the booze. With his throat raw, Ryck started to edge his way to the tables, anxious to be one of the first in line as soon as the governor declared the ceremony over.

A huge crash made him jump—not startle, but actually jump. He spun around to a sight that at first, just didn't register. Four PICS Marines had entered the hall. Around each one was an enormous leopard skin—Ryck didn't realize fabricators could make skins so large—and under each PICS' left arm hung a huge kettle drum.

The 22 Marines broke their position to beat out a "Forward, march!"

The four PICS Marines started forward, their long legs quickly closing the distance, one of the other drummers keeping a cadence. Within moments, they reached the rest of the drummers, and somehow spun around in unison on one leg, the other leg up in the air and splayed out.

A PICS was an amazing piece of fighting gear: strong, powerful, and fast. But it was not really nimble, and Ryck's mouth dropped open at this display of dexterity. Ryck didn't think he could do it, but right then and there, he vowed he would try as soon as he could.

With the four PICS drummers facing the crowd, they started a booming tattoo that Ryck could feel in his bones. The other drummers moved to form a semi-circle behind them, and their beatings, so powerful before, seemed like that made with child's toys.

Ryck had never seen, had never heard, of PICS in a corps of drums. They were just too unwieldy. They were combat units, not musical units. But then again, all Marines were "combat units."

What amazed Ryck even more was the juxtaposition between the PICS and the other drummers. The normal drummers in the back were crisp and robotic in their movements, mechanical. The four PICS drummers were fluid, more like dancers who had been on the stage earlier. While pounding on their drums, they swayed and moved with the beat. They were the human drummers and the others were the mechanical ones.

This time, when the finale approached, there was no question. The combined pounding of 26 Marines, four of them augmented by their PICS, simply blew the huge hall away. Ryck wasn't sure what he was hearing and what he was feeling. All he knew was that this was the best beating he'd ever attended.

Someone pounded his back, but he was too into the moment to even look to see who it was. He was a Marine. He'd been led in combat, and he'd led men into combat. That's what Marines did. But somehow, this beating, something taken from Marines long past, transcended the "job" of a Marine and touched on the *soul* of a Marine. Just as ancient homo erectus sat with hollowed logs around a campfire, this set off a sympathetic beating in his very DNA. At this very moment, he was not a man who was a Marine; he was the Marine Corps. A small cell in the bigger organism, to be sure, but still, he was the Corps.

The Corps of Drums stopped with a deafening silence—at least that was how it felt—a silence that was almost painful. The cheering erupted once again as the drummers marched out, Sgt Horatio the only one keeping a steady cadence. Up on the dais, the governor was pounding LtCol uKhiwa's back. Ryck knew that the battalion had made an impression on the people of Sierra Dorado.

The *Inchon's* CO, Captain Rotigue, was flushed and smiling as he quit clapping and leaned into the podium mic. "Sailors and Marines, there is nothing I can say after that except the bar is open!"

This was one grubbing amazing beating!

KAKUREGA

Chapter 9

"Another corporate police mission," First Sergeant Hecs grumbled. "We might as well put on company uniforms."

Ryck had to agree. He had taken an oath to protect the Federation, not break up labor strikes.

"Come on, First Sergeant. If the people on Kakurega are rioting, don't you think that is a public threat? And what if PI is burned down or something. You heard the brief. Look how much the company makes. I've seen you munching on Paradise Bars. What are you going to do if you can't get your ice cream?" the XO asked.

"He's got you there, First Sergeant. You take more of those bars out of the chief's mess than anyone I know, and guess who makes them? Cool Swiss is a Propitious Interstellar brand," Sams said with a chuckle.

"So I like my ice cream bars," Hecs said. "Big deal. The point is that our mission is to protect the Federation, not to act like some corporate jimmylegs.[10]"

"I'm with the First Sergeant on this," Ryck interjected. "But ours is not to reason why—"

"Ours is just to get shit on," the first sergeant interrupted.

Ryck involuntarily looked around his small stateroom, packed with his five lieutenants, First Seregeant Hecs, and the gunny. He wouldn't put it past the Navy's political division, or even the FCDC, to have had the stateroom bugged, and he didn't want the conversation to get any further into something actionable.

"Be that as it may, we've got our marching orders. XO, I want you and Gunny to start preparing an equipment and supply list. We could be on the planet for months, maybe even up to the end of our deployment."

---

[10] Jimmylegs: slang for corporate security

"You don't think they'll extend us, do you sir?" 2dLt Gershon Chomsky asked.

Gershon had gotten married just prior to this deployment, and the XO had told Ryck that the young lieutenant was not taking the separation well.

Get used to it, Lieutenant, Ryck thought, but responded with "We don't know. That's a possibility, but I would imagine that if it got to that, another battalion would be relieving us.

"Platoon commanders, I want you to start briefing your men. We need to get them in the proper mindset. This isn't like the *Julianna's Dream*, much less the Trinocular War. The people on this planet are Federation citizens. They are not our enemy. We'll protect ourselves, if need be, but we are not going in to kick ass and take names. The ROEs *will* be followed to the letter. Am I understood?"

There was a chorus of "yes, sirs," in response.

"This is going to be more a show of force than anything else. At least that's what I hope will happen. We need to be prepared for anything, though. I'm not about to lose any Marine to a labor strike."

For a brief moment, he recalled the CO's admonition on being too cautious.

Screw him, he thought. *He's never lost most of his men in combat.*

That wasn't fair, he knew. He still respected the CO, and it wasn't his fault that his units had never been in combat, but Ryck still smarted from the CO's dressing-down. Besides, this was not going to be combat. This was a police action, nothing more, and he'd be damned if he lost a single Marine to it.

Suddenly in a sour mood, he decided to end it at that. The platoon commanders had work to do anyway, and it was time they got on to it.

"That's it. Get you men briefed, then let's get them ready. I want us to look professional when we make our grand entrance. XO, I want that list in three hours. If there's anything else we need from battalion, we've got to get that submitted.

"This may not be the mission we wanted, but we're going to conduct it like Marines. That's going to take every one of you to make it so.

"Let's get cracking. Dismissed."

Chapter 10

The stork swooped down low, and Ryck's stomach rose in his throat. Null-G was easier on him than these atmospheric acrobatics. He wished he was on one of the shuttles used to take his company to their temporary (he hoped) home at the old refinery. But the CO wanted all his enlisted and officers to make a grand entrance over the city. He wanted there to be no question that the Marines had landed, and that meant the MAU's four Storks were to come in from various directions and then meet for a synchronized landing at the city stadium.

Ryck looked out the windows to both keep his mind off of his stomach and to get the lay of the land. The city was like any other industrialized city he'd seen. While it was bigger than his own home town of Williamson, and it was much greener with vegetation, it still wasn't impressive. Generic high rises formed the center of the city, bisected by the River Tay.

Ryck craned his neck to try and look upstream. The refinery was about 15 klicks from the city. He'd seen the photos and holos, of course, but he wanted to see his new home with his own eyes. Unfortunately, the Stork swept to its right and the river swung out of view.

Bravo and Weapons Companies were going to be with the CO at the stadium. They were the point of main effort and would conduct most of the local operations. Charlie was going to be at the refinery, ready to react as needed as well as provide a force on the main route from Tay Station to other cities. Alpha was going to be independent at Dundee.

If Charlie wasn't going to be the point of main effort in the city, he wondered if it might be better to be completely away in Dundee. He wouldn't have the CO breathing down his neck on a daily basis. The point was moot, however. The decision had been made, and the refinery was where he'd be.

John Levin brought the Stork over the wall of the stadium, flaring the bird perfectly at its designated landing spot. Ryck got a glimpse of one of the other Storks flaring in about 40 meters off the port side. It looked like at least these two pilots nailed it, coming in together. Ryck imagined that the other two were synchronized as well.

They didn't rush out as if this was an assault. The Storks shut down, and the Marines took their time to unbuckle and stand up.

Top Forrest stood at the back ramp, waiting for the CO's bird to commence debarking. Ryck wondered if all the choreographing was necessary, but it was not that big of a headache, so he let it slide.

The Top suddenly stepped back and spun one finger in the air. It was go time!

Major Tschen was the senior man on the bird, and he led the rest out and to the right where they had a truncated formation. This was going to be a top-heavy formation as most of the main body was taking the shuttles. Ryck wondered if this plan had been a good idea. If the intent was to impress the natives, then possibly a bunch of officers and senior staff were not the best choice at looking good in formation. A couple of platoons of infantry would fare much better.

It didn't turn out quite a bad as Ryck had thought, but it was still a bit of a gaggle as the Marines moved into formation. Luckily, there was no marching, no pass in review. It was just get into formation behind the CO and his senior staff officers, then wait for the CO to report aboard.

In the first row of spectators' seats, a small entourage awaited the CO. Ryck knew that the Governor and Federation administrator had arrived from Dundee, and with them, the Propitious Interstellar CO would be accepting the report. He kept his eyes forward, but he could see the worthies standing up.

"Battalion, Atten . . . HUT!" the CO shouted out, his voice reverberating nicely within the stadium.

Ryck thought everyone was already at attention.

The CO conducted an about face, then shouted out, "Sir, First Battalion, Eleventh Marines, "The *Tiburónes*," reporting for duty!"

A voice responded, but too softly for Ryck to make out the words. The CO responded with, "Aye-aye, sir." Then after conducting another about face, "Commanders, carry out your orders!"

And that was that. Ryck had to admit that the Storks had probably been a nice touch, but the so-called formation was sort of a joke. The people they were trying to impress (read, to cow them) couldn't even see into the stadium. Holo cams had been recording, of course, but still, they couldn't make emeralds out of farts.

Ryck looked around for Hecs. He and the first sergeant had to catch a ride to the company, and Ryck hoped the brotherhood of senior enlisted had rustled something up.

He saw his first sergeant and started over to meet him when a woman's voice called out, "Captain Lysander, may I have a word with you?"

Jonathan P. Brazee

He turned to see an immaculate woman fitted out with a designer suit. She had a small directional mic on her lapel, and a man with a bulky holo cam trailed her. He kept a smile plastered on his face while he inwardly groaned. The ship's PAO had warned him that his presence within the battalion was not a secret, and the press had already reported his imminent arrival. Ryck had hoped that he might escape media attention, at least for awhile.

First Sergeant Hecs smiled and mouthed out "Better you then me" from over the reporter's tailored shoulder.

Ryck steeled his nerves. This might take awhile.

"Yes, ma'am, how may I help you?" he said, ready to do his duty.

Chapter 11

"So this is our home for the next whatever," Ryck said as he looked around the old refinery.

The refinery had once been used by the early settlers to crack organics from oil and natural gas. When Propitious Interstellar had taken over the planet, the cracking was moved to more efficient company plants. The old refinery, located downstream from Tay Station, was not abandoned. The cleared area so close to the River Tay itself was a good spot to grow the algae that was so vital to a significant percentage of Propitious Interstellar's fabrication. The company's genpatent for its line of algae was for "Blue-99," which Ryck knew only from the brief. Like most people, he gave little thought to the products that came out of the big fabrication companies. As he looked over at the racks and racks of tubes where greedy algae soaked up the sun and fresh water, it was somewhat hard to realize that the company made everything from steaks to cosmetics to chairs from it.

For the hundredth time, he wondered if Charlie had been exiled to this position. Preston's Alpha Company had been sent to Dundee, the planetary capital. Donte's Bravo Company and Jasper Yeoung's Weapon's company were the main forces in Tay Station, the financial and population center of the planet. Charlie, on the other hand, was positioned in this out-of-the-way refinery. Ryck's AOR[11] was larger than any of the other companies', but there was not much there. The main highway between Tay Station and Dundee was his main concern, but other than the refinery, the local park, and a few scattered farms and homes leading to the outskirts of the city, there wasn't much to oppose the company.

Maybe it's better this way, he thought. *This mission sucks, and I don't want to play riot police.*

While Ryck didn't think the mission was in keeping with the Corps' charter, he knew there was precedence. During his own career, he'd been on operations that seemed more in line of keeping internal order than protecting the Federation. And on Ellison, before Ryck was even born, to be sure, the Marines had been used to put down a worker's rebellion.

"I don't know how long we'll be here," Ryck told his staff. "Gunny, let's get the men settled in. Hook up with the PI liaison and

---

[11] AOR: Area of Responsibility

confirm just where we're allowed to set up our barracks. Make sure we've got water and power."

"Roger that, skipper," Sams said as he stepped away, motioning for Sgt Contradari, his police sergeant.

Ryck turned back to the rest of his staff, knowing that Sams would get billeting and logistics squared away. "Jeff, I want your patrol out within 30 minutes. Ephraim, I want your men bedded down. You've got the next patrols in eight hours."

Ryck didn't expect that there would be any security issues out here in the booneys. Even in the cities, there hadn't been much of anything concrete. But Marines did not live to ripe old ages and retirements by being complacent. Ryck had to make sure the area was in fact secure.

"You two," he said, pointing to the other two lieutenants, "The first sergeant's got the duty roster. Until we get a regular rotation set up based on the situation, you two've got security."

Ryck could see the disappointment flicker across 2dLt McAult's face and made a mental note of it. Hog McAult didn't want his Third Platoon to be relegated to standing guard around the camp.

"This is only temporary," he told them. "We'll be getting frags from battalion, I'm sure, and once we have the lay of the land, everyone will be rotated in and out of camp security and whatever other mission comes up.

"Any questions?" he asked. When neither lieutenant had one, he added, "Then let's get going.

"First Sergeant, XO, let's take a little walk around our new home. I want a warm and fuzzy that we know everything, and I mean everything about this place. I don't want any surprises to come up and bite us in the ass."

Chapter 12

The battalion staff watched silently as the company liaison made his way out the hatch. As the door closed, the silence was broken as chairs shifted and they turned to the CO to see what he would say.

LtCol uKhiwa held up his hand to quiet everyone, then said, "So, Captain Ward, two of your Marines damaged one of the company hovers, and that has upset our *hosts*. You should have trained your Marines to get out of the way of hovers quicker. Did you hold jumping-over-moving-hover training? No? I thought not. I am extremely, extremely disappointed with you, Captain. Consider yourself duly chastised, something I am sure has shaken you to your very soul."

Laughter broke out. Propitious Interstellar, the very company they had been sent to protect from virtual hordes of angry rebels, had made it their practice to submit demands for compensation for imagined or even real damage to company property done by the Marines. In this case, a small two-man company hover driven by one of the company senior management had run into two PICS Marines. The Marines had barely been moved, but the hover had been totaled.

Ryck had been the first on the chopping block for one of PI's claims. In order to power up the barracks, he had authorized the re-routing of power transmitters, something he had done only after the company liaison had authorized it. When the bill was presented to the battalion, Ryck had expected the CO to use it as an excuse to ream him, but the CO had gravely listened to the battalion liaison, then shit-canned the demand as soon as the liaison left. The CO had asked him if the re-routing was necessary, Ryck said yes, and that was that. Nothing more was said. Over the next two weeks, this had almost become a routine, and whoever was responsible for the company getting its collective panties in a wedgie would be heartily scolded, much to the amusement of the entire staff. There was now even an unofficial contest between the five company commanders to see who could rack up the highest dollar amount in claims.

Ryck still didn't like the CO. He respected him to an extent, but he didn't like him. But he had to admire how this little act of faux punishment was forming a bond within the officers and senior SNCOs. That was something that Ryck filed away in the back of his mind to use later when and if it became appropriate.

"Well, now that my duty as commanding officer has been fulfilled—uh, Lieutenant Tuapao, make sure you note that in the battalion log," he told the adjutant as an aside, "let's get down to business. Two, what do you have for us?"

First Lieutenant Maurice "Mary" Abd Elmonim, the battalion intel officer, stood up to begin his brief. Ryck settled down and attempted to pay attention. As always, though, he had to wonder how the big S-2[12] had acquired his nickname. Even the CO, who was careful with military etiquette, occasionally resorted to calling him by it.

If Ryck had thought that being out at Camp Joshua, the name Ryck had anointed the old refinery after his brother-in-law, would give him time to act on his own, he was sorely mistaken. Each and every day, he had to make the trip into Tay Station for the battalion staff meetings. The CO demanded his physical presence as well. No conference calls would be accepted without a very valid reason. At least he wasn't Preston. Dundee was too far for a drive, so he had to fly in each morning for the meeting.

And not much was said. He'd heard Mary's brief more than a dozen times now, and it rarely varied. After the first initial problems in Dundee, things had quieted down. There were protests, but these were minor affairs. The company spies kept reporting that people were organizing, but not much had transpired.

Ryck took a quick glance at his watch. The meeting would drag on for another hour or hour-and-a-half. He'd grab a quick bite in the mess hall, which had better food than they had at Camp Joshua, then make the trip back. Say 1630, and he'd be at camp, so 1700 could be his brief. It wasn't lost on him that as much as he thought the constant meetings were a waste of time, as soon as he would be back, he'd have his own meeting with his staff.

The battalion meetings were long and boring, but usually there were several pertinent pieces of information that had to be disseminated. They served a function, Ryck knew. He just wished he could attend via conference call.

Lost in his thoughts, Ryck hadn't realized that Mary had stopped talking about ten minutes too soon given his previous briefs. Master Sergeant Wojik, the comms chief, had come into the meeting and was quietly speaking to the CO. Everyone else in the room had his eyes locked on the two Marines, wondering what was going on.

---

[12] S-2: A designation given the Intell officer. "S" is for a staff officer at the battalion level. "2" is for intel. 1 is for admin, 3 is for operations, 4 is for logistics, 5 is for civil affairs.

The CO glanced at the XO and sergeant major as if he wanted to speak to them alone, but instead, said, "No, pipe it here. I want everyone to see this as I do."

Lieutenant George, the top's[13] boss, tried to catch Wojik's eye, but the master sergeant was keying in something on his PA. Evidently, George was in the dark on whatever this was as well.

"Gentlemen, it seems as if something has just come up. This was just broadcast a few minutes ago, and I'm seeing it for the first time as well," the CO said, nodding at the top to start whatever it was he had to show.

A holo flickered into life over the conference table's platform. This wasn't a true 360-degree holo, but the type recorded by news teams. With all the Marines around the conference table, that would leave the ones in the back looking through the "rear" of the recording, but built in compensators refracted the recording so that each Marine was presented with the head-on view.

What they saw took a moment to register. Some sort of cosplay heroine stood in the middle of the recording. A redhead, she stood tall and had a rather remarkable physique, and the pseudo-military costume left nothing to the imagination. Behind her, in a rumpled bed, a young girl, obviously naked, but with a sheet covering her front, sat, head down. What caught Ryck's attention, however, was the naked, subdued-looking young man just to the cos-play woman's right. Something about the man screamed "Marine."

"Shit, he's mine," Donte whispered, confirming Ryck's fear.

The woman stared into the holo cam and started, "I am a member of the Free Kakurega Militia. We have been formed to protect our rights under our Federation Charter, rights that have been abrogated by Propitious Interstellar Fabrication, Inc. Not only have they broken the charter, but they have brought in Federation Marines to crush our legal right to protest.

"Today, we have stopped one of their Marines, Lance Corporal Thane Regent, from abusing a free citizen of Kakurega."

Donte held up a hand and pointed back down on himself, letting the CO know the Marine was from Bravo Company.

"The Federation Marines have the power here. They killed three of our citizens when they arrived. They are enforcing martial law. And now they take our citizens for their own perverted pleasure."

---

[13] Top: slang for a master sergeant

At the word "killing," a murmur of protest erupted from around the room. Three civilians had died that second day in Dundee, true, but that was hardly the fault of the Marines. Some civ a-hole had decided to make a Molotov Cocktail, filled with who knows what, to throw at a line of Marines. The bottle ignited before he could throw it, engulfing ten of the closely-packed protestors. Preston's Marines managed to get the flames out on seven of them and get them off to medical care, but three people—two men and one woman—were too badly burnt and were killed at the scene. The idiot who made the bomb was among the three killed. Whatever he put in the bottle was wickedly effective and was difficult to put out. The irony was that even if he had thrown it before it ignited, simple flames would have no effect on Marines in PICS.

The woman continued. "It is up to you, people of Kakurega. Will you stand for this? From First Families and all Free Citizens, from employees and indentureds, this is our home, and Propitious Interstellar cannot break the charter as they deem fit.

"If you agree, on this Saturday, at 9:00 AM in the city, we urge all of you to take to the streets. We are not advocating violence. We leave that to the Marines and Propitious Interstellar security forces. But let your voices be heard. Let the Federation know we will not stand for this."

With that, the woman swept one hand back to indicate the naked girl whose sobs were shaking her body. The holocam lingered on her for a few moments before the recording cut out. The assembled staff broke out into talk, and the CO had to hold his hand up for silence.

"Captain Ward, prepare your men. I want Regent located, and we will recover him with whatever force is required. Sergeant Major, I want everything on this Marine. Lieutenant Commander Pillbury," he said to the Navy staff judge advocate attached to the battalion from the *Inchon*, "please brief Captain Rotigue and prepare for a General Court Martial if this Marine was abusing that girl. XO, the company and the government are going to be screaming about this. Calm them down and tell them we are acting. Principal staff, stay put. I want a course of action in 15 minutes. The rest of you, you're dismissed. You've got things to do."

Ryck jumped up and rushed out the door, signaling Private Çağlar on his PA to get the hover running. He had to get back to Camp Joshua before everything exploded.

Chapter 13

The crowd was large, and its mood was aggressive. Company spies reported that the camcording of the "Red Athena," as she was being called, had galvanized the population against both the company and the Marines. Flash-surveys showed a majority of the population now resented the Marines' presence and wanted them off the planet.

Lance Corporal Regent had been guilty of nothing more than falling in love. Interviews with the so-called victim confirmed that. He had broken regulations by sneaking out for his nooner, but that did not demand a formal court martial. He was trotted out in front of the camcorders after numerous rehearsals by the Navy, Marines, and Propitious Interstellar handlers, but unfortunately, the young Miss Osterson refused to go on cam, afraid for her family's safety. Ryck thought that without her testimony, the official rebuttal fell flat, but CAPT Rotigue, as the senior military in system, backed by the Federation governor, refused to allow the company to try and force the girl to speak. Ryck thought that was the right decision.

LCpl Regent was given restriction for a month for sneaking out, but nothing that would reflect on his record. Donte told Ryck that the young Marine had gained a sort of cult status among the other Marines for actually snaring an attractive local sparrow.

Ryck stood motionless in his PICS behind the lines of Marines, who were in turn behind a line of company security personnel. With the spies reporting that Camp Joshua was off the radar screens for the moment, the CO had ordered Ryck to attach two of his platoons to Bravo Company for the demonstration. Ryck left the XO in charge of the camp and accompanied his men. As the Bravo commander, Donte had nominal tactical control over Ryck's two platoons and Jasper's three weapons sections, but Ryck was not going to lose all control over his men. Besides, it was not as if Donte was in real command. If anyone thought the CO was going to stand back during any confrontation, then he was pretty naive.

Ryck wondered if the CO had made a mistake. If Ryck was to augment any company, perhaps Alpha, all alone in Dundee, would have been a more logical choice. Reports had just arrived that there had already been a confrontation in the planetary capital with some deaths reported among the protestors.

Ryck had his sensors on their highest resolutions as he scanned for any threat. If anything did threatened his Marines, he was going to act immediately regardless of the tactical chain of command. He'd apologize later rather than asking for permission first.

The crowd had a cheerleader sort, gallivanting around in front, his voice booming out as he changed the chants. The current one was "Red Athena, Red Athena!" and the crowd seemed to be enthusiastically behind it.

Exactly at 8:15, the cheerleader announced that it was time for the Propitious Interstellar anthem. The crowd booed, but as the music started playing, the crowd joined in with the most awful screeching and off-key singing Ryck had ever heard. He was glad he was in his PICS: it wouldn't be too appropriate for a Marine captain to be spotted laughing as the protestors tweaked the company's nose.

This rally was being staged by the WRP, the Workers' Rights Party, and Ryck was curious to see who would be leading it. The chairman of the party was actually a company spy. That secret had obviously not been as closely kept as the company had thought because this spy had been murdered the night before. Another man stepped up to the speaker's platform. Ryck didn't recognize him, but he knew surveillance cams would be sending his image to the company data banks, and they would have the man identified within seconds.

Ryck didn't like the fact that the Marines were working with a corporate security division, but the fact was that they had the best capabilities on the planet. If it took working with the devil to keep his Marines out of harm's way, well, that was a price he was willing to pay.

The speaker gave way to a camcording of Henry Jugos, the civil rights gadfly who was the bane of Federation companies. Ryck had listened to the man before, and while he usually made some good points, Ryck thought his methods were misguided. He seemed more inclined to listen to his voice than to get anything actually done. On Gallahad 3, Pelican Systems had actually come to an initial agreement with its work force until Jugos had arrived to throw sand in the gears. The agreement was rescinded, and the subsequent negotiations broke down as Jugos pushed for more than the company thought reasonable. As a result, Pelican pulled off the planet, costing over 100,000 jobs.

A local comedian was up next, but Ryck only figured that out from his outlandish clothes and the laughter of the crowd. He wasn't paying attention to the actual words as he scanned the area.

Ryck knew he should be further back with his Marines, who were the second line of defense if the crowd stormed the company headquarters. But from back there, he'd have to ask to slave into Bravo Company Marines' displays. He wanted his own where he could control what he was doing. So along with Private Çağlar, who had become his defacto bat boy,[14] he had edged up until he was behind one of Donte's platoons.

Çağlar pulled on Ryck's arm, directing his attention to the rear. Ryck had been so focused on what was going on in the front that he'd forgotten the entire battle sphere, a potentially deadly mistake in an actual battle and a very bad habit into which to fall. Luckily, this time, there was no threat in back of him but rather a big Propitious Interstellar T2000 forklift moving forward. Ryck stepped aside as it moved up to stop right behind the front line of Marines.

A civilian climbed on top of the forks, and the operator lifted him up above the Marines.

Ryck focused on the man and blinked twice. His AI identified the man as Dr. Keller, the Tay Station deputy mayor.

"People of Tay Station, this gathering is illegal and you are ordered to withdraw," he said over his bullhorn. "Despite no permits being issued, we have used patience as a show of good will. That good will has been exhausted, so as law abiding citizens, you must go home.

"If you have reasonable grievances, you may come down to the city offices during normal working hours and file them.

"As a member of the city council, I am issuing the order to cease and desist as per City Proclamation 19.815.3062, the previously declared imposition of martial law. Failure to do so can result in arrest and imprisonment for a period of no more than ten years."

Ryck's AI caught something arching up out of the crowd, and he tensed for a moment as the round, red object sailed from the crowd and arched over to strike the deputy mayor on his thigh. It was a tomato, and it had been ripe enough to splatter, covering him in juice and seeds. The crowd roared with laughter and the deputy mayor hurriedly motioned for the forklift operator to lower him.

"Second Platoon, prepare to advance," was passed over the tactical net.

"Jeff, get ready," Ryck passed to his First Platoon leader.

First platoon was the Bravo Company's Second Platoon's back-up, and Ryck wanted them ready to move in an instant if needed.

---

[14] Bat Boy: a term of an all-around assistant to an officer or senior SNCO.

The crowd's laughter broke off and faded to nothing as the company security forces, who had been lining B Street, split in the middle of the line and marched smartly to each side of the street, leaving the center open. A few people moved forward as if to enter the opening the jacks had made.

"Advance and hold," the command came over the net, and the Bravo Marines started marching forward.

All three ranks of Marines passed through the jimmylegs and formed up in front of the crowd, looking menacing. Some of the people tried to back up, but with many more behind them, the press of the crowd kept them locked in place.

"This is your last warning. Leave the square now and return to your homes or you will be forcibly evicted," an amplified voice reverberated over the crowd.

"Move your men up," Ryck ordered Jeff on the P2P, "but stop on my position. Do not enter the square."

"Roger that, sir," his platoon commander replied.

Ryck focused on what was happening in front of him at the same time as he watched First Platoon's icons on his display start moving up from behind him.

The crowd was not evacuating the square, but Ryck didn't think the people could. There were just too many people packed in it. He started to report that back to the Three[15] when the order came over the net.

"Bravo-Two, move to Phase Line Lilac," came over the command circuit.

In battle, phase lines were used to control movement and area. This was not a contested battle over vast tracts of land, and Ryck thought the use of the term "phase line" was a little grandiose for what was merely the far side of the square. But military habits died hard, so "Phase Line Lilac" it was.

The PICS Marines started moving forward. As a sergeant, Ryck had led his Marines forward against a crowd on Alexander to evacuate a Legion negotiating team, and he knew how effective a line of PICS Marines could be. There was nothing a crowd without heavy weapons could do to stop them.

In this case, the people in the front could not move out of the way fast enough as those in the back realized what was happening too late. It takes time to overcome inertia, and as those in the rear turned to flee, many of the people in the front were stuck in front of the advancing Marines.

---

[15] Three: the S-3, the Operations Officer

With nowhere to go, quite a few were trampled by the Marines, only to have eager jimmylegs pounce on their broken bodies as the Marines passed over them. Those still moving bore the brunt of the jimmylegs' batons.

Ryck steeled himself as he witnessed that. These people were out of the fight, if a fight it even was. There was no reason to beat them. Part of him wanted to march forward and take the batons out of the security forces' hands and break them in two, but he held his position. His mission was to wait and react only when ordered to.

Within a few minutes, the Marines were at Lilac. Ryck thought they had slowed down as the people offered no resistance, but he was not privy to what might have been passed on a Bravo Company P2P. Except for a dozen or more broken bodies littering the square, it was empty of protestors. The jimmylegs scurried around, collecting the wounded. At least Ryck hoped they were only wounded. He hoped no one had died here this morning.

He wasn't supposed to worry about that, he knew. He was a Marine, and he followed orders, orders that went up the chain of command all the way to the Federation Council. It was the duty to which he had sworn to uphold.

Still, these people had not been a threat. They were Federation citizens, too, people he was sworn to protect. What was a Marine supposed to do when there seemed to be a conflict in his sworn duties?

Ryck felt dirty. He was glad that no Charlie Marine had actually gotten involved—yet. Hog and his Third Platoon were with Jasper's Weapon's Company, and Ryck didn't know if they were facing anyone.

Ryck was suddenly happy that he'd been exiled to Camp Joshua. No one had bothered his Marines there. Routine patrols might not be exciting, but they were good enough until they were recalled off this grubbing planet.

Chapter 14

Ryck and the first sergeant were making the rounds. He tried to stay out of the barracks, preferring to leave those areas to the SNCOs, but frankly, he was bored. This whole mission sucked hind tit, but if the battalion was going to sit on this cesspit, he wished that they'd do something.

He was glad they hadn't really gotten involved with the latest protest in Tay Station, but the routine patrols along Route 2, along the river, and at Ledges Park were getting old pretty quick. They'd encountered a big fat zero as far as any trouble. That was good, of course. No trouble meant all his Marines were safe. But Marines did not have sitting on their ass in their DNA. Marines were meant to do things, to be aggressive, to take it to the enemy.

Ryck wasn't even involved with the day-to-day running of the company. Because of the daily briefings, most of that had been ceded to the XO and the first sergeant. Today, however, there was a top-level meeting with the Federation governor and company CEO, and that was way above Ryck's pay-grade, so he had a day off. He was going to use it to get out among the Marines.

"We're getting better bedding in here, compliments of Gunny Coudry," Hecs was saying as they entered the barracks.

Gunny Coudry worked in the armory, but he was a scavenger extraordinaire. It seemed he could get anything.

"Attention on deck!" a voice called out as the two came into sight of the Marines in the squadbay.

Ryck was about to put them at ease until he realized that about a dozen of them were gathered around a rack, most looking guilty. He held off and walked up to them. Several looked about ready to pass out or go into seizures.

"How are we doing today, Marines," he asked, trying to see beyond them.

He received a chorus or "Fine, sirs," and "Ooh-rahs."

He put one hand up against Corporal Sympington's shoulder and gently pushed him aside from where he was blocking Ryck's view of the rack. Ryck thought Sympington rolled his eyes ever-so-slightly, but he did not resist.

On the rack was a simple Sanyo film screen. The screen could be folded up or rolled into a small package, then unfolded when it was needed. With a simple press of the power button, it got rigid and became a display screen for flat vids, photos, documents, or whatever.

Ryck picked it up, then almost dropped it. The screen displayed a woman, obviously naked. Only, not everything was shown. The screen had been broken into 320 small sections, and almost half of them had been filled in. This deployment was scheduled for 320 days. This was a shortimer's calendar.

Most of the borders of the pic had been filled in, as had most of the model's face. Enough of her arms and legs had been filled in so give Ryck an idea of what was still hidden. Number 320, the last small section to be filled in was strategically placed over the model's most private part.

"Whose is this?" Ryck asked.

"Uh, mine, sir," Cpl Sympington managed to get out.

"And who is the young lady?"

Sympington hesitated, and Hecs had to prompt him to answer his company commander.

"My wife, sir," he blurted out, face red.

Ryck swallowed hard and placed the screen back on the rack. Pornography of any kind was expressly forbidden in the Corps. But soldiers going back to the Babylonians had probably kept little mementoes of what, or rather who, they were fighting for.

"Well, Corporal, I'm not so sure that this is really a group calendar. Why don't you put this back in your seabag and fill it in when you have a bit more privacy," Ryck offered.

"Yes, sir! Aye-aye, sir!" Sympington shouted, grabbing the screen and powering it down.

Ryck turned around, and with Hecs beside him, walked out of the squadbay.

"They're pretty hard up for excitement, aren't they?" Ryck said as they left.

"Not much to do here," Hecs said. "The patrols are it, and they're getting pretty routine."

"Routine isn't a word I want to hear about Marines on patrol. We need a break, something to shake it up," Ryck said.

"Battleball?" Hecs offered.

"My thoughts exactly, First Sergeant. My thoughts exactly. Say on Sunday? Not full platoons, but ten-man teams."

"I'll take care of it," Hecs said.

As they made their way back to the CP, Ryck asked, "Do you think I did the right thing with that?"

"Ah, if you nailed Sympington, you'd have to nail half of the company, I'm thinking. I dare say even some of the senior Marines might be guilty of a little flesh collection. Sympington is no different, except that he shouldn't be letting his Marines partake in it. I'll have Sergeant Rios talk to him about it."

The first sergeant was right. Ryck knew others had their little reminders of home, starting right at the top. The big difference was that Hannah's pic, with the same strategic placement for number 320, was 10-level password protected on his PA. Ryck's shortimer's calendar was for his eyes only!

Chapter 15

When Ryck had set Sunday for the company battleball tournament, he'd forgotten about A-Day, Adjustment Day. Officially, everything in the Federation went by Greenwich Mean Time back on Earth. And while most inhabited worlds in the Federation were within spitting distance of a 24-hour rotation, none were exact. Small doses of synthetic hormones kept people attuned to their planet's particular diurnal cycle, but nothing was going to force a planet to match the Earth's rotation exactly. So, depending on each planet's rotation, a day was either added or subtracted as required from the calendar as a rough way of keeping the planets in synch. For Kakurega, that meant adding an A-Day every 23 planet days or so. An A-Day was usually a day of rest on most planets, so the battleball tourney was moved to that day. Sams had arranged for a BBQ with the best steaks and links Propitious Interstellar manufactured, and somehow, he'd even put together cheerleaders from two Tay Station universities.

The patrols were still out, but for the bulk of the company, this was going to be a day to let off some steam. And Marines being Marines, battleball was the perfect way to do that.

Battleball's origins were somewhat lost in time. Some said it came from rugby, some from American football, some from world football. The first recorded game was shortly after the Federation was formed. A battalion made up from mostly ex-British Royal Marines played a battalion formed up from mostly Chinese Marines. Almost immediately, the game caught on and became part of the new Corps' DNA.

The allure in the game was probably in its simplicity. Teams lined up across either end of the playing field. A large, three-meter inflatable ball was placed in the middle. At the ref's whistle, both teams tried to push the ball into the opponent's goal line. That was about it. Rules were minimal. If the ball went out of bounds, play stopped until the ref brought the ball back in and commenced play. There was no striking of another player. Other rules were up to the ref to enforce as he saw fit.

The game was a game of brute force. Oh, there was always someone pushing some strategy or the other, but basically, it was which team was stronger and more aggressive. This was the penultimate Marine game.

Games could be and often were brutal, and regen was always a possibility for some players. Several times, the top brass had tried to ban the game, and General Fitch, the 13th Commandant actually did ban it—until General Maracopa, the 14th Commandant and a huge fan and player in his day, brought it back.

Ryck wanted his men to shake off the complacency, and the game was only one part of the day's activities. But he had to remember that they were on combat footing, even if there hadn't been any combat. He could handle a couple of sprained ankles or cut lips, but massive amounts of injured Marines needing regen could not only land him in trouble, but more importantly, diminish the company's ability to perform a required mission. So he limited the size of the teams to ten men and drafted Bravo's gunny, Dove "PICS" McTanish, to ref. Dove was 2.3 meters of rock-solid Marine. No one was going to argue with Gunny PICS, and the gunny understood that he was to keep the violence to a minimum.

The mood was pretty good before the first game between First and Second even started. Sams was in fine form with an old-fashioned chef's hat he'd acquired from God knows where. He was supervising the firing of the hickoryoak, something he'd managed to get donated by Propitious Interstellar. The smoke wafting over the playing field had gotten Ryck's stomach churning. As the senior Marine at the camp, however, he would be the last one fed, so he tried to banish the thoughts of those charbroiled steaks from his mind.

Ryck didn't know what was taking more of Sams' attention: the grill or the cheerleaders. No, strike that. This was Sams, after all. The cheerleaders. A good half-a-dozen of them were gathered around him as he explained, or probably bullshitted them, about how to grill a perfect steak.

At 1100, Gunny PICS pushed the battleball to the center of the field and called the first two teams to their places. Without any stands, Marines surrounded the sidelines and climbed onto the roofs of the surrounding buildings. The gunny blew his whistle, and the tournament was on.

With each platoon limited to only ten men, Ryck thought the biggest and strongest men from each platoon would have been selected. He was surprised, then, that Second Platoon had LCPL Summers on the team. Taking nothing from Summers, but he was barely 1.6 meters and maybe 60 kgs soaking wet. Lt Chomsky's selection of the Marine became clearer when Summers immediately locked his sights on Jeff and tackled the big lieutenant, much to the delight of the watching Marines. Each time Jeff struggled to his feet, pushing the smaller Marine away, Summers was back in the attack, grabbing and hauling Jeff to the deck.

Without their leader being able to lead, First Platoon suffered a surprising defeat, falling to Second 10-6. After the battleball was pushed over the goal for the tenth time, the entire Second Platoon rushed the field and lofted the battered, exhausted, but smiling Summers on their shoulders.

The steaks started coming out after the first game, and Ryck tried not to stare. Sams had put together a pretty big grill, and he had three assistants, but he could only get out so many steaks at a time, and while the PI links were pretty good, he knew, Ryck wanted beef!

Around the field, the cheerleaders were getting more than their fair share of attention from the men. It was like a pack of orca surrounding the mackerel. Battleball, as simple as it was, seemed to be beyond the cheerleaders as they hadn't done much cheering during the first game, but the Marines didn't seem to mind that as they tried to chat them up. Some evidently thought the quickest way into their panties was through the girls' stomachs as there was a never-ending line of Marines bringing food to them.

"Let's keep an eye on that," he told Hecs as the first sergeant walked up sipping on a Bolt Cola. "We don't want another LCPL Regent here."

The first sergeant nodded and held out the Bolt to Ryck, who grimaced and shook his head. Aside from the fact that Bolt was sickly sweet, he wasn't about to swap spit with him. Ryck really wanted a tried-and-true Coke, but with Propitious Interstellar making Bolt, that is what they had, along with their even sweeter Grab-On and Utopia.

Grab-On? What vile programmer came up with that shit? Ryck wondered.

Gunny PICS called together the next two platoons and started the second game. This was a much closer-fought affair. Lt McAult was the central cog for Third, and SSgt Menlo Nomchaikut, the Heavy Gun Section leader, essentially ran the game for Weapons. The score was tied at six apiece when PFC Quita went down, almost immediately followed by Lt Davidson. Down eight men to ten, Weapons scored only one more goal before Third reached ten.

Ryck glanced back at the grill. Smoke was pouring up into the crystal clear air, forming a nice plume that rose 40 meters high. The XO was standing by, watching the grill like an osprey over a quiet lake. Ryck had to smile.

Get used to it, son, he thought. *The men always come first.*

There was a lull in the action as Third needed a break. Over on the other side of the field, Chomsky was getting his men ready, and once again, he surprised Ryck. Instead of using the same Marines, an entirely new group was getting ready. The lieutenant was spreading the wealth. It might not get him the win, but it was in keeping with Ryck's intention of breaking the monotony. Ryck wished he'd thought of that earlier and made it a requirement.

Beside Ryck, several members of Third's team were sitting on the ground, sucking air. They needed more time, and Ryck wondered if bringing in fresh players might have a strategic basis. Was Chomsky that calculating?

With the delay, Marines were losing interest, especially those who'd already been served. They were gathering in small groups to shoot the shit. The mood was still good, but Ryck didn't want to lose them just yet.

"Lieutenant de Madre!" he yelled out to Jeff at the spur of the moment. "You up for a challenge?"

"Sir?"

"I asked, are you up for a challenge? Or are your Marines too tired?"

"What, sir, against Weapons?" Sure, we're up, aren't we?" he asked his men who cheered back at him.

"Not Weapons. Headquarters."

"Sir? Headquarters?" he asked, sounding slightly confused.

Ryck understood why. Headquarters didn't even have ten Marines total. With the XO, the first sergeant, the gunny, the police sergeant, the comms chief, and the admin chief—and Ryck—that was seven Marines, three short of a team. Doc Kitoma and Corporal K'Nata were with the headquarters, but Kitoma was the official corpsman for the tourney, so he was off-limits, and K'Nata was back at battalion entering PDPs.[16]

He understood it, but pretended not to as he asked, "What, you're afraid of Headquarters?"

That brought a roar from the rest of the company.

Jeff had no other response possible but, "Bring it on, sir!"

"First Sergeant, get the headquarters together. That's seven of us."

"Thanks for the opportunity, oh captain of mine," Hecs said sarcastically. "Just as the SNCOs are getting their steaks, too."

"Oh, you love it. Admit it," Ryck said.

"Well, maybe I do, but you could have given my old bones a warning," he grumbled as he moved off to gather the others.

"Private Çağlar, where are you?" Ryck shouted out.

---

[16] PDP: Personnel Data Points

After a few moments, he heard a "Here, sir!" from the other side of the field.

"You're my driver, so I've drafted you into headquarters. Get your ass over here!"

Çağlar made his appearance as he started to run across the field accompanied by coughs that thinly disguised the "Brown-noser," "Captain's bitch," and "ass-kisser" that were being yelled at him.

"Corporal Patrick! I see you over there trying to make time with our guests," Ryck shouted to the Gun Team leader, who'd been one of the more active Marines attempting to make nice with the cheerleaders. "You're attached from Weapons Company, and that makes you part of Headquarters, so get your PFC and get your asses over here, too!"

Patrick was the team leader for the M54 Field Gun that had been attached to Charlie from Weapons Company. He'd been working out of Ephraim Davidson's Weapons Platoon, but Ryck used his command prerogative to make the two Marines part of Headquarters for the game.

There were more hoots and hollers that intensified when one of the cheerleaders reached out and briefly took his hand as he pulled away to come join Ryck and the rest of Headquarters. Sams was the last to arrive, his chef hat still on. Battleball was played in "utes and boots," and old phrase that meant the utility trousers, combat boots, and t-shirt, and Sams frankly looked ridiculous with the towering chef's hat on, but that was Sams. Ryck just shook his head and addressed his team.

"Sorry for the lack of preparation, but we've all played before. We know the drill. Let's kick some First ass, OK?"

"Uh, have you looked over there, Skipper?" the first sergeant asked. "I'm guessing they outweigh us by 15 kg apiece, and they can't average over 20 years old. Even with our ringers here," he continued, pointing at Çağlar, Patrick, and PFC Yarby, the M54 A-gunner, "I'd say they're six years younger than us. They're going to be full of kick-ass, so I think we need to be crafty sons-of-bitches and use our vast experience."

The first sergeant had the crux of the matter. Jeff had been able to choose the ten best players in his platoon to face Headquarters. Ryck had to make do with what he had. To tilt the odds further against them, Ryck, Hecs, and Sams were all in their 30's, and the others were mostly older than the other team as well.

"Speak for yourself, old man. I'm reckoning I'm more than a match for any of those young boys," Ryck said, going into a flex pose, which elicited a roar from the Marines who were gathering on the sidelines to watch.

Ryck had participated in normal PT before, but this was the first time the Marines in the company would see him in this type of activity, and he knew they would be evaluating him. Ryck wondered if this was a mistake. Having a good showing would stand him in good stead in the company, but if he were embarrassed, that could plummet his credibility.

Too late now, he thought as Gunny PICS pointed to each end of the field.

Before the two teams were in place, someone shouted out "Incoming Air!" Ryck looked up to see a Stork arriving. The big bird circled the field, which was also the LZ for Camp Joshua.

"Clear the LZ!" Sams shouted as he ran back and forth, motioning for everyone to move back.

Who the grubbing hell? Ryck wondered. *We don't have anything scheduled.*

The Stork flared and landed, and Ryck's heart fell when the CO and sergeant major stepped out.

What now?

Ryck rushed up to the CO as the Stork lifted off. "Sir! I wasn't expecting you. Can I help you?"

He felt self-conscious in his utes and boots, sure that the CO wasn't going to like that.

"Carry on, Captain. The sergeant major told me about your field day here, so we thought we'd come take a look. You do have all your patrols out and security manned, correct?"

"Yes, sir, we do," he assured the CO.

"And I take it you are about to play yourself?"

Ryck wasn't sure if there was a note of displeasure in the CO's voice or not, but he was committed, and he was standing there in his utes and boots. Hard to deny that.

"Yes, sir, Headquarters is getting in one game."

"Well, unless Gunnery Sergeant Samuelson is the only chef, perhaps the sergeant major and I can get a steak and watch?"

"Certainly, sir." Ryck looked around and spotted Chomsky's platoon sergeant. "Staff Sergeant Kondo, please have someone rustle up the CO and the sergeant major a plate."

Gunny PICS was not going to let the CO's presence keep him from his sacred duty, and he was impatiently motioning for both teams to get in position.

"Don't let me keep you, Captain. Gunnery Sergeant McTanish is ready to kick this off."

Ryck ran to his team's goal line, where Hecs asked, "Anything up with that?"

Ryck just shrugged his shoulders. He couldn't change anything, so he might as well enjoy the game. Gunny PICS blew the whistle, and Ryck joined the mad rush to get to the battleball first.

It had been a number of years since Ryck had played, and in his rush to be first, he launched himself at the ball, hitting it a little high just as several Marines from First hit it on the other side. For every action, there is an opposite and equal reaction, and Ryck's reaction was to get bounced backward up in the air to land on his ass three meters back. He could hear the roar of the crowd as he scrambled back up—only to be taken down hard, his breath knocked out of him.

"Sorry 'bout that, sir," a ginning Sergeant Joab Ling said, looking down at him.

"Grubbing hell, Ling," Ryck said to one of his long-time Marines. "*Et tu?*"

"All's fair in love and war—and *Battleball!*" Ling shouted as he rushed to join the rest of his team pushing the ball.

At least Ling wasn't going to birddog Ryck, à la Summers and Jeff. Ryck struggled back to his feet again, then ran to try and join the defense. It was too late. The big ball had momentum, and within a minute, it was First: 1, Headquarters: 0.

The next score went to Headquarters. The ball had bounced out to the side, and Sams, Çağlar, and Sergeant Singh, the admin chief were in position to take advantage of it, pushing the ball on a breakaway down the sidelines. Two Marines from First converged on them, but when Sams' chef hat began to slip down, and he reached up to right it, the two First Platoon Marines couldn't resist and took him down, letting the other two score.

"Still got it!" Sams shouted as he got up, hat securely in place.

Ryck was in on one score, and more importantly, he took Ling down hard, eliciting hoots from the crowd. With the score 4 to 3 in favor of First, Singh, quickly followed by Yarby, went down to injuries. Neither was serious, but this was not do-or-die, so both Marines left the game. With no one else to pull, Headquarters had to go on short-handed. Within two minutes, the score was 6 to 3. It was going to be a blow-out.

As Gunny PICS was setting up the battleball again, the CO walked out on the field and approached him.

Is he going to call the game? Ryck wondered.

Sure, they were getting trashed, but Marines don't quit. Ryck started to get angry. This was not the message to send.

Jonathan P. Brazee

The CO walked off the field, but Gunny PICS didn't blow the whistle. It wasn't until then that Ryck noticed the CO and the sergeant major were taking off their blouses. When the two trotted out to join Headquarters, it became clear. They were going to play.

"I hope you don't mind us joining you. I spoke with Gunny McTanish, and he agreed that as part of the battalion headquarters, we were eligible to join you. If you'll have us, that is."

"Hell yeah!" the XO shouted. "I mean, yes, sir, but it's up to the skipper."

Not really, Ryck thought.

But he said, "Glad to have you with us, sir. And you, Sergeant Major."

Then Gunny PICS blew the whistle, and matters were OBE.[17]

The CO was immediately in motion, and the rest of the team was a half-step behind. LtCol uKhiwa was short and broad-shouldered, and he hit the ball low a split second before a couple of Marines from First reached hit. Hitting it low, the CO managed to launch the big, heavy ball into the air, where it hit Jeff and LCpl Hotchkins in their faces, surprising them and knocking them flat on their backs. The CO didn't stop, trampling Jeff in the chest as he kept the ball moving. The entire headquarters team joined in, and with two men trying to get back up, First couldn't gather themselves, and Headquarters got a quick goal.

The Marines on the sidelines were going crazy. Several ran out on the field and fell to their backs in fake swoons as Gunny PICS screamed at them to get off the field.

"Sir, that was awesome!" Ryck shouted, pounding on the CO's back.

"That's how you get it done, Captain," the CO said, a grin running ear-to-ear and a trickle of blood running from his nose.

He wiped the blood with his hand and seemed to be surprised to see it. He probably hadn't known he'd been hit, Ryck thought. When the CO looked at the Marines close to him, he smiled and made a show of licking the blood off of his hand. Which, of course, drove the on-looking Marines wild again.

The rest of the game was more even, both teams trading goals. Ryck got one breakaway, and he leveled Ling again, putting him one up on the sergeant. The CO got zeroed a couple of times, but he gave more than he received. Jeff got up limping after one nasty hit from him, and Ryck knew he would be going to Doc for some nanos that evening.

---

[17] OBE: Overcome By Events

84

With the score tied at nine-all, the final push broke down into a long, drawn-out exhibition of brute force. Ryck was exhausted as he tried to hold back the inexorable force that pushed them back, step-by-step. The CO was beside him, his lungs heaving like bellows. Several times, the XO went low, under the ball, using his body as an obstacle to make the opposing Marines stumble. This bought them time, but the young bodies on the other side were just too much for them. Ryck wanted to win badly, but when Gunny PICS blew the whistle signaling a score, he was almost relieved.

Both teams lined up for the handshake. As each team filed past each other, Ryck pulled in Sgt Ling.

"Don't think I'm going to forget that cheap shot there, Sergeant of Marines," he said into Ling's ear.

"Oh, shout it loud, sir, I think you more than got me back," Ling said with a rueful laugh.

Ryck pounded Ling on the shoulder, and they filed past each other. The crowd clapped through the handshakes, and as the exhausted warriors reached the sidelines, Marines stood there with full plates to give to them. Ryck needed a few moments to catch his breath, but the steak did look delicious, and finally, he was going to get a bite of each.

Ryck was appreciative of the gesture, even if he knew it wasn't entirely altruistic. While Ryck had to wait to be the last person to eat, no one could get seconds until he'd been served, and Marines were hanging around like vultures at the lion's kill, waiting to descend on the serving line again. Ryck cut off a small piece of steak, then sniffed at it, taking in the aroma. He turned the piece around on his fork as if admiring it. He started to take a bite, but then stopped, as a groan swept through the Marines.

"Oh, you want me to eat this?" he asked innocently.

"Yes, sir!" came the chorus.

Ryck put the steak into his mouth, and there was a mad rush for the line.

Private Çağlar, I'm not sure you now qualify for seconds, seeing as you lost your first serving on the field, so go get yourself another helping," he said.

Çağlar reddened, probably embarrassed. He'd lost his meal five minutes into the game. He hurried off, though, to get some more.

"Good game, First Sergeant, don't you think?" he asked.

"As you say, it was 'grubbing righteous,'" Hecs replied excitedly. "Did you see when me and the sergeant major crushed Oppenheimer?"

"No, but I'm sure he deserved it," Ryck said with a laugh.

Hecs was glowing. He'd really gotten into the game. He might have been putting on a show of complaining, but a Marine was a Marine, and they wouldn't, *couldn't* back down from combat in any of its forms.

Ryck was relieved that his decision to play had worked out. He'd had fun, and he'd gotten some of his own stress relieved, but more importantly, he thought they'd acquitted themselves well. They'd earned their cred. And he had to admit, the CO joining in had been brilliant. To the average Marine, a battalion CO was some far off, impossibly high personage, beyond mere mortal concerns. He was a concept, not a real person. By getting dirty and mixing it up, he proved that he was a real Marine, one of them. He'd gained his own cred, and one which had elevated his position among the men.

Ryck took his plate and started circulating among the Marines. He noted the CO was doing the same. Marines didn't seek either of them out, but they knew where the two commanders were at any time, and they seemed genuinely pleased when either of them stopped to talk.

Ryck had to keep in mind what it meant to a Marine when his commander talked with him. In many ways, Ryck was still Recruit Lysander in his mind, and Hecs was Drill Instructor "King Tong" Phantawisangtong. Although he was now a captain, the rank had become the new norm. Colonels and above were the unreachable ones. But when he was a private, or even a sergeant, a company commander was someone important, and a chance comment from a captain could thrill him or send him into the depths of worry. Ryck really had to fight to keep in mind how what he said and what he did would be perceived.

When Second and Third fought for the championship, Ryck joined the CO and watched. He tried not to be biased, but it was impossible not to cheer. He just tried to cheer both sides equally. Second Platoon won, something Ryck would not have foreseen. The CO surprised Ryck when the sergeant major pulled out a trophy from his assault pack and gave it to the CO to present to Lieutenant Chomsky. That was a really good touch, and it was something he should have thought of.

The CO gave a small speech, thanking the company not only for a good time, but for the great job they were doing. The speech was short and sweet, but it received a very loud chorus of "ooh-rahs."

Ryck felt a warm glow, despite the fact that he knew the company hadn't done much. Most of the action, what there was of it, had been met by the other three companies. Weapons Company had done more than Charlie, a line company. He'd thought the colonel had arrived perhaps to chew his ass, but the man seemed happy. That brought him to his thoughts of a little while before. He guessed he was no different from his Marines. While they might want Ryck's approval, Ryck wanted LtCol uKhiwa's approval.

He was surprised when the CO said, "Come walk with me, Captain," after the trophy presentation. Was he in trouble after all?

"So, did this field day accomplish what you wanted?" he asked.

Grubbing shit, he thought. *Was this a bad idea in a combat situation?*

"Yes, sir. I thought the men were getting complacent. I needed to snap them out of it. Complacency kills," he answered.

"Hmm," the CO said.

"Hmm?" What the hell does that mean?

"We'll see. But I wanted to pass you some intel. Nothing concrete yet, but you need to be aware of it. There has been some chatter that you, you and Charlie Company, might be a target."

That caught Ryck's attention.

"Due to your position in the public eye," he began, one of the few times Ryck had heard him refer to Ryck's status as a so-called "hero," "it would be a coup for the dissidents to be able to inflict some damage on the company, particularly if they could kill or capture you. Captain Rotigue has been fully integrated into the situation, and as you can imagine, he said this will not happen. Just so you know, there was talk of pulling you back to the ship, to get you out of harm's way."

Ryck's heart dropped. The *Inchons'* CO was in overall command, and if he wanted Ryck relieved of command, it was his call.

"Marines don't run from threats, though, so you still have the company for now. But I assured the CO that we would take precautions. I'm sending the Three over tomorrow to go over how you set up your security here, and as more detailed intel is released to us, we'll be working on a course of action. For now, keep your patrols running. And I don't want you coming in for each day's briefing. I want you and Captain Knickerson to attend via conference call from now on unless otherwise specified. If you do need to come in, try and frag a bird first, but if you are taking ground transport, I want you with more than just your driver for security. I am not sure the dissidents can mount any real action against your position here, but a snatch and grab against you is within the realm of possibilities."

Ryck tried to take all of that in. Mostly, he focused on "you still have your company" and "for now." Losing the company scared him more than facing any number of dissidents. And while the CO hadn't said it, there was no doubt in his military mind that he was the one who had fought CAPT Rotigue. Ryck knew that it wasn't because the CO thought so highly of him but rather that the Marines could not be seen to back down to threats. Still, he was grateful.

"You can brief your staff, but for now, until we know something more, I want you to keep this from the ranks. Keep doing what you're doing now, but get your mind working on the camp's defense. Make good use of Lieutenant Peltier-Aswad. He's got a good tactical mind."

Sandy? The XO was a good Marine, a good manager, but the CO thought more of him than that? Ryck wondered why, but then put that out of his head to focus on the issue.

"That's all I wanted to pass to you at the moment. There may be nothing to this, but I wanted to bring you up to speed," the CO said, looking at his watch. "The Stork's coming back in 15, but I think there's enough time for one more of those excellent steaks. I'm not sure how Gunny Samuelson managed to beg them from Piss Interstellar, but I intend to enjoy one more."

"Piss Interstellar?" Ryck wondered.

The CO had shown several sides to him that Ryck hadn't seen before: during the game, bringing out a trophy, fighting to keep Ryck in command.

But "Piss Interstellar?"

Ryck couldn't help but laugh out loud as he followed the CO back to the chow line for another helping of food.

Chapter 16

Ryck shook his head and inwardly sighed as the battalion operations officer Major Kjartan Snæbjörnsson (the "Viking"), Mr. Tanaka, a company rep, and Captain Herod Bey from the FCDC argued. After two days, it was obvious to Ryck that he didn't have much say in anything.

It hadn't started well from the beginning the day before. Mr. Tanaka had immediately objected to the "Camp Joshua Hope-of-Life" sign at the gate. He stressed that this was Propitious Interstellar—Ryck couldn't help but to keep hearing "Piss Interstellar" in his mind—property and the Marines were only guests. He then proceeded to object to most of the improvements made to the camp to bolster its defense. In particular, anything near the river and the banks of algae tubes was a non-starter as far as he was concerned.

Captain Bey was another matter. He obviously had a mongoose up his ass about the Corps. Fair enough; very few Marines gave the FCDC any credence, with "Gestapo" being perhaps the most civil nickname Marines had for the service. "Fuck-dicks, (FuCkDiCks) was a more common term. But Bey seemed particularly antagonistic.

As far as Ryck was concerned, this entire operation should have been an FCDC mission. Civil control was their bread-and-butter despite the "Development" in their name. But it wasn't the Marines' fault that the Federation authorities wanted the more recognizable—and probably more positive—image the Corps had in order to quell the situation on the planet.

Bey kept clashing with the Three, despite the Viking being a rank higher than him. He seemed to be under the impression that only the FCDC knew how to handle unruly civilians, and everything the Marines had done so far was worthless.

Ryck didn't know much about riot control, but he did know how to defend a camp, and that was what he'd done. He'd tried to point that out the day before, but he was completely marginalized as the Three took over. So for two days, he and the gunny followed the joint team around, ready to answer specific questions, but offering no ideas of their own.

Captain Bey was off again on one of his pet ideas of luring any possible dissidents in by leaving the gates open and having no presence along the river and algae banks. To him, identifying the dissidents seemed to be the top priority. Mr. Tanaka was having none of it. He wanted the entire refinery walled off with no possible unauthorized egress.

"Skipper, we've got an incident," Hecs said after hurrying up and pulling Ryck aside. "We've got two Marines hit at the park. Ling and LCpl Smith."

"Sir, I've got an issue to take care of," Ryck told the major, his heart racing.

Ling!

As a commander, Ryck knew that all Marines were equal to each other. Ordering Joshua to his death taught him that horribly difficult lesson. But Ling was one of "his" boys, his posse. Ling had saved his life on the *Marie's Best*, and he was one of the Marines Ryck had been slowly gathering around him.

"How bad is it?" he asked, not sure he wanted to know.

"They blew down half of a mountain on them. Smith's buried in the rubble, but he's fine, but Ling's fucked up. His PICS shut him down, and he's probably in for a long regen. Doc Kitomo will give us an update as soon as he gets on the scene."

"Get the reaction—"

"Already done. The XO ordered it out immediately, and Lieutenant de Madre has secured the area."

"Who did it?" Ryck asked as the two rushed into the company CP.

"No clue yet, sir. Kashmala and Tuarez were right on the scene and reported chasing two individuals down some sort of access tunnel, one too big for them in their PICS, and with the situation uncertain, he didn't think it would be a good idea to molt and chase them."

"No, he was right. And this could still be a diversion. I want everyone on 100% alert now, and recall all patrols until we figure this out. Have we notified battalion?"

"Yes, sir. We did that immediately. They want the Three to take over, but I wanted to tell you first," the first sergeant said.

"Thanks, I appreciate that, but better send a runner to fetch the Viking now," Ryck told him.

Ryck pulled out his handheld, a screen that was slaved to his PICS command center. With it, he could observe and message anyone just as if he was in his PICS instead of back at the CP in safety.

Every ounce of Ryck wanted to rush out, to join the QRF, the Quick Reaction Force. He wanted to make sure Ling was going to make it. He wanted to track down whoever had the bright idea to hit at two of his Marines. But he was no longer a sergeant. He was not even a lieutenant. Ryck was the company commander, and his place of duty was back at the CP, where he could best exert command and control.

The Three rushed in the CP, pale face flushed red. Ryck nodded at the XO, indicating that he should brief the major. The XO took the hint, and rushed forward to intercept the Three as Ryck immersed himself in the various feeds, bouncing from one to the other, as his Marines rushed to the aid of their fallen brother.

Chapter 17

Ryck watched the camcording for the third time. He had to give her grudging credit. She might look like a cosplay queen, but there was a sense of earnestness about her that Ryck knew would resonate with the public.

The recording flickered, then smoothed out with Miss MacCailín standing tall over Ling, prone in his PICS, one foot on his chest like an old-time big game hunter. She slightly nodded at whomever was doing the recording, then began.

"My name is Michiko MacCailín. Some of you know me as The Red Athena. I was born and raised here on Kakurega, and this is my home, a home under siege. Propitious Interstellar has not only broken the charter, but they have murdered our citizens, not the least being my fiancé, Franz Galipoli. When we resisted, they called in the Federation to rescue them with the Marines. Make no doubt about it, we have been invaded, and we must fight back. The Marines are not invincible, as you can see. We can win. All sons and daughters of Kakurega, rise up and throw the invaders off our home!"

Just as she was saying "home," a brief noise became noticeable. That would be Sgt Kashmala and PFC Tuarez arriving at the scene. The recording cut out.

"Run it again," Ryck ordered.

Michiko MacCailín was a First Family woman, descended from the Scottish and Japanese who settled Kakurega before the company arrived and received the charter. From previous briefs, the First Families were vested in the status quo, so it seemed odd that this child of privilege was the face of the dissidents, first as the "Red Athena," and now under her own name. But the FCDC report forwarded to the company only 20 minutes after the camcording was aired on the undernet confirmed Miss MacCailín's statement about her fiancé, a major player in the workers' rights movement being killed, gunned down at a rally. The assailant was still unknown, but the FCDC put the probability at 87% the assailant was a company operative.

"Ling's never going to live this down," the first sergeant said as they watched the recording again.

"I won't let him," Sams said with a chuckle.

Ryck didn't laugh.

Sgt Ling was going to be fine. The lower half of his PICS had suffered severe damage, and the suit had gone into emergency mode, shutting Joab's body down. Anytime a Marine was shut down required regen to repair the damage the shut down itself caused above and beyond any injuries. Ling had soft-tissue damage to his legs, and his pelvis had been broken, so he was going to be in regen for six to eight weeks, but there would be no lasting issues. It could have been much worse, though. Ling could have died, and that sobered Ryck. He'd sworn he'd bring back every Marine, and he'd come close to failing to uphold that oath.

He knew Ling would be the butt of jokes for some time to come. As a PICS Marine, the ultimate fighting man the Federation possessed, he'd been taken out by some graphic novel heroine. It had also been reported that Miss MacCailín was most likely the woman who'd been earlier spotted at the scene in the romantic company of a man. So not only had Ling been taken out by a cosplay queen, but by one who had been getting it on. Marines being Marines, they were not going to let the sergeant forget that.

Aside from Ling's embarrassment, the mere fact that the two Marines had been taken out of action with a primitive home-made explosive device was sobering as well. If Miss MacCailín or her partner had thrown the explosive device at the two Marines, there would have been no damage or injury. The on-scene analysis confirmed the chemical make-up of the explosive, would have caused an explosion much too slow to damage a PICS. However, slow, powerful explosives were perfect for moving large amounts of dirt or rock, and the sheer weight of the rocks had buried Smith and crushed Ling's legs. Someone out there understood how to make use of his or her resources. And that made him or her dangerous. This was no longer a simple mob—this was a group that had the resources to threaten his Marines.

Chapter 18

Ryck was the Charlie Company commander in name only, at least in his opinion. The Three had pretty much taken up residence at Camp Joshua, and both Propitious Interstellar and the FCDC had teams there. Between them the three groups were determining Charlie's fate, Ryck's wishes be damned.

Immediately after Miss MacCailín's little manifesto, protests had broken out, protests that spilled into violence as a crowd tried to attack Alpha Company in Dundee. At least 80 people had been killed as Preston led his company in defending itself. That stark reminder of the Marines' capabilities put a damper on violent protest, but non-violent protests had cropped up in both Dundee and Tay Station.

When Alpha was attacked, the CO had led the QRC himself to support Preston, but by the time he'd arrived, the attack was over, smashed. Word was that CAPT Rotigue had had a piece of the CO's ass for leaving Tay Station, and that was probably the only reason he wasn't at Camp Joshua himself. Having the Three there was bad enough, but if the CO had been there, too, Ryck would have been totally instead of merely 90% marginalized.

At least the Three was a Marine. Ryck resented his presence because it took away from his own ability to command, not because of the major's personality, but he detested both Capt Bey and Mr. Hortense, the assistant-vice-chief-spy-whatever jimmylegs. Ryck wanted to wipe that smug look off his face, the look that seemed to be permanently cemented on the man. Hortense loved to brag about his spy network, the network that had brought to light the coming assault on Camp Joshua. On Charlie Company. More specifically, on one Captain Ryck Lysander, UFMC.

Ryck had felt guilty that his presence had targeted Charlie. But when he found out that Piss Interstellar and the grubbing FCDC had actually orchestrated the attack, using him as bait, he'd about lost it and had to be restrained by the XO and first sergeant from performing his own assault on his "allies."

Yes, those worthy organizations thought Ryck was the perfect catalyst to bring the dissidents out into the open where they could be crushed. Their people on the inside—people supposedly high up in the dissident command, particularly in the National Independence Party, the most activist dissident organization on the planet—brought the idea forward and pushed for it. In other words, the coming attack did not originate with the dissidents but rather with the FCDC and Piss Interstellar.

The Three had let Ryck know that both the CO and CAPT Rotigue had fought against the plan, but they had been over-ruled by the Federation command. Ryck appreciated their efforts, but it was more than a little upsetting that the Federation thought setting up the company as bait while it actively tried to coerce Federation citizens to attack, them was a proper mission.

Whether he liked it or not, whether he thought that the Federation should be encouraging an attack or not, didn't matter much at this stage. If Hortense was correct, and Ryck had to think the asshole was, in a few days, Camp Joshua would be attacked. And Ryck had no input in regards to how to defend his Marines. That plan had been handed to him *in toto*.

The ops order was not exactly what Ryck would have developed, and he thought it did not take into account the specific and even personal capabilities of his Marines. But it seemed adequate, not that Ryck had any choice. This was the ops order that would be put into effect.

The dissent battle plan, which had been developed with the help of company operatives, was fairly simple. A large force of about 2,000 men and women would initiate what was supposed to look like a frontal assault. It would stall well away from the camp, but when Ryck's Marines were fixed in place by that assault, another team, using commercial diving gear, would walk across the river bottom and attack the camp from the rear. In the resultant confusion, the frontal assault force would commence the attack for real.

The dissidents would have had very little chance for success even if the Marines had not been privy to their plans. However, they had three Donaldson 25mm field guns. The guns were squarely in the economy class for private and local armies, but still, a direct hit on a Marine in a PICS could be deadly. Mr. Hortense assured the Marines that he had a solution for the guns, but Ryck would rather take out the guns before they could fire. He'd actually brought the point up, but both the jimmylegs and Capt Bey objected, saying that if the Donaldsons didn't initiate fire, the attack might peter out before it even commenced—which was a good thing to Ryck. Better a fight that never started than one that could go haywire.

He looked up at the Three while the two men were giving their reasons that the field guns had to be allowed to fire. The Three caught his eye and gave a slight shake of his head. Ryck knew then that he wasn't going to win the fight. He swore to himself, however, that if one Marine was hurt by the Donaldsons during the fight, he'd make Hortense pay.

Chapter 19

"They're on the move, sir," the XO said from where he was monitoring the surveillance and acquisition team from battalion.

Ryck looked up and walked over. The five Marines had their equipment spread out in the CP, and the main display showed large numbers of contacts on the move.

"How many does it look like, SSgt Manley?" he asked the team leader.

"I'd say about what we expected: around 2,000. Do you want me to run a tally?"

"No, no need. The rough count is fine," Ryck responded.

The CO had wanted to augment the company with more firepower, but he'd been vetoed again from on high. The powers that be did not want to tip off the dissidents—rebels, they called them—that the Marines expected anything. Any sudden surge in manpower or weapons would have been noted.

But having the surveillance and acquisition team was something they couldn't argue against, and both Hortense and Bey were avidly watching the displays, although both seemed more interested in the live feeds from the ground-based sensors and the overhead—collected by both Marine drones and the *Inchon's* space-borne sensors. Ryck thought he could see a blood lust in Hortnese's eyes as he awaited the fight, although he realized that could be just a projection of his own dislike of the man.

Ryck touched his XO on the shoulder and motioned him to follow.

In the back of the CP, out of hearing range of the others, he quietly said, "OK, I'm going out to forward CP. You know what I want, right?"

Lieutenant Peltier-Aswad took a quick glance back at the others crowded in the CP, and then just as quietly answered, "Yes, sir. Keep an eye on our guests, and don't let them give any orders. Our orders come only from you."

"Or Major Snæbjörnsson. He's the task force commander. And if anything happens to him or me, you're in charge. Do not let any jimmylegs or FCDC gopher take command for any reason."

"Roger that, sir. I've got you covered."

With that assurance, Ryck quietly left the CP to where LCpl Jaquinto from the armory had his PICS waiting for him. He squirmed in and powered up. His PICS could not directly display the feeds from the surveillance and acquisition team, which was a major liability, in Ryck's estimation, but it could pick up the signals from the field repeater. He couldn't switch feeds on the repeater, but he could have the XO manually switch the feeds being broadcasted. The Federation had settled vast swathes of space and could communicate instantaneously over its domain, but a combat commander could not control himself what feeds he wanted to receive.

Ryck felt the familiar mini-vibrations as his PICS came online. He'd been in PICS for a good chunk of his career, and it was in the combat suits that he felt the most comfortable. For a moment, he could forget Piss Interstellar, the Fuck-dicks, the S-3 coming to take command. He was just a combat Marine, ready to do battle.

He had no real bone to pick with the dissidents and their causes. In some ways, it seemed as if they were merely demanding their rights as Federation citizens. And he felt their coming attack had been a sort of entrapment. But entrapment or not, they were willingly coming to try and kill his Marines, and that made them his enemy. He could sympathize with them in some ways, but when they decided to take on Charlie Company, they chose—unwisely, he knew—their path. Now they would have to pay the consequences.

His display clock showed 12 minutes before the river assault force entered the water and 32 minutes before the bulk of the dissidents started their feint. What the dissidents didn't know, though, was that First Platoon was also underwater, ready to scoop up the river force. A PICS was not designed to fight underwater. However, it could act as an effective, if cumbersome EVAvacsuit, so it was airtight. A Marine could easily ford most rivers and streams in a PICS, staying underwater for up to about four hours without any modification. When the morning "patrols" had gone out, the purpose had been two-fold. It had kept up the routine, and it also allowed the patrols to double back into the river and form a line of defense. Jeff had his men simply standing on the river bed, their low frequency sensors piercing the water as they waited for their prey. The First Platoon Marines would be slightly outnumbered. But dissidents in commercial diver suits would be no match for combat Marines. Ryck didn't expect any problems on that front.

"You ready for this, Gershon?" he asked his Second Platoon commander on the P2P as he moved into the forward CP.

"Yes, sir. Ready to be flybait," Lt Chomsky responded.

If Ryck detected a slight bit of chippiness in Chomsky's voice, he let it go. Ryck understood the feeling. He'd rather be out there himself, either with First or Third, but his job was to command, not fight, and with either of those platoons, he wouldn't be commanding the company. Like First, Third was underwater, just off Route 2 to the south of camp. Of any of them, it would be Third that would see real action. The assault section made up of Second and Weapons had the mission of seeming like a full company going about its daily routine. Marines from Second moved back and forth outside of their PICS and kept up a normal chatter. The gun sections of Weapons were hunkered down, each man armored up and with weapons ready, but on emissions silence. When the assault began, the Second Platoon Marines would scrambled into their waiting PICS, and if Third ran into any problems, it would be thrown into the breach. However, Ryck doubted it would come to that.

Ryck was well aware of Clausewitz[18] and the "fog of war," and that no battle plan ever lasted past the first shot fired. However, in this case, Ryck had never been so sure of the final outcome. What concerned him was the chance of Marines getting killed while achieving that outcome. He had over 30 Marines wandering back and forth in the camp in their skins and bones, not PICS, and there would be incoming in half an hour. Even in a PICS, a direct hit by the dissident's guns could be fatal.

Ryck became more nervous as the display counted down the seconds. Sitting and waiting was worse when he didn't have a mission.

He knew that wasn't accurate. He had a mission, a vital one. He had to command. But he didn't know what that would entail. As a junior Marine, all he had to do was close with and destroy the enemy. That was easy to conceptualize, and he knew how to do that. As a commander, he kept running through a multitude of possible scenarios, and what he would do for each one.

It was a relief when the first report was passed that First Platoon had gathered up the river assault force like fish in a net. No one, Marine or dissident, had been hurt, and only two dissidents had managed to escape the trap. Trucks were moving in from their staging area to pick up the prisoners while the *Inchon* blanketed out the river site to block any transmissions back to the larger ground assault force.

Just a few minutes after Ryck received that word, the first salvo from the dissidents' Donaldsons opened up.

"All hands, armor up!" Ryck immediately passed as he asked his AI to plot the trajectories of the incoming rounds.

To his surprise, the first three rounds were projected to impact in the agricultural land just on the other side of the river. Ryck

---

[18] Carl von Clausewitz, a 19th Century Prussian military strategist.

turned to look as the rounds impacted, sending up nice gouts of smoke and dust. He realized that to observing forces, the rounds would probably look like they were impacting inside the camp, and it might take them a few salvos to realize their mistake.

Both the jimmylegs and the FCDC had assured the Marines that the guns wouldn't be an issue, and Ryck had to give them credit. However they had messed with the firing data, though, as soon as the dissidents realized the error, they could manually make the corrections. What this did, however, was allow Second Platoon to get into their PICS without the threat of incoming rounds.

There was the outgoing report of the M54 firing kinetic rounds. Although the M54 was still attached to Charlie, the Three, as the task force commander, had pulled Ryck out of the loop and ordered it to fire. The first round landed just at the crest of Route 2's raised roadbed as the first of the frontal assault force crested it. Bodies were blown back down the other side and out of sight.

As more dissidents showed themselves, the automatic gun teams opened up, kinetic rounds impacting on the roadbed and zipping over it—or into the bodies of dissidents as they ran forward. Several dozen fell before the rest retreated back on the other side.

Ryck and the Marines knew this was a planned retreat. The dissidents, thinking they had fixed the Marines defenses, would wait for the upcoming river-based assault from the rear before re-commencing their assault in earnest. Only they wouldn't get the chance. Now, while they were bunched up on the far side of the roadbed, was the Marines' opportunity.

"Taco-Charlie-Three, commence your assault," Ryck ordered over the command circuit.

Lt. McAult didn't respond, but slaving off his lieutenant's display, Ryck could see him emerge from the murky water, hundreds of dissidents stretching along the roadbed. Even with McAult's feed taking up only six square centimeters in the bottom right of his display, he could see the panic of those dissidents nearest him as they realized that the trap had been sprung.

The Marines opened fire, which Ryck could both see on the feed and hear in real-time. Dissidents opened fire as well, but they were poorly armed for a fight with PICS Marines, and each of Third Platoon's avatars remained a bright, healthy blue.

Ryck watched as the blue avatars moved forward. He could barely see the tops of some PICS over the roadbed until McAult ordered one of his Marines up onto the roadbed itself. The gun teams from Weapons all had the Third's avatars plotted, and each gun ceased firing as Marines entered that teams sectors of fire. Lt

McAult evidently was taking no chances, making sure that the gun teams knew where his Marines were. The M881 12 mm guns fired a round that had the potential to damage or even take out a PICS, and no one wanted a friendly fire incident.

Ryck juggled his displays, trying to grasp the situation. From an overhead live feed, he could see that the Marines had swept through half of where the dissidents had taken cover. Bodies littered the ground, and groups of people were either surrendering or running. The Donaldsons were silent, and Ryck felt the threat had been broken.

"Cease fire, cease fire. Respond to any aggression, but do not initiate any further firing. Restrain and capture all combatants, but deadly force is no longer authorized unless attacked. All hands, acknowledge," Ryck passed on the open circuit.

The acknowledgements started lighting up his display as the firing slowed to a halt.

"That is negative. That order is not authorized. All you Marines, keep firing your guns and kill every rebel!" a voice blasted out over the same circuit.

His AI didn't identify the speaker, only that it was a Piss Interstellar "Security Team." A jimmylegs—who had no authority here. The only person here who could overrule Ryck was Major Snæbjörnsson.

"This is Taco-Charlie-Six Actual, belay that last unauthorized transmission. There will be no more firing unless you are threatened.

"Mike, do you copy that?" he asked Lt McAult over the P2P.

"Roger that, sir. I take my orders from you, not some flipping fat-ass jimmylegs. The dissident attack is broken, but I need some help. I've got a shitload of POWs, and I think some are slipping away."

"You've got it, Mike. I'm sending Gershon out now. Good job. Six, out."

He turned to the Second Platoon commander and said, "OK, you've got a mission. Get your men out there and help gather up the prisoners. I don't have to tell you that you are to protect yourselves at all times, but unless attacked, I don't want any more killing."

"Aye, aye, sir!" Lt Chomsky shouted as if his comms needed the extra input.

He started passing orders, and his platoon started moving over the open area to the roadbed.

Ryck hadn't been happy to turn the entire planning over to the Three, and he would have done things differently. But it was hard to argue with success. An assault of over 2,000 people had been turned back without a single Marine being hurt.

That was something he could live with.

Chapter 20

"I'm proud of all of you. Great job, Charlie Company!" Captain Rotigue told the assembled Marines, receiving a chorus of "ooh-rahs" in return.

Ryck joined in the clapping, but not too enthusiastically. He still hadn't digested the action that morning. The *Inchon's* CO—and task force commander—had made the trip down to survey the scene of the battle. Approximately 625 of the dissidents had been killed, although that number could edge up a bit as the forested area was swept and more bodies discovered. That was a huge number of dead, and all were Federation citizens, citizens who professed merely to want Piss Interstellar to heed the existing charter. This number was not even close to the same magnitude of the massacres on Ellison and Fu Sing, but Ryck wasn't comfortable having his name linked to any mass killings of citizens. Yes, they attacked, and they paid the price for that idiotic decision; still, Ryck hoped history would stress that and not the outcome.

The battalion was formed up on the LZ, where the battleball games had been held just a short time ago. Things had changed. Out beyond the gate and across the open area leading to Route 2, Ryck could see trucks lined up to take the over 800 prisoners back to Tay Station. FCDC troops were tasked with that evolution, and Ryck was happy to let them have it. The Marines had repulsed the attack; now let the Fuckdicks play policemen to their hearts' content.

CAPT Rotigue stepped off the platform and started pressing the flesh among the Marines. That struck Ryck as very politician-like, and he took another look at the CO as if seeing him for the first time. The captain was competent enough, but for Navy officers, things were a little different. If a captain was selected for flag rank, that could be the next step of a journey that could end in the very highest levels of the Federation government. Ryck wondered if this mission could be the stepping stone for Rotigue to earn his first star. A command *and* a successful mission in support of a large corporation—that could earn him some friends in high places.

Ryck was glad the Marines didn't have to play those games. Well, to be more accurate, they didn't have the *opportunity* to play those games. The Marine Corps was not above politics, and trying to earn a star did have its own checkmarks. But no Marine was ever going to be the Chairman, and only one Marine had ever served on the Council over the past centuries.

"Hey, you with us?" Donte asked as he put his hand on Ryck's shoulder.

"Oh, sure, just thinking," Ryck said as he was pulled back to the present.

"Dangerous thing, that. You thinking."

"You've got that right," Ryck said with a chuckle.

"You know, it's bullshit, you not being put in for an award. It's your bleeding company," Donte said, his indignation evident.

"Ah, forget it. I'd rather not be considered," Ryck said, and he was only slightly surprised that he meant it.

During CAPT Rotigue's speech, he'd mentioned that Major Snæbjörnsson, Lieutenants McAult and del Madre, and Sergeant Abramowicz would be put in for awards. No mention was made about Ryck, not that he needed any more medals. And, to be honest, not that he thought he deserved any recognition. The plan had been the major's, not his. All Ryck had done was watch it unfold and stop the killing once the field of battle was won.

But he appreciated Donte's concern. He'd known Donte ever since they were both midshipmen at NOTC, but they hadn't been close until they'd served together in 3/1. Now, Donte was one of his closest friends. There were officers who were stand-offish with their peers or even worse. It was more difficult to get promoted the higher a Marine rose within the ranks, and the bottom line was that with seven captains in the battalion, their evaluations with respect to each other would be a factor considered in future promotion boards. Some officers could never forget that, could never overlook that, in some ways, it was a competition with each other.

Not Donte, though. There wasn't a jealous bone in his body, and Ryck knew Donte wished him only the best. He was a good Marine and a good friend.

"It's bullshit, that's all, my man. But you done good. Stopping the slaughter was the right move. We were all monitoring the fight back at the CP, and there were some high-fives when you countermanded that chicken-shit fuckdick."

"Well, like you said, it was time to stop. The dissidents were broken."

"Keep fighting the good fight, Ryck. I gotta fly now, though. The big boss looks like he's done, and I've got to catch a ride back with him to the CP. I don't want to have to catch a hover back," Donte said.

"Welcome to my world. I was riding back and forth every day for awhile," Ryck said, taking Donte's hand in a firm shake.

"Keep your head down," Donte shouted over his shoulder after shaking Ryck's hand and then sprinted to catch up to the command party as it started to load the Stork.

Ryck turned to go back to his company CP. With the Three leaving, he was back in charge. And he was feeling better. Donte's short talk had done that for him. He may not have liked the mission, he may have regretted the loss of life, but he had performed it to the best of his abilities. Charlie Company had broken the attack without a Marine or sailor getting hurt, and once the attack was broken, the company had ceased using lethal force. Ryck had done what had to be done. That was a victory.

Chapter 21

"OK, here we have General Loski Sonutta-Lyon, one of the two operational commanders of their assault," First Sergeant Hecs, said, reading from his PA.

"Really? This is the genius who came up with that plan. We should have put him on the payroll for how easy he made it for us," Ryck said.

"Come on, sir, be nice. We did have pretty much their entire plan before they launched."

"So you're telling me that if we didn't have the plan, they could have succeeded?" Ryck asked in surprise.

"No, not succeeded. But they could have made it hairier for us. The river assault force wasn't a bad idea, and we didn't really have the area adequately sensored," Hecs went on.

"Something that has been rectified now," Ryck muttered. "Oh, well, let's get this done."

Despite his tone of voice, Ryck had requested the duty from the CO. The Marines considered the 813 prisoners as POWs. They had been in uniform and had openly attacked them. It was cut and dry as far as the Marines—backed up by the Navy—were concerned. Both the FCDC and the PI security, however, considered them criminals and not subject to the same rights and protections that were afforded POWs.

The CO could not keep the FCDC nor the jimmylegs from accessing the prisoners, but he could send in Marines on command visits to ensure the prisoners were being treated according to law. Ryck felt a degree of responsibility for the prisoners as it was his men who'd captured them, so he'd volunteered to come into town to do the visit. Even the FCDC major thought it was a good idea when he'd heard about it, although Ryck thought that had more to do with rubbing into the dissidents' faces the fact that Ryck was still alive.

The jimmlylegs jailor put his eye to the scanner and the cell door opened. Ryck, Hecs, and Sgt Singh stepped into the cell. On a bare metal rack, a broken man stared up at them. He'd pretty obviously been subject of some rough treatment, treatment that Ryck was sure didn't come until after he'd been captured.

"General Sonutta-Lyon," Ryck said, stumbling slightly over the name, "I am Captain Lysander. I trust you know who I am?"

The battered face, only partially visible in the low lighting of the cell, nodded.

"You are now a Prisoner of War, and as such, I am here to ascertain your treatment. Have you been treated humanely as a prisoner?"

The man said nothing.

Come on, Ryck implored in his mind. *Give me something to nail the bastards!*

Instead, he merely repeated the question.

Ryck thought the general was going to remain silent, but he croaked out, "I've been treated well enough, given the circumstances."

Then he turned in his bed to lie facing the wall. They'd been dismissed.

Ryck stared at the back of the man for a moment, then shrugged and led his team back out to the corridor.

"He's scared," Hecs said, stating the obvious. "He thinks we can't protect him after we're gone, and whoever did this to him will take it out on him if he speaks up."

Ryck was about to respond when he saw the jimmylegs trying hard to look like he was not listening. He'd take this up later with the CO, out of PI security or FCDC hearing.

The jimmylegs unlocked the next door, and the three Marines walked in. A woman was on the metal table, a FCDC warrant officer standing over her, and another FCDC PFC was standing back near a table.

Hecs looked at his PA, then said, "Michiko MacCailín. She's a general in the NIP."

"I'm aware of who she is, First Sergeant" Ryck said. "I saw the camcordings."

Ryck had recognized the woman despite her being naked and rather worse for wear. The fuckdick warrant officer was a surprise, and Ryck's distant response to Hecs was more for the warrant officer's benefit than for either of his two Marines.

"Can I ask you what you are doing here, sir?" the chief warrant officer asked.

"Merely checking on our prisoners, Chief," Hecs said.

"Well, as you can see, I'm in the middle of an interrogation, so if you could come back later, I would appreciate it."

"I can see what you are doing, and no, we'll check now. The captain is a little busy to arrange his schedule around yours."

Ryck moved forwards and looked at Miss MacCailín. She'd pretty obviously been wounded, probably in the attack, although Ryck hadn't been aware she had been part of the assault as anything more than a figurehead. The wound had not been treated, which was against the Universal Charter for the Treatment of Prisoners of War. More than that, she had also been pretty badly treated after her capture. Ryck was disgusted, but he swallowed that down.

He looked over her, then turned to the chief warrant officer and asked, "Why has she been abused?"

"Wasn't me. The jimmylegs got a little too enthusiastic. Besides, that arm wound was your boys' doing," he said, pulling out his PA and handing it to Hecs.

The first sergeant looked it over, then nodded and handed it to the captain and simply said, "He's right."

Ryck looked it over, then handed it back before asking, "So you didn't do that, but why hasn't she been given medical treatment?"

"There's no requirement for me to do that, sir, as you know. She's an insurgent, and a free citizen. If she was a Class Four, the company here would be required to provide the treatment, but as a Free Citizen, she needs to provide her own."

"And did you offer it? Did you contact her family? It doesn't matter. As a *prisoner of war*," Ryck said, emphasizing the words, "we are required to provide full medical treatment."

"She's an insurgent, a common criminal, sir, not a prisoner of war," the FCDC chief warrant officer protested.

Ryck turned toward the chief warrant officer and snarled, "She was wearing a uniform, right? She headed an army, right? She's a grubbing POW, and I *really* don't think you want to fight me on that, Chief!

"First Sergeant Phantawisangtong, get Doc Botivic over here to check her out. I want the letter of the law followed here."

"Aye-aye, sir," the first sergeant said before speaking into a throat mic.

HM1 Botivic was from the battalion aide station, and he'd joined the XO and Private Çağlar while they assisted Ryck by checking other prisoners being held.

"With all due respect, sir, this is an FCDC matter, not a Marine concern. I'm in charge of interrogation, and you can't be interfering in that. If you have a complaint, you can register it with my major," the chief warrant officer said.

"Do you know who I am, Chief?" Ryck asked.

"Yes, of course, sir. But—"

"But nothing. I'll have your ass if you fight me on this. I'm going to get her treated, then you can interrogate her to your heart's content."

"Why the hell do you care? She jumped two of your Marines, brought a whole cliff down on them. She attacked your company?"

"I don't care about her, Chief. I care about us. We're on a dirty mission here, and I intend to keep us as clean as possible despite that. And it didn't do her a lot of good, did it? Not one Marine killed."

"I killed one of your Marines," Miss MacCailín stammered out, the first words she'd uttered since the Marines had entered the cell.

All five men in the room turned to look at her, the Marines with bemused smiles on their faces.

"I killed one of you bastards. Me!" she asserted.

"I think she means Ling," the first sergeant said.

"Oh, so you killed Sergeant Ling?" Ryck asked, stepping up to stand over her.

"If that was his name," she tried to say with a snarl. "I crushed him in the Ledges."

"Yes, Sergeant Joab Ling. He's been with me quite awhile. Well, after he gets out of regen, I'm sure he would like to meet you," Ryck said with a condescending laugh. "Not everyone gets to meet his killer."

"Oh, you messed him up but good, girl," the first sergeant said. "And he's going to have to live that down. I think half of the Corps sent him stills of that camcording you made with your foot on him like some big-game trophy. But no, he's gonna be fine. All you got was his pride."

Her face fell as that registered.

Not so easy there, missy, is it, taking on Marines? Ryck thought with a tiny bit of vindictiveness. *Payback for Joab and for LCPL Regent, huh?*

"Um, Captain? Take a look at this," Sgt Singh said, speaking for the first time.

He had picked up the doser, and now he held it out for the Ryck who looked at it, anger taking over as he saw what the next dose was.

"Propoxinal, Chief? You know that is proscribed!" he shouted at the fuckdick.

"Not for her, sir! I can use whatever means I deem necessary. Look the frigging regulations up, if you want," the chief said.

"For insurgents or terrorists in the course of an operation, yes. For listed groups like the SOG. But not for prisoners of war! POWs can only voluntarily offer information, not be coerced, and certainly not by proscribed drugs! You are breaking about a thousand treaties on this!" Ryck yelled, spittle flying from his mouth.

Jonathan P. Brazee

"I'm going right to my major on this!" the chief screamed, not backing down.

"Tell your fucking major whatever you want! I'm telling you now, Chief Warrant Officer, if you value your career and if you don't want to spend time in the brig, you will cease and desist. You will not attempt to interrogate her. I will be checking back, and if you fight me on this, your pathetic life, as you know it, is over. Do you understand?"

Ryck could see the anger warring on the chief warrant officer's face, but the man bit it back down and said, "I understand."

"Len, I want you to stand here until Doc arrives," he told Sgt Singh. "Get her treated. Then I want someone in here every day to check up on her. First Sergeant, come with me. Let's see who else in this hellhole thinks he's above the law."

"Grubbing son-of-a-bitch," Ryck said to Hecs, oblivious to their jimmylegs escort. "I want that chief's name. He was about to use propoxinal on a POW! The Brotherhood or the Confederation would have a field day with this if it leaked out. We're checking every single prisoner, then we're going to the CO with this. We're Marines, and by God, we're going to make sure the law in this shithole is followed!"

Chapter 22

"Did the prisoners all get transferred?" Ryck asked Sams as the gunny came into the battalion CP.

"Got them all, Skipper. There were some pretty pissed off fuckdicks, but what could they do?"

"You cut it pretty close, but we had to do something," Ryck said.

When the new orders came for the battalion to leave Kakurega for a mission to PPL-7, Ryck had gone straight to the CO. He argued that without the Marines, the FCDC would revert to treating the POWs, men and women captured by Marines, however they wanted. And that would not be within the guidelines set up by the treaty.

The CO told him that was out of the Marines' jurisdiction, but when Ryck told him his plan, the CO relented and scheduled Charlie to be the last lifted off the planet.

What Ryck had done was to make liaison with the city government, a government that seemed to be chaffing somewhat under the heel of the all-mighty Piss Interstellar. The mayor welcomed the opportunity to accept all the POWs into the city jail both to uphold Federation law, which he was sworn to do, and to do a favor for the famous Captain Lysander. Ryck also knew that while the mayor wouldn't admit it, he probably wanted to tweak the nose of the company CEO.

When the CO gave the OK, Ryck swung into action. First Platoon, along with Sams and Sgt Contradari, went to the prison and forcibly took the prisoners to the city jail. And now, with the last shuttles arriving in less than 15 minutes, the Marines had returned to the stadium in time to make their pick-up.

Ryck knew that moving the prisoners to city control might not be a long-term solution, but the mayor seemed willing to fight, and Ryck had every intention to contact a few higher-ups in the chain of command to make sure there was pressure from the Corps, and hopefully the Navy, to keep the POWs protected up to the level afforded them by intergovernmental treaties.

"Skipper, the first shuttle is landing. You're manifested for it," the XO said, poking his head in what had been the CO's office.

"No, put me on the last one," he replied.

The XO scurried off to run the retrograde. Ryck had dumped the movement in his lap, and Sandy had done well.

"He's a good lieutenant, Skipper. Reminds me of you," Sams said.

"Him? He's organized, I'll give you that, but he reminds you of me?"

If any of the lieutenants reminded people of him, Ryck had thought it would have been the personable and dynamic Jeff de Madre, not the XO.

"Yes, him. I know you don't think much of him, but he's the best of the bunch, and you should give him a little encouragement, you know?"

That took him aback. He respected Sams' opinions, but this time, Ryck thought his gunny was mistaken.

He quickly put the thought out of his mind as the second shuttle landed outside. The company and gear would be lifted on three shuttles, and he was about to get off this nasty little planet and its nasty little games.

"Let's diddiho, Gunnery Sergeant of Marines. I never thought that the close quarters of the *Inchon* would be such a welcome place."

"Damned straight, Skipper. Damned straight," Sams said as the two Marines took one last look at the CO's old office and went out into the early morning darkness to board the shuttles.

SUNSHINE

Chapter 23

Ryck spotted Donte ahead of him. He hurried to catch up and then clapped his friend on the shoulder.

"Hey, congrats, Major-Select Ward!" he said with enthusiasm.

Donte turned around, a huge grin threatening to split his face in two. "You, too, Major-Select Lysander. You, too!"

Both Ryck and Donte had the same date of rank for captain, so they had been up for major on the same board. Making major was a huge milestone in an officer's career. Unless they screwed up somehow, they now had job security until retirement. Neither Ryck nor Donte was a Marine for the pay, but as both had families, mundane matters such as job security became more relevant.

There had been little doubt that either officer would make it. This year's selection rate was over 55%, and both Marines had made names for themselves. Still, having that message when they reported in for work today had been most welcome news.

Not everyone made it, however. Virag Ganesh, the battalion's S-3A had also been in the zone, but he was not selected. Ryck hadn't seen Virag since they'd gotten back to Sunshine, and now he wasn't sure how he should act when they did meet up. Virag had one more promotion board next year. If he were not selected for promotion then, he'd be forced out of the Corps.

It would still be some time before Ryck and Donte actually pinned on their oak leaves, but the thought of having to leave Charlie Company made his promotion something of a two-way sword. Majors typically had the worst jobs in the Corps. They were too junior to get command of a battalion but too senior to remain a company commander.

"Do you think the CO'll give Virag a company to try and make him better for the next board?" Ryck asked Donte, giving voice to his concerns.

"Don't know, but if he does, then I hope Virag does a good job. All I know is that by this time next year, I'll be back at Camp Charles. I'm getting Range Company," Donte said, if anything, his grin getting impossibly wider.

"What? How the hell do you know that?" Ryck asked. "We just saw the board results today!"

Range Company ran the training ranges for the recruits, and it was one of the very few commands in the Corps for a major. Getting that billet was a plum position, and Ryck felt a pang of jealousy. He was happy for Donte, but that was a billet he'd have done almost anything for. A command, and good steady hours. He'd be home every night for three years, watching the twins grow and spending time with his wife.

"I called Colonel Ketter and asked him. Most of the new billets have already been assigned."

"He's our new monitor?[19]" Ryck asked needlessly as that was who the colonel had to be if he had Donte's next assignment.

"Yep. He's the O4 monitor. Just got off the comms with him. Nice guy, too. I bet he's already got you pegged, too."

"What time's it there?" Ryck wondered aloud, looking at his watch.

Like most watches, the local time was foremost in the display with GMT in small numbers above local. He pushed the function button three times and got Tarawa time where the majors' monitor was stationed.

"Sixteen-twenty," Ryck said. "He'd still be at work, right?"

"He was 15 minutes ago, my man. Go for it," Donte told him.

"Yeah, maybe I will," Ryck said. "I've got to run if I'm going to catch him. Meet up with me at the O-Club after, and I'll let you buy me a beer while I tell you what great job I've been assigned."

"I'm already on my way there now, Ryck. And the first beer's on you."

Ryck hurried to the comms shed. The battalion had six hadron communicators, three of them twinned to Headquarters on Tarawa. There were plenty of commercial communicators on the planet, but the Marine comms were secure, and while Ryck's future billet was hardly a state secret, Marine business was always done over the secure circuits when possible. Ryck hoped he wouldn't have to wait, and to his relief, two of the comms lines were open. As a captain, he didn't need any authorization. He simply signed in with the clerk, and moments later, his instantaneous transmission was connected with the Headquarters comms AI. A few moments later, and a civilian woman was asking him what he wanted.

"I'm Captain Ryck Lysander, ma'am, and I'm on the select list for major. Captain Ward, that's Donte Ward, is out here with 11th Marines with me, and he said—"

---

[19] Monitor: an officer in charge of assigning billets for all officers or SNCOs within a specific grade.

"Let me see if the colonel is free," she interrupted, the visuals switching to some sort of quiet mountain stream.

Ryck stared at the stream, watching birds flit through the tree branches. He idly wondered if the image was real or some construct. A minute passed, then two. Ryck wondered if the colonel might have already left for the day when the woman came back.

"Colonel Ketter will see you now," she said as the feed flickered once and opened on a thin-faced colonel, sitting behind a large wooden desk.

"Captain Lysander, I'm Colonel Ketter, the O4 Monitor. Congratulations on your selection. I imagine you would like to know what your next duty station will be," he said with a tone that hinted he'd been receiving calls like this all day.

"Uh, yes, sir. I would, sir," Ryck said.

"Well, I see you've had a successful tour as a company commander," the colonel said, looking down at his PA, "so you've checked that box. We try and move new majors out of their current duty station, and with two years on station by the time you'll pin on your leaves, your qualify for a PCDS[20] move."

"Yes, sir," Ryck said, wondering where he'd be assigned.

Hannah wouldn't be too happy, having to pull up stakes again after only two years. She had a pretty important position, and while she wouldn't lose any seniority due to the move, her work would have to change. But it didn't sound like the colonel was going to assign him anywhere on Sunshine.

Ryck was hoping against hope that he'd be heading to recon. There were nine recon companies in the Corps, and these were the only combat commands available to a major. Surely his experience in recon as well as his Federation Nova would hold some weight in getting him one of those companies.

"You're expected to be promoted on Novewmber 1st, and on November 28th, you are to report to the Federation Training Center in Zurich."

What? Earth? Ryck wondered, entirely confused.

"After your 12-week intensive course in diplomacy, you are to be assigned to the Federation Embassy on New Mumbai."

New Mumbai? In the Confederation? There were the Marine Guards at the embassy, but they were enlisted.

"Uh, sir, at the embassy? In what billet?" Ryck asked.

"I would think that would be obvious. You are being assigned as the assistant naval attaché."

---

[20] PCDS: Permanent Change of Duty Station

Ryck's heart fell. Not only would he not be getting a command, but he wouldn't even be with the Marines. And he was supposed to be a diplomat? Not grubbing likely. He was a warrior, not some schmoozing pogue.

"Uh, sir, if I may, I don't think this is a good idea. I'm not, well, the diplomatic type," he began.

"Well, it really isn't up to you now, is it? This is your next assignment."

Ryck felt the anger begin to rise. He'd been hoping for a command, and he thought he deserved it. And they wanted to stick him in some sort of diplomatic post, and in the Confederation of all places? No way!

"I don't think you understand, sir. I'm not going to take this assignment. There are others much more qualified than me for it."

"I don't think you understand, *Captain*. These are your orders."

With the colonel's emphasis on "captain," Ryck blew up.

Who the grubbing hell does this skinny admin puke think he is?

"Do you know who I am?" Ryck asked, actually rising from his seat as if he could physically lean in through the screen.

"Yes, I know who you are, Captain. I have your file right here. Do you know who I am? Obviously you don't. I am the O4 monitor, and I control who goes where based on the needs of the Corps. I decide, and majors salute smartly and march off."

"I'm not just any major, sir. I know people, important people, and we'll just see about this," Ryck said, his face red with anger.

Colonel Ketter just stared at Ryck over the light years of distance, then calmly said, "You have fulfilled your obligated service and can refuse any orders, Captain, and be released from the Corps. These are your orders, and you have until tomorrow at 0900 GMT to acknowledge them. Out," the colonel said, cutting the transmission.

Ryck wanted to scream at the obstinate asshole, but he was staring at a blank screen. He gathered himself, then spun around and walked out of the comms shed. He was a grubbing Marine Corps hero, and he'd pull in favors until these stupid orders were canceled.

Chapter 24

"The Confederation? Why not send me to the Trinoculars instead? I fought them, too," Ryck exclaimed, sticking a beer in the cooler.

He put the timer on ten seconds and waited silently, still fuming, as the beer cooled down. The cooler dinged, and he removed the beer and took a long swallow. He had promised to go meet Donte at the O-Club for a beer, but he'd been so upset that he'd gone straight home to tell Hannah.

The *Inchon* had only returned to offload the battalion the evening before, and tonight, for his first home-cooked dinner since getting home, Hannah had dialed up pot roast, one of his favorites. But she stopped her rare foray into domestic endeavors and sat down as Ryck came in the door, listening to him rant.

Ryck came around the kitchen island and took a seat on the couch. He took another long swallow, and that helped calm him.

"So do you know what I said to him? I asked him—"

"Do you know who I am?" she interrupted, her voice gravelly in a poor imitation of him.

"What?"

"You probably asked him if he knew who you were," she said.

"Well, yeah, but how did you know?" he asked, puzzled.

"Because that's what you usually say," Hannah responded.

"No, I don't," Ryck protested.

"Hecs told me you said that to that FCDC officer on Kakurega. And you said that to the mechanic for the Hyundai before you left."

What? Hecs and Hannah were talking, and Hecs said that? I didn't tell that asshole fuckdick anything of the sort.

But then he thought about it. Well, maybe he had said something like that in the jail, and maybe he'd told that idiot mechanic in town. But he didn't really think that way. He'd just said it to get the hover fixed before he deployed. Did Hannah think he was leaning on his medal?

"Well, I never meant it like that. Sometimes, you've got to use what resources you have to get things done," he said. "Right?"

"I'm not criticizing you, Ryck. You're one of the few living Marines who have proven themselves as you have. I be proud of you."

"Then why did you say that?" Ryck asked, his righteous anger at Col Ketter fading as he worried about Hannah's opinions.

"I'm not meaning anything by it. It just came out," she said, getting up from her overstuffed chair to come sit by Ryck on the couch. "If you don't want this posting, then you know better than me what you should do about it."

"I mean, it's probably not even an accompanied tour. That means three years away from home, away from you and the twins," he said, trying to bring her on board with his thinking, even if that wasn't really the reason he'd objected to the assignment.

"If it isn't accompanied, we'll be managing ," Hannah said, taking his hand in hers, "like we be doing before. The twins be starting school soon, and they'll be fine."

Ryck sat there, staring at her hand. He turned it over, noting how soft and fine it looked. Hannah took great care in her manicure, and he appreciated her attention to detail.

Forget about her hands! he told himself. *Does she think I'm being an asshole about all of this?*

"Uh, what do you think? I can call General Ukiah, and I'm sure he can fix this."

Hannah shrugged, then said, "Yes, I'm sure Hank would help, if you ask him."

Ryck didn't think she seemed too enthused with the notion,

"But should I?" he asked, looking into her eyes.

She wouldn't meet his eyes, but instead looked down at their hands and said, "That be your choice. It be your career after all."

She wasn't voicing her real opinion, Ryck knew

"What would you do, if you were me," he asked, pressing the issue.

She hesitated as if wondering what she should say. Ryck was going to ask again, but Hannah took a deep breath and began.

"Do other Marines have godfathers that they can call to get their orders changed?"

"No, not most Marines. But I am not most Marines."

"True, you be not most Marines," she said, slipping into her old Torritite speech patterns, something she did when deep in thought or under stress. "And I be so proud of you. But you will be serving with your fellow Marines for years. What be they thinking if you get special treatment, if you go outside procedure when you be wanting to?"

"But this is not because I don't want the job," Ryck protested. "I'm not suited for it. I'd be a detriment to the mission."

Ryck tried to convince himself, only partially successfully, that that was his only reason for objecting to the orders.

"Maybe they be knowing more about you than you do," Hannah said quietly. "You always be second guessing yourself, wondering if you be good enough. And each challenge, you rise to it, and you succeed. Just maybe, you be the right man for this job."

Ryck tried to take that in. What Hannah had said hit home. It was true—he had a deep-seated fear that he was a fraud, that he wasn't up to being a leader of Marines. Every success he'd had was more a matter of luck than any particular skill he possessed. He could fight, and that was about it. Soon, someday, his weaknesses would be exposed, and everyone would know him for the fraud he was. This new assignment could very well be the one to expose him as a lucky, but basically incompetent street brawler.

He didn't want to disappoint anyone, especially Hannah. He couldn't bear the thought of being a failure. But he didn't want her to think he was some egotistical a-hole, either. He knew she could accept a failure better than a character flaw. He needed some more feedback.

"Uh, Hannah, how long before dinner?"

"Charise is bringing the twins back in about 30 minutes. So right after that."—

"I think I need to make a call, if that's OK," he told her.

"Of course. I'll just get the table set and call you when the twins get here."

Ryck kissed her forehead and went upstairs to the extra bedroom that served as a home office. He went online and connected through AT&T to Tarawa. It would be late there, but Bert wouldn't mind.

This wasn't official business, so there wasn't a need to use an official line, and Ryck didn't want any scans that might draw attention to his conversation. So he was willing to pay for a commercial call.

Major Bertrand Nidischii' answered the call. He was dressed in a very old and ratty black t-shirt and had a cup of what was probably tea in his hand. He was in his living room, so at least Ryck hadn't woken his friend up.

"Ryck, good to see you. You got back yesterday, right?"

"Yeah, last night here on Sunshine."

"I heard good things about your deployment. It went over well with the general staff," Bert said.

Bert was probably the closest Ryck had to a brother in the Corps. Donte and others were friends, even good friends, but Bert was the Marine in whom Ryck could confide. Ryck respected Bert tremendously, and he respected the major's opinions on just about anything.

"Uh, not so great, really. I don't think the CO likes me, and the—uh, I can tell you about that later," he said, remembering that he was on a public transmission, not a secure line.

Ryck's opinions on their Kakurega mission would have to wait until he could speak freely.

"Hey, Bert, sorry to bother you in the evening like this," he began as Bert waved off the apology, "but I need to talk to you. I'm on the list for major—"

"Yes, I saw that. Congratulations."

"Well, yeah, thanks. But I just found out my orders. I'm going to—" he started before pausing, wondering if he could say that on a public circuit.

It would all be a matter of public record, though, so he thought it would be OK.

"I'm going to be the assistant naval attaché to New Mumbai."

"Yes, I know. I was asked about that before the decision was made."

"They asked you?" Ryck said, surprised.

"Colonel Ketter did, yes. He's just on the deck above me at Headquarters."

"What did you say?"

"I said you were a fine Marine, of course. What did you want me to say?"

"That's just it, Bert. I don't think I'm the man for the job. I mean, think of it. Me, a grubbing diplomat?"

Bert shrugged but said nothing.

"You had a recon company as a major. I think with my record, I've shown that would be where I belong, not in some embassy."

"So you want a company?" Bert asked, his voice steady.

"Hell, yeah! You wanted one, and you got it."

"Yes, I did. And now I'm pushing papers at Headquarters that will never see the light of day."

"But you had your command as a major, and that's going to stand you in good stead when you are up for a battalion," Ryck said.

"Or hurt me. Maybe the command board looks at that and says I already had my chance, so now let's let someone else have a command."

Ryck hadn't thought of that possibility, and that gave him pause as he considered it, but only for a moment.

"Look, I'll crash and burn as some sort of diplomat. You know it—"

"No I don't know it," Bert interrupted. "Give yourself more credit."

"So I was thinking I could contact General Ukiah, or maybe General Praeter. He's retired, but he still keeps in touch. I think either one could call that pencil dick Ketter and get my orders changed," Ryck said, ignoring Bert's comment.

"Hey, Colonel Ketter's good people, Ryck."

"That skinny pogue?"

"I'm a pogue now, too," Bert said with a little steel in his voice. "And you remember the *FS Hudson Bay*?"

Of course, Ryck knew about the ship, an ore freighter that had been one of the first taken by the SOG.[21] A Marine platoon had boarded what looked to be a derelict ship, only to be surprised by the SOG with a long and difficult battle. The Marines prevailed, but it had been a close thing.

"Sergeant Ketter earned a Navy Cross in the fight," Bert told him.

Colonel Ketter had been in on that fight? Ryck thought, feeling a little guilty now for the pogue comment.

Still, the billet was the wrong one for Ryck, one he didn't want, Ketter being a righteous warrior or not.

"Bert, what do you think? I know this is a mistake, and I can get it fixed."

"You probably could," Bert said with an obvious lack of commitment.

That took Ryck aback. He'd hoped that Bert, a fellow fighter of note, would back him up and validate his feelings. It didn't sound like Bert was totally on-board.

"Uh, I spoke with Hannah a few minutes ago. She seemed to infer that I've been maybe pushing my medal around, using it to get my way."

"And?"

"Well, do you think so? I mean, you've got a Navy Cross. Do you ever use it to tip the scale sometimes?"

"No," was Bert's simple answer. "I'm just a Marine major, and that's what matters."

"But, I don't think I do it, either, unless it's important."

Bert didn't say anything, but he pursed his lips like he was pointing back at Ryck. This was a habit of Bert's using his lips that way in the manner of the Navaho people. Ryck knew Bert was singling him out, challenging him.

"Do you think I do?" he asked Bert.

---

[21] SOG: Soldiers of God, a terrorist group that uses piracy to fund their operations

"Do you want the friend supporting you answer, or do you want the truth?" Bert asked.

That didn't sound good, Ryck thought as his heart fell.

"The truth," he said with resignation.

"I love you, Ryck, and you are a hell of a Marine, a hell of a warrior. But, well, your reputation is that of a difficult prima donna. The top brass likes you, or they like using you, parading you around like a trained monkey. But your peers, and those just above you, well, they aren't so kind. They might respect you, but they don't like you."

Ryck took that in, stunned. He'd never thought he was unpopular with his peers.

"Couldn't that be jealousy, or just being competitive with me?" Ryck asked.

Bert tilted his head and looked back with an expression of disappointment on his face.

"I . . . I never thought . . ." Ryck started, not sure where he was going with that train of thought.

"Look, Ryck, you don't have to be liked to be a good leader. Some of our best leaders were total assholes. Look at General Andropov. He was a total flaming asshole. His staff hated him with a passion. Hell, the entire Corps hated him. But he transformed the Corps—for the better— more than any other commandant.

"But remember, if you alienate your peers, well, these are the Marines who will be on your flanks in the next battle. You are going to have to rely on them, and Andropov aside, it is hard to go it alone."

"Ryck, Charise is here with the twins. Dinner's ready," Hannah called out from downstairs.

"I hear your boss is calling," Bert said.

"Yeah, I gotta go. But what would you do," Ryck asked.

"Not my call, Ryck. It's your decision."

"OK, thanks. I'll call you again to let you know," Ryck said, cutting the connection.

He got up and made his way down the stairs to where Charise had brought the twins back. Charise was the wife of a Navy petty officer, and she did the daycare for the twins while Hannah was at work.

"Daddy!" Esther shouted, dropping her mother's hand and rushing him.

Ryck swept her up in his arms and squeezed her tight. "I missed you snuggle bunny!"

"I was completely out-of-line, and I hope you can accept my apology.

"I felt, and still feel, for that matter, that I am not qualified for such a sensitive billet, but I am a Marine, and if you think I am right for this job, then I will give it my all. I think it was my duty to express my misgivings, but once expressed, it was also my duty to salute and march on. To threaten you, and that is exactly what I did, no getting around it, was deplorable and not what a Marine does. I can't tell you how sorry I am, and as one Marine to another, I hope you can forgive me."

There, I said it, he thought, glad he'd gotten most of what he wanted to say out.

Col Ketter just stared at Ryck for a moment before he gathered himself and said, "Well, Captain. I must say you surprised me, especially given your, well, your reputation."

That comment cut Ryck to the bone.

How the grubbing hell did I ever let it get to that? How did I not realize what was happening?

"But I am relieved to hear that, and let's forget that conversation ever happened. I certainly have not relayed it to anyone yet. So apology accepted," the colonel said.

Ryck let out a breath of air he hadn't realized he was holding. He'd been in the wrong, and the colonel would have had every right to take action. Medal holder or not, he couldn't survive being on the wrong end of that. He'd probably still be promoted to major, but his reputation would be officially trashed, and his career would peter out with make-do billets.

"Can I ask you something, Captain?" the colonel asked.

"Certainly, sir."

"If you had gone to someone higher up, as you threatened, who would it have been?"

The question surprised Ryck, but he answered truthfully, "Probably General Ukiah, sir."

A smile came over the colonel's face. "I thought as much. He's known as one of your godfathers. Do you know, though, that he was the one who selected you for this billet?"

"General Ukiah? Not you, sir?" Ryck asked, caught completely off guard.

"I'm just a colonel, son. For sensitive positions like this, assignments are well above my pay grade. I just issue the orders."

And take the grief, Ryck thought. *Another officer would have passed the buck, but Colonel Ketter assumed all responsibility.*

"Oh, if you had gone to him, he'd have gotten the orders rescinded. He said you probably would not like them, but he felt you were the right Marine for the job," the colonel said.

"Well, Captain, I've got work to do. Your actual orders will be issued in a few hours."

"Uh, thank you sir. I mean, for understanding."

"Understanding what? Nothing happened as far as I'm concerned."

"Uh, yeah, thank you, sir," Ryck got out before the colonel nodded and cut the connection.

Ryck sat, staring at the blank screen as he thought about what had just happened. The colonel could have told him the first time they had spoken that General Ukiah had selected him for the billet. That would have saved a lot of grief. Ryck could have called the general and rationally discussed the assignment. Instead, Ryck had blown up at a full colonel, one just doing his job.

The colonel had stood fast. Both the colonel and Ryck knew that he could have gone to another general, and depending on who it was, that could have caused the colonel some serious headaches. But he let it play out by the book.

Had this been some sort of test? he wondered.

He didn't think so, but it could have been.

Ryck left the comms shed, told Sgt Smith to secure it, then wandered over to his company CP. He slowly got into his PT gear for an early morning run.

He'd let Hannah know after work. She wouldn't be happy, but at least she could stay put for three more years. The twins were four, almost five. He'd be gone for three years, almost as long as they'd been alive. He hoped they would understand

Ryck did not want to leave them, but more than that, he wanted them to be proud of him. He didn't want them growing up knowing their father was a royal asshole, disliked and resented.

And he had been an asshole. He realized that now. As he walked out the hatch and lurched into his run, he swore things would be different from here on. It would be difficult, but he had to change that perception.

And no matter what, the words "Do you know who I am?" would never cross his lips again.

Chapter 26

"Oh, nice shot, XO. But you're killing me," Ryck said as Lt. Peltier-Aswad's drive arched over the fairway to land and roll some 250 or 260 meters away, a short iron shot to the green. "You do know that evals are coming up, and 'loyalty' is one of the categories?"

Ryck, the first sergeant, the XO, and SSgt Grimes made up the foursome, and after 12 holes, the XO had pocketed the ante for ten of the holes. Ryck hadn't taken a single hole yet.

The battalion was on half days for a week following its return from deployment. With Hannah working and the twins with Charise, Ryck had accepted the XO's invitation for a round of golf. It felt good to get out on the course, the first time he'd golfed in at least five years.

"Sure do, sir, but I think loyalty to the integrity of the game counts, doesn't it, First Sergeant?"

"Yes, I imagine it does, XO," the first sergeant agreed as he teed up.

"Your eval comes up next month, I might remind you," Ryck said just as the first sergeant started his swing.

It didn't matter. First Sergeant Hecs' drive was almost as pretty as the XO's.

"You need more than that, Skipper," Hecs said as he put the driver back into his bag.

"Yeah, like a game," the XO said, causing the other three Marines to break out into laughter.

Ryck shouldered his bag and stepped off. At least SSgt Grimes was struggling, and Ryck's drive on the hole wasn't the worst. This was a good day, and Ryck felt great. He'd submitted the award recommendations for the deployment. He'd forwarded a number of Battle Commendations for the CO's approval, and had recommended three Marines, including SSgt Grimes, for a Distinguished Meritorious Service Medal, which had to be approved by the Awards Board back at Headquarters. Giving out awards, or, in this case, merely recommending them, always put him in a good mood. Add the beautiful day and his three companions out on the course with him, and yes, it didn't get much better than this.

But it could get worse. Almost simultaneously, all four Marines' tethers sounded recall.

"Crap, what now?" Hecs asked.

Ryck pulled his tether out of his pocket, but no explanation was given on the readout. This was a Class A recall. They had less than two hours to have the company formed up and ready for whatever. Ryck rather thought it was just a drill, to make sure Marines could be recalled, but you never knew.

"OK, let's head her up. XO, make sure the lieutenants are responding. First Sergeant, get confirmation from the SNCOs."

Both men got on their PAs as the four Marines walked back to the clubhouse. The XO gave Ryck a thumbs up after only a minute or so. First Sergeant Hecs was not as quick to give confirmation.

"Got everyone?" Ryck asked as they made their way to the parking lot.

"Sams," Hecs grunted out. "He said he'd be in his quarters, but he's not responding."

"OK, the SNCO quarters are on the way back. Let's just sweep him up along the way."

The four Marines got in their hovers and pulled out, starting back to the battalion area. Ryck and Hecs made a detour at the SNCO quarters, pulling in at Sams' building. Both Marines got out and climbed the stairs to the second floor, the first sergeant knocking on the hatch. There was no answer, and he knocked again. They could hear faint movement inside, and the hatch finally opened, exposing a naked and tousled Tara Samuelson. She motioned her thumb over her shoulder and casually walked to the cooler, where she dialed down a fruit drink.

Ryck tried not to stare at her as the two Marines entered Sams' quarters. He'd seen Tara naked before on GenAg 13, but that was in a combat situation. This was different. This was in Sams' quarters, and it was obvious that the two had been enjoying some carnal pleasures.

Sams wandered out of the bedroom, equally naked and equally tousled.

"What's up, First Sergeant?" he asked, then, "Oh, hi, Skipper."

Hecs threw him a pair of trousers that were lying haphazardly on the couch, among other pieces of clothing, both male and female.

"We've been recalled, or didn't you hear your tether?" Hecs asked.

"No shit? A recall? I didn't hear. I sort of stuck my tether in my sock drawer for a bit of time, you know, so we wouldn't be interrupted."

"A bit of time? That's an understatement," Tara muttered as she found her panties and slid into them. She sat down at the couch.

"We're still technically deployable, as you well know," Hecs admonished Sams. "You can't be hiding your tether, or turning off your PA."

"Yeah, you're right. My bust. Look, we've still got an hour and forty minutes. Let me get dressed and cleaned up, and I'll meet you at the company," he said, looking hungrily at Tara.

"No, I think you're coming with us now," Hecs told him.

Sams sighed, but went back to his room, coming out again in two minutes, uniform on.

"I'll probably be back in a couple of hours," he told Tara. "If it's longer than that, just let yourself out if you have to go."

Tara waved over the back of the couch as she turned on the holo.

"You do know the meaning of 'ex-wife,' don't you?" Ryck asked Sams as the hatch closed.

"Well yeah, of course I do," Sams said.

"Yet you're in there screwing your ex?" Hecs asked.

"Hell, yeah! I mean, so we can't live together without killing each other. That doesn't mean we can't fuck. Why punish ourselves like that?" he said, sounding perplexed.

Ryck just shook his head. He'd known Sams almost his entire Marine Corps career, and just when he thought he understood the gunny, something else came up.

Fifteen minutes later, the three Marines pulled into the company headquarters. The XO was getting the counts in and seemed to have things well in hand, so Ryck changed into the spare uniform he kept in his wall-locker and left for battalion. Hopefully, the drill would end soon, and he'd be home before the twins were brought back.

Donte was walking to battalion, too, and Ryck caught up with him.

"You hear anything?" Ryck asked.

"Nah. Just another drill, I'm guessing. Bad timing, too. I had the steaks on the grill—real steaks, not fabricated ones. Had to take them off and come down."

"Real steaks? What, you win the lottery?"

"Marry rich, my man, marry rich. Caitlan's parents brought them over. They've been visiting for the last month while we were deployed. They'll be leaving next week, thank goodness."

"Hey, send them my way if you want. I'll put up with any in-laws if they're packing real steaks," Ryck said with a laugh.

The two captains entered the battalion CP. There was an air about the building. Ryck's combat sense picked up the vibe. He had a sudden feeling this might not be just a drill.

Virag Ganesh came down the passageway. When he saw the two other captains, he changed direction and came up to them.

"Better get into the conference room. The CO's calling a meeting in fifteen," he said.

"Why, Virag? What's up?" This is just a drill, right?" Donte asked.

Virag looked around as if trying to see if anyone was listening. "No, this is the real deal. We're going back on the *Inchon*. The Confederation has taken over one of our disputed systems, and we're going to get it back."

"But we're not deployed anymore. 3/11's on the *Sevastopol*, and they're operational." Donte protested.

The *Sevastopol* was the fourth *Falklands* Class IAT, and with 3/11 onboard, it had taken over the reins from the *Inchon* two days before the *Inchon* arrived back on Sunshine. If there was a contingency, that task force should respond to it.

Virag's voice got lower as he leaned in. "Word has it that the Marines and Navy have not meshed well, and the Navy command doesn't think the *Sevastopol* is up to the challenge. We're a proven commodity, and they want us. The commandant agreed, so we're back into the breach."

They'd only been back for five days, barely enough time to get reacquainted with friends and family. Post-deployment leave hadn't been scheduled for another week-and-a-half, so at least the battalion was at full strength. Even Sgt Ling, out of regen, had met them upon their return, completely restored to full-duty status.

After Kakurega, Ryck had still wished for a real mission to wash the nasty taste of that one out of his mouth. Their mission to PPL-7, the one that had pulled them off of Kakurega, had been a letdown. Upon their arrival in orbit, the disputing parties, well aware of what had happened on Kakurega, had come to the table and settled their differences. This was a huge victory for the Federation. They had used the Marines as a threat, and without any real action, had diffused a problem.

Ryck knew this was perfect use of the Marines, but he wasn't suited to be simply a threat. He, like most Marines, wanted action.

Ryck had just gotten back, and part of him wanted more time with his family, but deep within his DNA was the desire to march to the sound of guns. His heart raced as he followed Donte into the conference room.

He was going back into the fight!

CYGNI B SYSTEM

Chapter 27

"You ready for this?" Preston asked the other three company commanders and Drayton Miller.

"Born ready," Donte said as he slowly sharpened his Hwa Win on a whetting stone.

The combat knife was already sharp, but the routine act probably helped keep Donte calm as they waited for H-hour. After Ryck had told them about using his Hwa Win to kill a trinocular in hand-to-hand combat, Preston, Donte, and Drayton had ordered their own knives. Only Jasper thought knives were obsolete in the modern battlefield and refused to fork out the 350 units a Hwa Win cost. He held that his Marine-issued multi-tool would be good enough for any cutting that might have to be done.

The five Marines were crowded in Donte's stateroom. They'd received their last briefs, and while Ryck wanted to watch his Marines do their final preparations, he knew his presence would be a distraction. After telling his lieutenants to make themselves scarce as well, he had left the company to the SNCOs to let them do their jobs unhindered. He'd wandered to Donte's stateroom to find Jasper already there. Within 15 or 20 more minutes, Preston and Drayton had wandered in as well.

Drayton would not be leaving the ship, but the tension back on the *Inchon* was high enough as it was. The Confederation had capital ships, ships that could fight, so no one was without risk on the mission.

Seven days before, a Confederation task force had entered the disputed Cygni B system and landed an Army cohort on HECLA-3, the base of operations for the Federation mining company in the system. The 2,000 Federation citizens did not resist, and there was no fighting. They claimed this was in direct response to the Federation incursion into CF-32 to rescue the *FS Julianna's Dream*.

The Cygni B system was a valuable, if difficult to exploit piece of real estate. HECLA-3 (Cygni B-3 until the Federation had granted HECLA the charter) had no atmosphere, and the company personnel were housed in two domes. Terraforming, if it was ever to be done, was a long, long way off. What brought HECLA to the system was the Telchines Asteroid belt composed of a moon that had probably orbited the giant Cygni B-5 before it had been somehow destroyed. The moon had been made up of valuable metals that were ripe for mining.

Still, without the geothermal power source on HECLA-3, mining the asteroid belt would have just been too expensive. With Federation assistance (the Federation wanted at least squatters' rights to the disputed system), HECLA had erected the domes and constructed the processing plants.

When the Confederation had seized the domes, the Federation had wanted to take them back immediately, but HECLA, fearful of damage to the domes, suggested just taking the asteroid belt instead. It wasn't as if a full-out war would do much more than make big pieces of rock smaller pieces of rock, something the company was doing anyway. So the *Inchon* Task Force was going to bypass the planet and seize the Telchines. Without them, the Confederation would have no use of the system and could be (hopefully) brought to the negotiating table.

A Marine recon team had been dispatched aboard a Navy Circe picket-skiff. While the skiff remained in far system orbit passively collecting data, the recon team had actually been able to take position on one of the planetoids and had reported back that there was only a century holding the belt, most taking position in the main HECLA sorting ship.

The enemy order of battle was a cohort (minus) on HECLA-3. Subtract the 80-man century in the Telchine Belt, and that left about 400 soldiers on the planet. The converted transport that had brought them into the system was still in orbit around the planet, but the only capital ships were a corvette and a frigate.

The Federation military force consisted of the *FS Inchon*, with 2,000+ Marines embarked, the *FS Tallyday*, a destroyer, the *FS Kuala Lampur*, a frigate, and the monitor *R-445*. On paper, this gave the overwhelming advantage to the Federation forces.

Ryck's old ship, the battle cruiser *FS Ark Royal*, had been considered to lead the task force, but the politicians thought that might be overkill and lead to a wider confrontation. Ryck thought that was ridiculous. If you were going into a fight, you took all you had with you to win. Period.

Ryck checked his watch. It would be another 45 minutes before the Marines would start to move to their debark stations.

"You got another whetstone?" he asked Donte.

Donte merely grunted and opened a drawer in his desk, taking out another stone and tossing it to Ryck. Ryck pulled out his own Hwa Win and started sharpening it. The knife, with its tempered durosteel blade, didn't need sharpening, but Rycks nerves could use the diversion. There was something almost mesmerizing about the process, and Ryck could imagine his blood pressure falling.

Soon enough, he would be in the shit again.

Jonathan P. Brazee

Chapter 28

The first rank of rekis launched, almost immediately followed by Ryck's rank. One again, the *Inchon's* new technology had enabled her to come out of bubble space almost on top of their objectives.

Neither the *Tallyday* nor the *Kuala Lampur* had the same capability, but those two ships were there to hold off the Confederation ships, and they had emerged from bubble space at a more normal distance. Two Gryffyn monitors were needed for the assault, so the *Inchon* had held them with a tractor beam through the entire voyage. This could have been tricky. Sometimes a lampreyed ship lost contact in bubble space, and when the mother ship arrived at the destination, the lampreyed ship was lost for good. But when the *Inchon* came out of bubble space in the Cygni B system, the monitors were still attached, and they began firing on the last known positions of the century.

They were so close to the action that Ryck could see the explosions as the monitor's rail gun hit hard rocks, vaporizing chunks of the planetoids away. Of course, "close" was all relative. They were still over 50 klicks from leaving their rekis and joining in battle.

The entire Charlie Company was assigned to take T-486, a 1.5 kilometer-wide planetoid where a Confederation deca had been last reported. Ryck's 180 Marines should have no problem rooting out ten Confederation soldiers, but he was still glad the monitor would be pounding the rock with its rail gun in the meantime.

While Ryck was seizing the rock, codenamed Johnnie Walker, Preston would be taking Campari, about 90 klicks sunward, and Donte, with Jasper's Weapon's Company in support, would be seizing the sorting ship, codenamed Blue Barrel. Preston's Alpha Company had the additional mission of re-enforcing Bravo if needed. Both Alpha and Bravo had already debarked the *Inchon*, which had then moved to give Charlie less of a distance to cover.

Ryck's display had a number of pre-loaded reports. As his last rank of rekis left the Inchon, he blinked up the "Crossing Phase Line Guava" report. Using his eyes to command his AI was getting to be second nature to him. He'd hated it at first, but he was beginning to see how it allowed him more time to process the huge stream of information available to him.

Ryck barely noticed when Bravo crossed the FCL[22], which essentially meant Donte was into the assault. Ryck had his own concerns, and he continually monitored his men as the rekis brought them into the belt. From space and on displays used in planning, the belt looked like a jumble of rocks almost on top of each other. In reality, there was quite a bit of room between different planetoids. The reki coxswains had to maneuver the sleds around some of the larger rocks, but there was still plenty of open space within the belt.

As they neared Johnnie Walker, a single beam of light lanced out, glancing off one of the lead rekis. Almost immediately, there was a response as the monitor struck back in counter-fire.

Ryck pulled up that reki on his display. All Marines were nice and blue. Ryck let out a deep breath. The rekis were basically open sleds, and they only had a small shield attached to the front retaining bar. A direct hit with a high-powered weapon would blast right through the reki, hitting Marines in their EVA vacsuits. These weren't PICS. They offered very little protection against energy weapons, and while the modified bones gave them some protection from small kinetic weapons, a hit could kill a Marine if it wrecked the integrity of the suit. If a Marine were hit in the arm, for example, the suit could do nothing more than seal off the arm at the next higher joint. The arm would be lost, but the Marine himself could be saved.

As they hit the company FCL, the three ranks split, going into a complicated and confusing weaving pattern to approach the rock. "Pattern" was probably a misnomer. The AI's used chaos calculations to determine each reki's path to the rock, paths that were supposedly impossible to anticipate by enemy AIs. Another beam of light lanced out, missing one of Third Platoon's rekis.

Surprisingly calm, Ryck idly wondered why the Confederation used hadron and plasma beams that were visible to the naked eye. Federation beam weapons could not be seen in the vacuum of space, which was an advantage in small-arms combat. An enemy could not see where a shot came from and had to rely on AIs to analyze where the Federation weapon might be located.

Twice within less than 15 seconds, Ryck flinched as another reki seemed about to collide with his. This close to Johnnie Walker, the rekis were buzzing around like flies over a dead dog, and a collision seemed inevitable. But the AIs did their jobs, and the 28 rekis landed almost simultaneously.

Even before they landed, though, Marines from Third took a Confed position under fire. Ryck's AI struggled to give him a picture

---

[22] FCL: Final Coordination Line

Jonathan P. Brazee

of what they were firing at, but Ryck's reki touched down and he was vaulting out, holding the handrail to keep himself from floating up.

One key in EVA warfare like this was not to get too high where a Marine would be an easy target. Of course, a Marine wouldn't float away to drift off in space. EVA vacsuits had their own propulsion, so they could simply fly back. Being high above the surface of the planetoid, however, could bring a Marine under too much enemy fire.

Ryck couldn't see anything from his position. The heavy, iron and nickel-rich body of this particular planetoid interfered with comms, and without an atmosphere, the Marines could not bounce transmissions, so four of the rekis were to take geosynchronous orbits around the rock and act as relay stations. The problem was that they had just let the Marines off and were not in position yet.

"Gershon, form a perimeter," Ryck passed on a P2P to his Second Platoon commander.

Then Ryck, followed by Çağlar, let his propulsion unit lift him off and fly him around the horizon. He'd flown only 40 meters when his comms with Third were reestablished. His display lit up, all with bright blue avatars. But there was a fight going on.

"Jeff, commit the PICS to Third's position now," he passed.

"Roger that," came the immediate reply.

The PICS was an amazing piece of gear. It rendered a Marine almost immune to small arms, although it could still be brought down by field expedient methods, as Ling found out on Kakurega. It was not a good EVA fighting suit, though. With the strap-on M-722 Propulsion Pack, it could maneuver through space, if slowly and clumsily. It was too big for most spacecraft, too, so it wasn't particularly useful in ship-to-ship operations.

However, T-486 was primarily an iron-nickel chunk of space-rock, and that meant that the small magnetic slip-on soles, the same kind, if bigger, used in vacsuits, could anchor the PICS to the planet's surface. In other words, they could walk.

One squad of Marines had made the crossing in their PICS. Jeff had assigned Second Squad, Joab Ling's squad, to the mission. The last time Ling had been in a PICS, he'd almost been killed. Ryck knew he would be wanting payback, and any enemy was good enough to bear the brunt of that retribution.

Ryck flew forward another 300 meters, and the PICS Marines came into view. This had to be a surprise to the Confederation troops. Who used PICS in space?

A few beams lanced out, glancing off the Marines and doing no harm. As Ling advanced his squad, the deca leader opposing him must have realized his predicament.

"Hold your fire! We surrender!" came over the universal freq.

"Cease fire, cease fire," Ryck passed through the relay rekis on station so the entire company could here.

The Battle of T-486 was over.

Chapter 29

"Come on, Contradari," Gunny told the police sergeant. "We need to get that thing up.

"That thing" was a portable tiki hut, a tent-like structure that was air-tight and could hold pressure. The PICS could operate in a vacuum, but their time was limited far more than a vacsuit. Ling's squad had to get out of their PICS and into their vacsuits. The tiki hut was not huge, so only one Marine could go in at a time to make the switch. The *Inchon* was supposed to return well before the PICS reached their use-by date, but Ryck felt better being able to control that evolution.

Besides, no one knew how long they were going to remain on this rock, and while the vacsuits could sustain a Marine for up to a few days, that wasn't very comfortable. If he could cycle through a few Marines at a time, that would go a long way in increasing their endurance.

Doc Kitoma came loping up to Ryck in that oddly graceful stride that kept him low to the surface, but able to use his propulsion unit to move forward. Doc didn't have to be next to Ryck to report in, but habits sometimes made it easier to be close to each other.

"One KIA. No hope of regen. One WIA. Their vacsuits don't isolate limbs like ours do, and I'd like to get him out of his and into a ziplock," he told Ryck.

"Is he going to make it?" Ryck asked.

"If we get him in a ziplock, yes, sir, I think so."

"Gunny, before any of our guys use the tiki hut, Doc's going to take in one of the Confederation soldiers," he passed on the command circuit.

PICS were big, huge machines, yet Ryck swore he could see a few Marines slump as they heard him. Ryck rolled his eyes. They'd been in them for less than an hour, and another five minutes was going to kill them? Ryck would rather be in a PICS than his vacsuit. He'd always felt more comfortable in the far more capable piece of gear.

He looked around the planetoid, at least as far as was in his line of sight. Not a single Marine had been hurt, much less killed. Despite the monitor pounding the rock, only one Confederation solder had been killed with another wounded, and after seeing the Confederation fighting positions, Ryck thought that shot had been a lucky one.

The remainder of the soldiers were standing off to the side, having given their parole. None of them were hurt and would all be released soon. There were also five HECLA engineers that Ryck had not known about. They'd been dropping exploratory cores when the Confederation troops had arrived.

Their drill had given Ryck an idea. He did not know how long they would be stuck on the rock, but the Confederation troops had withstood some serious fire, and their fighting positions were rudimentary. With that big null-G drill, Ryck could make the rock into a fortress. It would probably all be for naught, but a busy Marine was a happy Marine—at least that was what they said. Having been a private, Ryck didn't know if he really agreed with that.

He'd gotten together with the head engineer, who had readily agreed to help the Marines. Now he and the XO were supervising the drilling of fighting holes and even a few bunkers around the planetoid. Ryck had listened in on them, and both of their voices threatened Ryck's ears with their combined excitement. Ryck switched circuits and left them to their mission.

Unlike Kakurega, and even to an extent the rescue of the *Julianna's Dream,* this had been a righteous mission. The Confederation had invaded Federation space and held Federation citizens. The Marines had responded. Several Marines from Bravo had been WIA taking the sorting ship, and 12 soldiers had been hurt, but the only KIA had been the soldier on T-486. A wrong had been righted without too much in the way of casualties.

The lack of casualties had been surprising. If the Confederation soldiers had fought harder or longer, the casualty list would have been much longer. The Marines were in vacsuit, after all, fighting in a vacuum. But the Confederate troops had surrendered pretty quickly, saving lives on both sides. This was probably Ryck's last mission as a company commander, and he was fine with that.

Chapter 30

Ryck looked around the chamber in awe.

"We're 14 meters deep, sir, and that's mostly taenite above us," the XO said excitedly.

Ryck had lost all connectivity as he flew down the shaft, but his AI had terabytes of stored data. He quickly looked up "tayonite" (which the AI recognized from the context) and saw that *taenite* was a hard, dense magnetic alloy of iron and nickel. On earth, it was found around meteorite impact sites, but in the reaches of space, it was a fairly common, if still valuable, metal deposit.

When Ryck had told the XO to honcho the building of the fighting holes, he had envisioned straight tubes into which Marines could drop for cover. He had no idea that the drill could turn corners and open up areas. This chamber, this *bunker* now, could easily hold half a dozen Marines, and was connected to the surface through a shaft just wide enough for a Marine in a vacsuit to fly up and down. With T-486's miniscule gravity, the EVA would have no problem getting back to the surface.

"How many of these do you have done?" he asked the XO.

"We've got enough here for Third Platoon, and Second Platoon on the other side. Give us another two hours, and the Pearson Drill will have the rest hacked out. Setting it up for each shaft is what takes the time. Chuck, that's Chief Engineer Chuck Haley, carved this out in less than five minutes."

Ryck reached out and touched the wall. His vacsuit would protect him from burns, but the temperature was cold. If the drill had just recently made this bunker, Ryck would have thought that it would still be hot.

"And get this, sir!" the XO said.

He pulled an external jack from his sleeve and hooked it into a small hand-held device.

"Taco-Charlie-Two, this is Six Alpha. Do you read me?" he asked

All of the metal surrounding them would effectively block all comms, Ryck knew, so he wondered what the XO was trying to prove.

"Six Alpha, this is Two-Actual. I read you," Gershon Chomsky's voice came over Ryck's speakers.

"See? This is HECLA's gear. Chuck told me it makes use of T-486's core as sort of an old fashion communications cable. The planetoid itself conducts the signals. Our comms won't work with it.

I've already asked. But he's got eight of these, and they're ours for the taking."

How those things functioned was beyond Ryck, but all he needed to do was know that they did—and he had eight of them.

"Good job, Sandy. I'm impressed. OK, this is what I want you to do. For First Platoon, we're going to need the shaft big enough for the PICS. I want half in one bunker, half in another. See if you can manhandle them down by hand. I don't want to get Sgt Ling's squad back in and out more than we have to. And get the tiki hut near the shaft of one of those bunkers. Where are you putting Weapons?"

"Right there, sir," the XO said, pointing down through the rock floor of the bunker and off at an angle.

At the same time, he sent Ryck a diagram showing the planetoid and each fighting hole and bunker. Next came the fields of fire based on those positions. There were some gaps on T-486's surface, but once out past about 20 meters, the entirety of space around it was covered by Marine weapons.

Ryck didn't want to stay below too long, out of comms with battalion, so he and the XO flew up the shaft and back out onto the surface. His EVA automatically darkened his visor in the bright light. Without an atmosphere to diffuse the light, the light was sharp and white, so the surface was either illuminated very brightly or was lost in shadows. The vacsuits' sensors were not as sophisticated as those of a PICS, and visuals were the prime method of spotting an enemy. With the gaps in the Marines fields of fire, if there were a counterattack and troops reached the surface, the shadows could give them a degree of concealment. Ryck tried to think how he could eliminate that weakness.

Not that he expected to have to confront Confederation troops. With the Federation in control of the Telchine Belt, the reasonable thing for the Confederation to do would be to come to the negotiating table. The Federation would deny that it had gone into Confederation space to rescue the *Julianna's Dream*, and the Confederation would insist that it was merely reinforcing its claim to the Cygni B System.

LCDR Pillsbury, back on the *Inchon*, had briefed them that most of this was for show. Most other governments would know they'd been in Confederation space, but most would agree that HECLA's facilities, which had been operational for over 20 years, gave the Federation the stronger standing there. A draw, and things would reset back to the starting line. Maybe not a draw for the family of the dead Confederation soldier, but a draw in the overall scheme of things as governments went.

"First Sergeant, can you read me?" Ryck sent via a P2P. There was no answer. The relay rekis would have reached him if he were on the surface, so he must be checking out the fighting positions, too.

"PFC Çağlar, please track down the first sergeant and bring him here," he told his shadow.

He wasn't sure why he still needed a body guard, but orders were orders. Çağlar was developing into a good Marine, but it was a relief not to have him hovering over him for a few minutes.

Ryck checked his watch. The XO said the HECLA engineer would be done in another two hours. Ryck would get his men into their positions, but then what? They might be sitting on this rock for days in their vacsuits, and he had to think of something else to keep them alert. He wondered if he could rotate a couple of rekis back to the *Inchon* for short breaks of real food and showers. He'd have to ask the CO.

Now that the Marines had prevailed, they had to revert to what military men going back to the Babylonians and before had to master: waiting.

Chapter 31

Ryck stunk. His nose had mostly adjusted, blocking the bulk of his ripe aroma, but it could still register the stink of living inside a vacsuit for two days. The suit's cleaning nanos processed his body wastes, but his skin itched, and he felt grimy. A hot shower aboard the *Inchon* sounded like paradise. Unfortunately, that would have to wait.

As with chow, officers went last. And with only 2/3 of the company having gotten out of their vacsuits for 30 minutes each in the tiki hut, Ryck didn't think he'd get his chance before they were back on the *Inchon*.

He'd even let the POWs have their 30 minutes. To Ryck's mild surprise, the POWs hadn't been picked up by the Navy. He guessed no one thought they had any intel. This was not real warfare—it was a political game, and the POWs were just bargaining chips. They'd get back to their cohort soon enough.

Ryck had placed them in one of the bunkers the HECLA engineer had dug, then pretty much left them alone. He hadn't even bothered to put a guard on them after their senior man had given him their parole.

Political maneuvering or not, Ryck had to get the company back on the ship in another 40 hours or so. Despite the very efficient scrubbers in the vacsuits, they would start running out of O2 right about then. Scrubbing the air took out CO2, but it did not produce additional oxygen. That has to be added to each vacsuit every 20-24 hours, and after two more charges, the Marines would be out.

Weapons and Bravo were at least in a ship, albeit a very crowded ship with close to 400 Marines in the two companies. They were on full combat alert, but they didn't have to live in their vacsuits. The CO had let Ryck know that before the company started running out of O2, if the mission was still on, he was going to have the two companies relieve Charlie and Alpha.

"You about ready to get out of these vacsuits, Skipper?" Hecs asked, coming up from behind to stand next to him.

Ryck instinctively turned to look at the first sergeant, and when he twisted his head, his left ear brushed the speaker inside his helmet. He'd done that a lot over the last two days, and his ear was sore. It was a minor inconvenience, but annoying just the same. A very simple med-nano injection could heal the ear in a few minutes, but no one had ever designed a simple injection port in the suits, an obvious need. When he got his turn in the tiki hut, *if* he got it, he'd ask Doc for a booster.

"You've got that right, First Sergeant," he told Hecs over the P2P. "I'm getting rather rank in here."

The Two Marines looked over the rocky landscape of T-486. Within 200 meters of him, there were over 40 Marines, but he couldn't see even one. Some would be resting, but the security watches would be just below the surface inside the shafts.

Ryck was just about to say something when his alarms went off.

"Confederation of Free States ships have just entered the system," his AI intoned while the figures flashed and ran on his screen.

"Threat Condition 1, I repeat, Threat Condition 1," Hecs shouted over the command circuit as he sprinted for the command bunker.

Ryck let him go. Even with the relay rekis sitting above them, with the Marines in the fighting holes, comms was spotty, and Ryck knew that Hecs would be grabbing the HECLA communicator to send the message to all hands.

Ryck tried to make sense of what was flashing on his display. Two, no now three Confederation ships had flared from bubble space into the system, still a long ways out, but closer than they'd shown the capability in the past. One was immediately identified as the R-23, a battle cruiser, which put it on par with a Federation cruiser. The next two were destroyers. Another ship, a corvette, appeared on his display. On paper, at least, the four ships outgunned the Federation task force. The *Inchon* was the newest class of Federation ship, but it was not a battle cruiser, like the old *Ark Royal*. Its systems were more advanced, but it did not have the pure firepower of the older ships.

It was almost 30 seconds before Charlie Company was put on Threat Condition 1 by battalion. Hecs had beat them to it. Ryck guessed the ship had more pressing concerns, but the delay left Ryck feeling slightly exposed.

The first sergeant popped his head out of the command bunker shaft and gave Ryck a thumbs up before disappearing out of sight again. The word had gotten out to all hands.

Ryck could see the tops of vacsuit helmets and the muzzles of weapons as Marines looked out of their fighting holes. It reminded him of the ancient kids game the twins has just started playing, Whack-a-Mole. The image bothered him. He hoped the analogy would not play through. He wondered for a moment if he should get his Marines out of the positions, to keep them more mobile, but he realized that would make them *very* exposed on this small rock.

The display on his face shield flickered ever so slightly, something Ryck had noticed when he was assaulted with multiple Flash-A messages. His AI had to listen to the messages before prioritizing them for Ryck to hear. Ryck would have thought that a simple manual override would be a nice tool to have. He wanted any battalion comms first, then he could worry about any other Flash-A's.

His AI fed him a task force message first. The three ships were pulling out of the system to re-group. Ryck's heart fell. They were being abandoned. Ryck had almost expected it when the initial report came in. That was a formidable task force the Confederation had sent, and the Navy commanders liked to go into battle in formations and with maneuver plans, not spread out over a star system.

At least the two Gryffyn monitors, the ones providing support to Charlie and Alpha, would remain on station. Without the gunners aboard the *Inchon* controlling them, though, they would revert to AI control, and in another stupid way to set them up, Ryck had no way to contact the monitor to request specific support.

Unless the *Inchon* and her escorts could drive away the Confederation ships, the Marines could be swept up like trash alongside the road. Ryck couldn't stomach the possibility of having to surrender his company, but in the political maneuverings that were taking place and the jockeying for an advantage, he couldn't see sacrificing Marines for a checkmark on a negotiating list.

It would have been nice to have the *Ark Royal* after all, but Ryck just hoped the *Inchon* would be able to take control back over the system.

The second message, this one from battalion, started immediately after the first and was limited to the command circuit. It would be going to the four company commanders and any senior staff not on the *Inchon*. "All commanders, this is Taco-Six-Alpha. The task force is pulling out in hopes the Confederation ships will follow. They will return. Your orders are to hold fast until then. The CO will be attempting a cast momentarily and will rendezvous at Blue Barrel. If he does not reestablish contact, I will assume command and issue orders as the opportunity allows. Taco-Six-Alpha, out."

Ryck involuntarily looked up as if he could see the *Inchon* leaving the system. The XO's comment about the CO not reestablishing contact was necessary. If the CO was going to attempt a cast from the *Inchon* while it was maneuvering for bubble space, he was taking a huge risk. If the ship entered bubble space before he cast in a shuttle or reki, he would be lost forever. While theoretically a reki or shuttle could launch as the ship gained speed, in reality, even before it was ready to enter bubble space, things tended to happen—bad things. No one knew exactly why, even if theories abounded. The bottom line was that in a reki, the CO had probably less than a 50/50 chance of a successful cast. In a shuttle, a little bit more.

Ryck needed to brief his men, so he flew to the command bunker shaft. Sgt Contradari was in the shaft, watching Ryck approach. There was no room for two men in the shaft at the same time, so Contradari came out, letting Ryck in.

Ryck briefed the first sergeant, Doc Kitoma, Çağlar, and the HECLA chief engineer, then picked up the HECLA communicator. Within a few moments, he had all his commanders on the phone, the XO listening in with Jeff and the gunny listening in with Ephraim.

With the *Inchon* task force gone, they had no Navy support, so Ryck's greatest concern was a spaceborne naval attack. He wanted all his Marines in their fighting positions where they would have the most cover.

Ryck had been without Navy support on Weyerhaeuser 23, but that had been because their ship, the *FS Intrepid*, had been caught up in the battle. This time, the task force had fled the scene, and that was a lonely feeling.

This wasn't the first time Marines had been in this situation over the centuries. Back in 1942, Old Reckoning, the United States Marines had landed on the island of Guadalcanal. The Navy, fearful of Japanese air and sea power, fled the scene before the Marine's supplies could even be offloaded. Four months later, the Marines were on the verge of starvation, but they fought on, often with equipment taken from their enemy. They would not surrender despite the odds stacked against them, and three months after that, when the US Navy had returned, the island was secured. Ryck had studied the battle as part of his history studies for his degree, and he'd been fascinated with the battle and the valor shown by the Marines. He'd wondered how he would have reacted had he been serving then. Now that he was in a similar situation, he hoped he would not be tested in the same way. He hoped the *Inchon* task force would return soon.

Ryck waited with his Marines, wondering what was going on out in the reaches of space. He waited for word from the CO, to hear that he had taken command of the situation. He waited for the Confeds to make a move. One thing was for sure—he hated waiting and would rather be instigating action instead of having it thrust at him.

After about an hour, his AI said, "Incoming hypervelocity M-883 missiles, targeting Johnnie Walker and Campari. Impact in approximately 20 seconds."

"Incoming!" Ryck screamed over the open circuit. "Take cover!"

Most of the Marines were already in their fighting positions, but a few, like Ryck, were standing outside. Ryck hoped they all made it in as he dove for his position, flying headfirst down the shaft. He didn't reverse fast enough, and slammed into the bottom before he could right himself.

His AI had the specs up on his display. The M-883 was a 500kg rocket capable of 6,000 meters per second. It didn't have a warhead but relied on the simple physics of mass times velocity to release huge amounts of energy. Only 22 centimeters across, it was a difficult target to hit, and even if intercepted and destroyed, the broken pieces of it would continue on and would wreck havoc on a ship.

On a ship!

T-486 was a huge mass of iron and nickel. As fast as the M-883 was, it wouldn't break the planetoid apart. The Confeds were targeting the monitors. So sure was Ryck of this that he started back up the shaft, Çağlar shouting at him to stop.

The space above the shaft flared with a blinding white light—but T-486 remained quiet. Ryck cautiously flew up the shaft, Çağlar on his ass, until he had outside comms.

"We have lost contact with the monitor. All indications are that it has been taken offline. The monitor assigned to Campari has also, with a high degree of probability, been taken offline," his AI reported.

A monitor was an extremely tough piece of gear, able to take a tremendous pounding. But the Confeds didn't have to destroy it, only destroy its ability to fight. The missile-strike most likely damaged the monitor's rail gun beyond internal repair, but more effectively, took out it's AI and ability to process targets and take them under fire. Destroyed or simply unable to compute firing data, the bottom line was that Charlie Company no longer had the monitor providing support.

Ryck scanned his display, watching for anything that could indicate a threat. Even without the monitor, there were numerous

Federation scanning assets keeping track of what was happening. There were unmanned active and passive scanners strategically placed around the system. Recon was out there, too, somewhere, watching and reporting.

Ryck knew something was coming, and it was almost a relief when one of the scanners picked up the threat, which his AI identified as a Confed ALC, an Atmospheric Landing Craft. The name was not important. The craft could maneuver in open space as well. What did matter was that it was a heavily armed, heavily armored, landing craft that could carry a century plus of Confed soldiers, or about 90 individuals.

Ryck would feel confident facing a century with Charlie Company—on an even playing field. But this was not even. The Confeds had the high ground, and they had an ALC that could stand off and wipe out the company.

"Çağlar, pass to the first sergeant that I want all hands inside their fighting positions," Ryck told the PFC.

His ever-present shadow was still right below him, and Çağlar flew back down the shaft a couple of meters until he had a direct shot into the bunker. Ryck could hear him pass the order, but the metallic walls of the shaft blocked the first sergeant's reply.

Ryck edged back up. He knew he shouldn't be exposing himself like that, but he had to know what was going on. Almost 30 minutes later, the ALC arrived on station. It did not land, though, to disgorge an angry century. If it had, Ryck had been ready to scramble his company and get them up on the surface to enter the fray. The first thing the ALC did was to quickly take out each of the waiting rekis, to include the relays. The only way now to contact the platoons on the other side of T-486 was through the HECLA comms, a capability that Ryck hoped was unknown to the Confederation troops.

Less than ten minutes after that, an explosion erupted 70 meters away. Ryck didn't need his AI to inform him that the ALC was bombarding them. Ryck edged back down the shaft and into the bunker.

Soldiers for centuries had been subject to long bombardments, but history showed that if those soldiers were dug in, a bombardment had little effect. It could break the will, as it had for the now disbanded Howard's Defenders on Silver Light. The Legion subjected the mercenary company to a week of heavy bombardment. Not one merc was killed, but their will was broken, and they surrendered without a fight when the Legion landed.

But disciplined troops could emerge from a bombardment as a fighting force, as the Japanese soldiers had done at Iwo Jima during World War II. They had been subject to intensive naval gunfire and aerial bombardment, but when the US Marines landed, they emerged from their tunnels to engage the Marines.

Ryck trusted his Marines. They were the best soldiers known to man. He knew they would endure this, then kick ass when given the order.

Ryck briefed each commander over the HECLA comms. He wanted each platoon to be reminded that they were not alone, that the entire company was in this together, ready to provide support. Then he simply moved to stand beside the first sergeant and wait it out.

The bunker shook with every strike, but the ALC's 30mm kinetic gun was having almost no impact on the company. The 30mm shell packed a huge wallop, and T-486 shuddered with each strike, but the planetoid, while small as celestial bodies went, was still a huge mass of iron and nickel. The Confederation gun wasn't making a dent in the surface. What was a bigger threat was the ALC's auxiliary hadron cannon that swept their positions. It wasn't penetrating the bunkers and fighting holes either, but it was keeping the Marines bottled up. If they stuck their heads out, they could get burnt off.

It was not as if any of the Marines within Third Platoon had a weapon big enough to take out the heavily armored ALC, even if they could hit it, which would require getting out in the open and letting a targeting AI triangulate the ACL's position. Getting out in the open was the key there, and a suicide mission.

"XO, still nothing there?" he asked on the HECLA line.

"No, sir. The sensors haven't picked up anything either, at least as far as I'm getting."

Just because there seemed to be only one ALC over them didn't mean that was the case. Something had fired the missiles that had taken out the monitor, and that was too big of a job for a single ALC. If Ryck had been planning this assault, he would have hit all sides of T-486 at once. Not doing so left the craft vulnerable. There were several weapons in the inventory that could be effectively used against such a craft—the problem was that Ryck didn't have any of those weapons.

The bunker flickered as the hadron beam passed over the entrance. The beam itself was not in the visible spectrum, but his AI informed him that the beam was interacting with the small amounts of phosphorous that was in the taenite. The interaction glowed like radiation was portrayed in the flicks, but evidently it was not dangerous.

Ryck dialed the code for Lt McAult, who was in a small bunker 150 meters away from Ryck, "You holding up OK?" he asked when the lieutenant responded.

"No joy, sir, no joy. But we're fine. Just anxious to hit back. Sitting here, just absorbing this, it's well, like—"

"I know. Same here," Ryck cut in. "Look, I'm worried about that dead space we discussed. An ALC is a personnel lander, after all, and it could be here to put troops on the ground." If there is any let-up, don't want for me. Check it out. You understand?"

"Roger, sir, I understand. We're on top of it."

"Third is ready to go," Ryck passed on the open circuit, which inside the bunker, meant only the other four men.

"How long do you think this is going to last?" Hecs asked, the first time he'd shown any degree of uncertainty for as long as Ryck could remember. Ryck realized that the claustrophobic nature of hiding in the tight space while lethal weapons kept them pinned down was getting to the first sergeant.

Ryck felt it too. He wanted to strike back. Sitting in the bunker like this went against every fiber of his very being.

So far, not a single Marine had been hurt, and Ryck was not going to change that by ordering some stupid, hopeless counter-assault. The CO had ridden Ryck for not being as proactive as he should be, but even the CO would have to agree with his decision here. Keep everyone alive for what could be coming down the pike next. If that was the *Inchon* coming back, then the little ALC that was keeping the company pinned would have to retreat or be blasted from space.

That "little" ALC was big enough, however, to keep Charlie Company hiding in their holes like frightened rabbits, and that gnawed at Ryck. He was so consumed with that thought that he didn't notice the change.

"Skipper, I think it's stopped," Hecs said.

Ryck looked around. The impacts had, in fact ceased.

"Çağlar," check it out, but be damned careful, you hear?" Ryck told the PFC.

Çağlar nodded, then edged to the access shaft. He looked back at Ryck before starting up—and came back down in a hurry.

"We've got company, sir, lots of them. I think they're setting up some sort of field gun, but it doesn't look like a weapon," the PFC said.

Not a weapon? Ryck wondered. What then?

He hesitated for only a moment, then moved to the shaft to go up himself.

"No, sir," Çağlar said, moving to block him.

Ryck looked at his PFC, not believing what he'd heard. Yes, he, as the company commander, was not supposed to endanger himself needlessly. That still ate at his core. He was a Marine, nothing more, no better than any other Marine. But it had been drilled into his head that while he may be "worth" no more as an individual, he was more valuable as a commander than a single rifleman was. This was not to demean Private Schmuckatelli as a person, but it was Ryck's training and experience that would keep Marines alive and ensure the mission's success. This had been a hard concept for Ryck to accept, and he was only lukewarm on it. But he had to see what they faced if he was going to be able to use that experience and training effectively.

"Çağlar, I need to know what's out there," he said, trying to step around the big Marine.

"Yes, sir, but I've got it," Çağlar said, tapping his face shield.

A moment later, Ryck's face shield flashed with an incoming notification.

Ryck realized what that was, and accepted the incoming, wanting to slap the side of his helmet. Of course, Çağlar had done a face shield shot, recording everything he'd seen. And what he'd recorded suddenly filled his own face shield display as if he was looking out at the scene himself.

Çağlar had known that not everyone had to expose himself, and the fact that Ryck had forgotten was not a good omen. He had to remain sharp and focused.

He patted Çağlar on his shoulder in thanks, then studied the scene. It was only two seconds long, so Ryck froze it.

Approximately 200 meters out, at the start of one of Charlie's dead spaces, there looked to be twenty or more Confederation troops. Four were on a weird contraption of which Ryck was unfamiliar. He blinked on a highlight and queried his AI.

"New Long Industries PR55C Field Fabricator with some modifications," the AI informed him, then ran a list of specifics along the edge of his display.

Essentially, the PR55C was a fabricator that could be taken to a field location and fabricate machine parts needed to keep construction or mining equipment functioning. Why the Confederation troops were setting it up was beyond Ryck, but it couldn't be good, and Ryck wanted to take it out before it could do whatever the Confederation soldiers wanted it to do.

But with the arrayed soldiers facing this group of fighting positions, as soon as one Marine tried to exit a shaft, he would be dead meat. The shafts were just not big enough to get more than one Marine at a time out, and even that was at a fairly slow pace. It was Horatio at the Bridge in reverse with the Etruscans keeping Horatio from exiting the bridge and taking the fight to them.

Ryck felt a slight shudder run through the bunker.

"Skipper, it's the XO. The ALC is over their position and bombarding them," Hecs said, the HECLA communicator in his hand.

Grubbing shit! They're going to keep us bottled up and get troops down to dig us out, Ryck thought. Not a bad plan.

The question was what Ryck was going to do about it. No one in Third could get out to take it to the Confederation troops facing them without getting taken out themselves as they exited the shafts. He considered Second or Weapons. No one was facing them yet, but with the grubbing ALC overhead, if he ordered them out of their positions to break up the assault here, they would be easy pickings for the ALC.

"First Sergeant, ask Second if they are covered by that gubbing ALC, and I want Chomsky to see if we've got any comms from battalion. I need to know when the *Inchon's* coming back," Ryck ordered.

He quickly went through his options. If First weren't under fire at the moment, he could order the PICS squad to assault. The ALC could take a PICS Marine out, but it was possible that some would get to this position, and even one or two could wreck havoc among the soldiers facing them.

He should have realized that an ALC, of all things, was not just going to orbit and fire at them. It was a personnel lander, after all. Of course, if he'd ordered the PICS squad into the assault earlier, then who would they assault? The ALC? There were no Confederation troops on the planetoid at the time.

But with the ALC over their position, that was a non-starter now. Ryck went through his options, and none were too good. All would result in a huge loss of Marines with only a limited chance of any tactical advantage. No option seemed good, and that left the status quo. The CO said Ryck was getting too cautious, and maybe he'd been right, but what else could he do?

"Lieutenant Chomsky says the ALC can fire on his position without moving. The orders from battalion still stand—hold our position. Nothing about the *Inchon* yet."

"Any great ideas coming to you First Sergeant?" he asked Hecs, only partly in jest. "You, Sergeant Contradari?"

He really could use some input. Ryck had a bad feeling about that field fabricator. The Confederation troops would not have landed it and be protecting it unless they thought it could be of some use.

It seemed no matter what he did, it would turn out bad. Dark thoughts began to whisper in his mind about the unthinkable: surrender! Marines didn't surrender. Sometimes they advanced in the other direction, as the saying went, but they never surrendered. Ryck didn't want to waste a single Marine's life, and if there was no possible way to prevail, anyone killed would have been a wasted life. His career would be over, and he probably would be court-martialed, but that might be the only realistic choice. Better his career than the needless death of even one Marine.

"Sir, it's Lieutenant McAult," Sgt Contradari said, holding the comms that the first sergeant had handed to him.

"Sir, something's happening. The top of our shaft, it's melting!"

Melting? What?

Then it hit him. The fabricator. It could take raw material and transform it into pretty much anything in its recipe banks. It couldn't make roast beef out of iron, but it could process iron into steel and tools. Or taenite. Normally, a field fabricator crept over the raw materials, spitting out the desired product. Ryck pulled up Çağlar's face shield shot again and saw the projector tube that had been jury-rigged to the front of the fabricator—the modifications his AI had mentioned. What they had managed to do was to propel forward the dissolution mechanism, the one that broke down raw materials into a usable form. It would be extremely inefficient, but it could breakdown the taenite around the lip of each fighting hole, sending what would act as molten taenite to drift to the bottom. They were making metal plugs to trap the Marines.

Ryck couldn't allow that. He could immediately order a full assault, but if the enemy soldiers were even half competent, each shaft would be covered. It would be suicide.

There had to be another option. Ryck hoped something would happen that would give him the opportunity he needed.

That something happened just seconds later. The space above T-486 flared bright white for a split-second, so bright that the light bounced its way down the shaft and illuminated the command bunker.

Ryck grabbed the comms and called Lt Chomsky.

"Sir, the ALC, it just blew up!" the excited lieutenant shouted before Ryck could even ask. "Something came fast and hit it, and my AI is trying to analyze it now!"

"It's gone? Completely?"

"Yes, sir. There's nothing left bigger than a fucking basketball!"

For all his worrying, Ryck didn't hesitate as the plan came to form in his mind. He immediately switched to First Platoon.

"Jeff, get the PICS squad out immediately. I want them assaulting the enemy at my position before they can regroup. Follow with the rest of your platoon in support. Do you understand?"

"But sir, they'll hit us as soon as we start coming up," Jeff protested. "We're under fire now."

"No you're not, Jeff. The ALC has been destroyed. You're clear. Get moving now before the Confederation troops can regroup.

"Are you sure, sir?" Lieutenant de Madre asked, a tremor in his voice.

"Yes I'm sure, Lieutenant, and I don't have time to argue. This is an order. "

"Aye-aye, sir," the First Platoon commander said.

Ryck had already switched to McAult. "Mike, I want anyone who can to reach up and fire out of their fighting positions. I don't care if they hit anything, so no use going completely exposed. Just hands and weapons. Keep the enemy occupied. First is coming to pull us out of this mess."

"Roger that, sir."

"Gershon," he told his Second Platoon commander. "I'm ordering Jeff with his PICS into assaulting the Confeds who are on our asses here. I want you to swing around left on the z-axis, then converge on our position. Let the PICS take the brunt of the assault, but be ready to jump in if needed."

That left Weapons. "Ephraim, I want all your Marines out of their fighting holes. Be ready to get back in if another unwelcome guest starts bombarding us, but be ready to move if I need you here."

He'd contemplated sending at least the gun section forward, but Weapons was the farthest away, and he hoped that First would have won the field by then. And if the Confederation had some nasty surprises, well, Weapons should be mostly intact to carry on the fight.

Ryck didn't have time to second-guess himself. This was happening now, and he was committed.

Çağlar, after hearing Ryck give the order to Lt McAult, had flown back up the shaft and was reaching out, his M99 pointed in the general direction of the Confeds as he let loose a burst. The platoon had a mixture of the 4mm flechette weapon and hadron beam projectors, but in a naked vacuum, both would be equally effective against EVA-type suits. If one of Çağlar's flechettes actually managed to find its mark, the Confed receiving it would be in a world of hurt.

Ryck kept waiting for First to kick off the assault. Five minutes went by, then ten minutes. Sgt Contradari relieved Çağlar in firing, then the first sergeant relieved Contradari. Ryck was going crazy not knowing what was happening.

Ryck wouldn't be able to hear the assault kick off, of course, in the vacuum of space, but he should be able to see flashes of light as they bounced off of the metal in the surface. He edged below the first sergeant, wanting to get up high enough to pick up any comms.

He knew the PICS Marines would have to be assisted up the shafts by the other Marines given the low output of their propulsion packs. But that should take only five minutes at most, and then it should take less than four or five minutes to make it to his position.

It was 15 minutes, though, before he saw the first flashes of reflected light. The first sergeant was just coming back down the shaft, so Ryck pushed past him and shot out to the surface.

Protocol be damned, he could not sit by while his Marines were in the shit. Ryck carried an M99 as well, and he swung around to face the Confeds as his PICS squad swept forward, weapons blazing.

Ryck was barely aware of the others popping out of his bunker and Marines from Third swarming out. Ryck was flying forward, a meter or so off the surface, firing his weapon. It looked as if the Confederation troops had been caught flat-footed. They were still oriented toward Third Platoon, and several of them were still firing at the platoon while 13 Marines in PICS came stomping in from their flank. At least one Marine fell limp, his momentum carrying him forward. Ryck gave the Marine a quick glance, and a kinetic round of some sort hit the Marine again, pushing his body into a slow spin.

A 7.5mm rocket flew past Ryck just a meter or two ahead of him. It had been fired from one of his PICS Marines.

"Watch your displays!" Ryck shouted over the open circuit. "We don't need to be shooting at each other!"

The rocket, unaffected by gravity, flew in a straight line above the surface until the planetoid curved underneath it and in flew into open space. Ryck knew it would keep going forever, its lethal warhead searching for a target.

Ryck could see the PICS Marines moving forward, their weapons blazing. Despite the confusion, despite the fight, his critical eye noted the professional movement of the Marines as if this was a casual walk-through at the battalion's training fields back home. He felt a surge of pride as his Marines converged fearlessly on the enemy.

The field fabricator exploded in a shower of sparks, taking two Confed soldiers with it as the PICS' heavier 8mm hypervelocity flechettes tore it—and the soldiers—apart.

Moments later, the surrender was shouted over the universal circuit. Several Confeds were still fighting, and the Marines didn't let up. Neither did Ryck. As long as the enemy was fighting, so was he. He fired a burst at a soldier who was trying to fire around a large boulder at the advancing PICS Marines, and several flechettes found their mark. The Confed soldier fell back and softly bounced off the rocks, his body floating away, but limp and motionless.

The surrender call was repeated, and this time, the surviving Confederation troopers stopped. None exposed themselves more than they had to as a couple of Marines still fired until numerous "cease fires" filled the circuits.

Ryck was breathing hard, but not from exertion. The assault had been a release, more mental than physical. He flew up a few more meters so he could survey the scene. More than half of the 20 or so Confed soldiers were down hard. The Marines were not unscathed, however. He could hear the calls for corpsmen on the open circuit.

The Second Battle for T-486 was over, and once again, the Marines had taken the field of battle. The question Ryck had to ask himself was if there would be a third battle.

Chapter 32

Ryck swept the area, Çağlar in trace. His display showed six light blue avatars and four gray. Six Marines were WIA, three from Third Platoon whose hands were taken off when they lifted their weapons to fire on the Confeds.

Three Marines, Sergeant Justin Ramikin, LCpl Terry Hyde-Organi, and PFC Chuck Playstatus, were dead, beyond hope of regen. All three had been in Third Platoon and had been at the forefront of the supporting assault on the Confederation troops.

Ryck wondered if he should have left the assault to Sgt Ling's squad in their PICS. Not one of those Marines had been hurt. He felt guilty, knowing that his decision had cost the Marine's their lives.

Was it really necessary? Did I fuck up? He kept asking himself.

Ryck went to each fighting hole. If a Marine had been hit and had fallen back or retreated into his fighting position, Ryck's AI would not be receiving that Marine's signal. He could have left this to Lt McAult to report back to him, but he was too anxious, and while the gunny was processing the POWs and the lieutenants were sorting out their men, he and Çağlar were checking each hole.

"Skipper," First Sergeant Hecs passed on a P2P. "The POWs are secure, and Doc's getting the last Marines and Confed WIAs treated. Four are going into ziplocs and frozen. What are you orders now?"

Ryck stopped and looked around, trying to spot his first sergeant. He saw that Marines were going down into each hole, and he realized he was making a very poor use of his time. The Marines would find any more wounded. He needed to be leading, not guiltily searching for them himself. Mistake or not, a sound tactical decision or not, what was done was done, and he had to get back into his leadership position.

"Platoon commanders," he passed on the command circuit, "after Doc has everyone treated, I want each platoon back at its positions, but not inside the holes. I want your Marines standing by and ready to take cover, but we can't afford to get trapped again."

He did a quick check of the status of oxygen among the Marines. Most had about 16 hours left, but a few were down to 12. Something had to be done about that.

"Look, we're getting low on O2. No more trips to the tiki hut."

That was a rough call. Being in the vacsuits for this long was not only mentally draining, but physically. But each transition in and out, then in and out of the vacsuit, wasted small amounts of air—amounts they could not afford to waste.

"Lieutenant McAult, how is your hole? Is it still usable?" he asked his Third Platoon commander.

"Not really, sir. That thing burned off a lot of slag, and that almost blocked us in. We were barely able to squeeze by as it was. Another three or four minutes, and I think we would be still there, stuck inside."

That caused a shudder to sweep through Ryck. The Pearson Drill that had made the positions, had been destroyed during the ALC's bombardment. Without that, the Marines had only some frogs[23] to try and burn through the slag and free the Marines, and just a touch of even a spark from a frog would burn right through a vacsuit and expose the Marine to the vacuum of space. In the confined area of Mike's command bunker, there was really no way a frog could have been used without hitting the Marines there. But if they stayed in the bunker, they would suffocate as their O2 ran out.

"OK, I want you to double up where you can get some cover. Everyone else, until further notice I don't want anyone more than ten seconds away from their fighting position. Go to it."

"What about the XO," Hecs asked him on the P2P.

"The XO? I don't know. Just tag along with First, I guess," Ryck said, dismissing Sandy from his thoughts.

Executive Officers at the company level didn't have much purpose in combat. They were there to take over if the commander got taken out.

"Word is that he led the assault and got it moving when Lieutenant de Madre hesitated."

"What? No," Ryck protested. "I don't believe it."

"That's what I hear from SSgt Grimes," Hecs continued.

That didn't make any sense. Sandy was a good Marine, a good organizer. But a leader? Jeff was a natural leader, something that Ryck had witnessed too many times.

"You don't give the XO enough credit," Hecs said quietly. "I don't think you do him justice."

The first sergeant cut the connection, and Ryck shook his head inside his helmet. Grimes was wrong, he knew. The staff sergeant

---

[23] Frog: the nickname for a small, hand-held incendiary device. Thrown like a grenade or attached to a target, it could burn through most substances.

wasn't aware of all the factors. Jeff had gotten the platoon moving, and that had broken the back of the enemy.

Chapter 33

An hour later, Ryck was discussing their O2 situation with the first sergeant when the open circuit blared with "Incoming personnel!"

It was a relayed message. The ALC had taken out the relay rekis, so Ryck had had to station Marines around the perimeter of T-486 so that anything could get passed line-of-site. He hated to leave Marines exposed like that, but he had to be able to receive all information on what was going on around them. T-486 was slowly rotating, and at the moment, Ryck was on the far side of the planetoid from the rest of the battalion.

"Who is it, XO," he asked Sandy on a P2P.

"He's got our codes, and he's coming straight in. He just passed a message for you, sir. He says 'Shart is coming in for a visit.' Do you know what that means?"

Grubbing right I do!

"Shart" was Sergeant—no, he had to be at least a staff sergeant by now—Flavius Gutierrez, a recon Marine from Ryck's old team on GenAg 13 when they rescued the civilians during the Trinocular War.

"Yes, I do," he passed. "How's he coming in?" he asked, opening up the P2P to Hecs as well.

"Flying in his vacsuit, I guess. We've got his comms, but we can't pick up anything yet."

Recon did not use the standard vacsuit. Their slate-grey vacsuits were designed for very long duration missions and had the most up-to-date stealth technology.

"Who or what is 'Shart,' sir?" the XO asked.

"He was on my team in recon. As soon as he arrives, send him over."

"Roger that."

"'Shart?'" the first sergeant started. "As in 'shit and fa—'"

"Right on your first guess, first sergeant," Ryck interrupted. "You don't want to know."

"Maybe not," Hecs said with a chuckle. Then more seriously, he continued, "You know what that means, right?"

Ryck had to hesitate for a second before it dawned on him. "The ALC!"

After the battle, Ryck had tried to piece together what had happened to the Confederation ALC. His AI, which had more processing power than any of the other Marines, had not been able to identify what had struck the ALC, only that it had been moving fast. Kinetic energy alone had destroyed the Confederation craft. There were unarmed missiles in the Federation's inventory which were essentially huge, very high-velocity bullets, but there hadn't been any Federation ships in the system when the ALC was taken out. Ryck and Hecs had discussed the possibility that the monitor had not been completely taken out and had fired off a GD-1905 that somehow hit the ALC, but the "GD" stood for "Gravity Dropped," and the tungsicle needed gravity to generate the force it needed. The side-mounted rail gun on the monitor could get it moving through space as well, but probably not at the velocity necessary to completely destroy the ALC, and even that would be dependent on the tungsicle being somehow guided to the moving target.

If it wasn't the monitor that had taken out the ALCL, it was something else, and with Shart showing up, it was pretty clear. Somehow, the team had used their coffin, the small two-man reki, as a missile.

The coffin was a very high-speed, low-drag, two-man version of the normal reki used by Marines. It was heavily shielded with stealth technology, and it was fast—very fast. A Marine or sailor in a normal vacsuit could not take the high Gs—up to 20 Gs—but the vacsuits used by recon teams could compensate for that. It was conceivable that a coffin could get in close to an ACL, which frankly, would not have the vast array of sensors that a capital ship would have, then accelerate right into the ALC.

Ryck felt goosebumps as his thoughts took him to the next level. The coffin would have to be guided, and only one Marine, Shart, was coming in. Someone had been the guidance system for the coffin to hit the ALC. Someone had sacrificed his life for the Marines in Charlie Company.

"Grubbing hell," he said to himself, forgetting for a moment that he was still on the P2P with Hecs.

"RIP, brother," the first sergeant said.

The two Marines started discussing the O2 situation again while they waited, but their thoughts wandered, and both went quiet as LCpl Griffith from First escorted a Marine in a dull-grey EVA up to them.

"Shart!" Ryck exclaimed, hugging his old teammate.

"Captain, good to see you, sir," Shart responded on the open circuit.

That took Ryck aback. He was "Toad" to his teammates. Recon always used first names. Then he realized that Shart and he were not longer teammates, and normal military etiquette took over, especially on an open circuit.

"Staff Sergeant Gutierrez, it's been a long time," Ryck said, switching to the more normal form of address.

"Still sergeant, sir," Gutierrez said. "I had a sort of issue on liberty on Vegas."

If Shart had had an "incident" in Vegas, the hedonistic resort planet where almost anything went, it must have been pretty serious.

"My AI can't connect to your P2P. Can you connect to me? And to First Sergeant Phantawisangtong here."

A moment later, the sergeant came onto the P2P, and Ryck saw Hecs on as well.

"Honored to meet you, first sergeant. The skipper here, he told me and the rest a shitload about you. More about your 'King Tong" days than your combat together, I have to say."

"I'd say the honor is mine, sergeant. I take it you had a hand in taking out the ALC?'

"Uh, yeah," he responded before pausing.

Ryck could hear him take a few breaths before continuing.

"Me and Igor, that's Lieutenant Albert, I mean, me and him were monitoring the situation, and we could see what was happening to you guys. We don't have any fucking weapons, you know, 'cepting our personal side-arms, First Sergeant, but when you was in the shit, Igor—the lieutenant—he said we had a weapon. He meant our coffin. He explained to me the math with time and acceleration and Newtons and shit. I told him I would do it, but he said no. It was his job."

He paused again. Ryck couldn't see through the recon vacsuit's face shield, but he could imagine Shart trying to control his emotions.

"I tried to fight him, but he said no. So we came in close and waited, all power off and silent-like. When the ALC swung our way, I got off, and the lieutenant, he aimed at that fucking ship and went to 20 Gs. Ten seconds was all it took, and that ALCL never had no chance. She lit up like fireworks."

Ryck's AI did some calculations. At 20 Gs, for ten seconds, a 300 kg coffin and Marine together would have hit at more than a million Newtons. Shart was right. The ALC and crew "never had no chance."

"So I came here. I ain't got no ride now, so I figured I'm better off here with you."

Ryck never knew this Lieutenant Albert, but when they got out of here, he swore to himself that he would get to know more about the man and see that he was nominated for a Federation Nova. Ryck and all of his 220 Marines probably owed their lives to him.

"Sergeant, we're happy to have you, and we're in your debt," Hecs said.

"Not me, First Sergeant. Igor."

Ryck would talk more with Shart later, but he knew the best thing for the sergeant was to get him back on mission.

"What intel do you have. Any word on the *Inchon* task force? We've been in contact with our other two companies, but no one knows anything."

"It's not good, Skipper. We've been upgraded in our comms, and the lieutenant, he had a hadron repeater with the major back on Zephyr Hadreson. Before he, you know, they told him the *Inchon* was hurt, but still in the fight. The *Kuala Lampur,* she's gone, but three more ships have joined up, and the Navy and the Confederation are playing cat-and-mouse. The ships have been ordered not to return until the fighting's over."

Three grubbing days, and they were playing cat-and-mouse? Ryck wondered in disgust.

Naval engagements just did not last that long in modern warfare. Politics was raising its ugly head, and Ryck could smell its stink. The problem with politics was that it would be the ground troops, the Marines—and the Confederation soldiers—who would pay the price.

"Thanks for the update. That sucks, but it is what it is," Ryck said. "Do you need anything? Anything we can get you?"

"No, Skipper. But if I can crash someplace for a few winks? I've been on stims for so long that they're losing their effects, and I could use a bit of downtime."

"I've got you covered, Sergeant," Hecs said. "You can use the command bunker."

Hecs took Shart over to show him the shaft, before coming back to Ryck.

"Not good news," Hecs said.

"Grubbing politics!" Ryck responded. "Meanwhile, we sit here running out of O2."

"Well, there is Blue Barrel," Hecs said.

The two of them had been considering taking the company to Bravo's Company's objective, the HECLA ship. It was a long, long way to go in a vacsuit, some 100 klicks, and neither the PICS nor the three Marines in ziplocks could not make it on their own. There were just too many things that could go wrong, and the chances were that not every Marine would make it. Preston had already been rotating his Marines across the 30 km from Campari to Blue Barrel, and one of his Marines had been hit by a piece of debris. He'd barely been able to get to the ship in time to be pulled in by his squadmates and put into a ziplock. Despite all the modern technology available, space was dangerous, not meant for the likes of man.

But man needed simple O2 to survive. As the clock ticked down, Ryck would have to do something. The vacsuits did not have great acceleration, but by going full out for ½ the way, then reverse for the second half of the distance, they should be able to make the trip in about 40 minutes. Giving the company two hours, the trip could be made in a more controlled fashion.

Ryck was counting on the fact that the task force knew how much O2 they had. They would not abandon them to die. No matter what political game they were playing, at least one ship would come to extract them. He hoped.

If nothing showed up at the three-hour mark, he couldn't wait any longer. If he wanted his Marines to live, he would have to get them to the HECLA sorting ship.

Chapter 34

"Taco-All-Stations, Blue Barrel is under imminent attack. I repeat, Blue Barrel is under imminent attack by a Confederation cohort."

Ryck immediately hit the open circuit with, "Charlie Company, assume defense posture bravo."

Half of his Marines should be scrambling for their fighting holes, the other half staying near, but outside on the surface.

By mutual agreement, chatter between the four companies had been kept to a minimum. Even if their transmissions were scrambled, the mere fact that there were transmissions provided the enemy with intelligence that could be analyzed. But this was a game-changer.

Ryck blinked to the battalion command circuit. Without the battalion command center on the net, and with the CO probably dead, the circuit had become a private circuit for the four company commanders.

". . . on our scans. No ships," Preston was saying. "I think they've been hiding in wait before launching."

A flood of information poured into Ryck's AI, and he tried to make sense of it all. A cohort of Confeds had jumped Alpha's Second Platoon as it was approaching the HECLA ship. All hands showed as grey—all KIA. Just like that, 34 Marines and a sailor were dead. The cohort was now advancing on Blue Barrel, using the scattered rocks as cover as they moved closer.

A cohort was about 500 soldiers, and facing them were about 350 Marines from Bravo and Weapons, holed up in the sorting ship, and now only 150 or so Marines from Alpha about 20 klicks away. In space, 20 klicks was nothing, just a milischosh. The Marine's side arms would reach that far in the vacuum. But in an asteroid belt, and the Marines in only vacsuits, that was a long ways.

"Any sign of more Confeds?" Ryck interjected.

"None that we can pick up," Donte responded. "But we never picked up these guys, either. We're not equipped with sophisticated scanners, and they've evidently upped their cloaking game."

For the same reason the ALC had not been able to detect Lt Albert in his coffin, the Marines had not detected the lurking cohort. They just didn't have the sophisticated scanning capabilities necessary to do so. If the *Inchon* had been on station, Ryck doubted the Confeds could have remained undetected despite any improvements in cloaking technology. But the *Inchon* was gone, so it was a moot point.

The question was if there were more Confed troops still hiding out there.

"Donte, how long do you have?" Ryck asked.

"I don't know. I think they'll hit us in about 20. We're already getting potshots taken at us, but until they emerge from the tailings field, we can't do much about them, and they can't really launch into anything, either."

"Any sign of heavy weapons?" Ryck asked.

An incoming image hit Ryck's display. It was a 20mm ballista, as the Confederation called their canons. The specs were listed, but Ryck was familiar with it. Deadly on land, in space, it was bulky, but packed a tremendous wallop. How they had kept that thing cloaked was something Federation analysts would want to now, but in the here and now, it was a huge threat to Bravo and Weapons.

Donte, as tactical commander at Blue Barrel and acting battalion commander with the CO missing, had to decide if he should abandon the small cover offered by the ship, or get everyone out and try to break up the assault.

"I'm coming," Preston said. "We're going to take out that ballista before it's set up. I think we can intercept their path."

Ryck could see as his AI started to fill in enemy positions that at least two centuries were maneuvering to block that move. Preston would have a hard time fighting through them, and Donte didn't have much time to get his Marines deployed and ready to meet the remaining Confeds. If Preston could take out the ballista, then Donte's best bet was to remain on the HECLA ship, which would offer protection against small arms. If the ballista were able to deploy, though, the ship could be a death trap.

"Charlie is coming, too," Ryck said, keying in the company command circuit.

"You're too far out," Donte said. "Too dangerous, and anyway, the fight will be over before you could get here. We can handle this."

"Not if that ballista opens up. And what if there are more of them? No, we're almost out of O2, anyway, so we're on our way. Watch for us at your 45 degrees Z, 80 degrees Y. We don't need you opening up on us."

Ryck was circling one finger above his shoulder as he spoke, telling Hecs to round up the Marines for a quick movement. The first sergeant rushed to comply.

"It's, that's dangerous, man," Donte said. "If there is another cohort hiding out there, you'll be caught dead to rights."

"If there's another cohort out there and they take you guys, we're next. Besides, look at their disposition. They don't expect us, either. They're massing to meet Preston."

"He's right," Jasper said, quiet until now. "Get your ass moving, Ryck, and I'll buy you a beer when all this is over."

"Done and done," Ryck said.

Ryck started to blink the company command circuit open to get things moving, but he heard Donte's, "Go with God, my brother, go with God."

Chapter 35

Only ten minutes later, the company was lifting off T-486, their home for the last three days. Each PICS Marine had two Marines in vacsuits, one on each arm, basically ferrying them to the battle. Three Marines had Marines in ziplocks attached to their backs. The POWs had given their paroles for the next 12 hours. After that, they could use their comms to effect their own rescue.

They had no weapons, but Ryck hadn't wanted to leave them comms, either. What if they told the cohort moving into attack Blue Barrel? He had their parole, but not everyone followed honor and integrity. In the end, though, Ryck had no choice. By international treaty, signed by both the Federation and the Confederation of Free States, he could not abandon them without the means to communicate for their rescue. Moral issues aside, Ryck was not going to be a war criminal.

It was eerie to watch his company lift off in silence from T-486. A few years back, a flick had come out about the end of days. When the final battle between good and evil was decided, the souls of the dead left their earthly bodies to rise up to heaven. His Marines lifting off the planetoid looked surprisingly like that scene. The connection to those people in the flick being dead gave Ryck the shivers. He was not superstitious, but his psyche didn't like the comparison.

They flew in a transmission blackout. Their vacsuits didn't have cloaking capabilities, but there was no use in simply announcing their presence. Ryck knew that silently flying along for 40 minutes could play hell with his Marines. It was claustrophobic enough for many Marines simply to be in their vacsuits out in the reaches of space. Not to be able to communicate or even see each other's faces would make them feel more isolated, and an isolated Marine could stew in his own thoughts and feel the fingers of fear nibbling at his brain. Marines needed to be kept active, but there was no way for Ryck to do that.

He glanced over to his right. Twenty meters away, Çağlar flew along, motionless. Not really motionless, of course—they were flying through space at a good clip now. But he wasn't moving his arms or legs, and he wasn't moving in relation to Ryck. Ryck was not given to the claustrophobia some Marines felt when EVAing, but he felt a small spark of comfort knowing his PFC was there with him.

He had his AI monitoring both the battalion command circuit and the open circuit. He kept expecting to hear that the Confeds had launched on Blue Barrel. But it was Preston and Alpha who initiated major contact. The two opposing sides—a depleted Alpha and two Confed centuries-- clashed and started exchanging fire with each other among the asteroid field. Ryck shrunk the battle display and moved it to the top of his face shield, noting when each blue avatar shifted to light blue or gray. Too many were making that shift too soon.

Charlie Company reached its halfway point and reversed their thrust. He was beginning to hope that he could arrive and take out the ballista before it could fire, but still five minutes out, the Confed weapon opened up. The first shot missed, but the second one scored a direct hit on the HECLA ship.

Thirty seconds later, as the ballista scored a couple more hits, beams of light reached out to touch the Charlie Marines. Four avatars turned gray.

Federation beam energy weapons did not display light in the visible spectrum, but Confederation weapons were designed for that. It supposedly helped the gunners deploy their weapons, but Ryck thought it was stupid. It gave every Marine a point of origin for that weapon, and within seconds, over a hundred Marines opened fire on the small rock from which the Confeds had fired. One more beam reached out before they all went silent.

The Confeds knew they were there, so transmission silence was lifted.

"First, drop your PICS and with the rest, swing farther left and loop up and curve back on the ballista," Ryck ordered.

"Left," "up," and "down" didn't have much meaning in space, but with their AIs linked, directions were relative to the company center and showed up on every Marine's face shield display.

They were still moving fast as they entered the tailings field. This was a dense rubble pile of the tailings, or the unwanted refuse expelled from the sorting ship. The field was almost four kilometers across, and Ryck immediately saw why it had taken the Confeds so long to get their ballista up and firing. This was some dense shit.

A Marine went light blue—not from enemy fire, but from slamming into a rock the size of a truck. Their relative speed was still too much.

Then fire started reaching through the rubble toward them. Ryck saw explosions of kinetic rounds on the tailings, and flashes from energy weapons as they hit the rocks. One beam flashed between Ryck and Çağlar.

As Ryck watched his display, his AI started filling in more of the enemy. They were shifting to meet the company. And that was causing a gap on the far left side.

"Jeff, push further out, past most of the tailings. I see a gap opening, and I want you to exploit it. Come in from behind and take out that grubbing ballista," he passed on the command net.

"Uh, sir, we're taking heavy fire. I don't think we can make it over there," Jeff passed back.

Confused, Ryck looked closer at his display. His AI might not have every enemy position located, but it could account for every weapon, kinetic or energy, fired. First was under no heavier fire than any other platoon. Only one Marine in First had even been hit yet. But Jeff was hesitating, even veering off while the rest of the company was pushing forward.

As their reverse thrust slowed them all down enough to start taking cover and bounding from rock to rock, First slowed to a halt.

"Jeff," he said, switching to the P2P. "What's going on? I need you moving now! We need that ballista out of action."

"Yes, sir, I understand. But we're pinned down. I almost got shot right now!" the excited lieutenant almost wailed.

Ryck was shocked.

What the grubbing hell was going on?

He was about to repeat the order when the XO came on the First Platoon command net with, "First, form on me. We're the PME,[24] and we're going to kick some Confed ass."

Ryck watched as the XO, who'd been moving with First, peeled off to the left and up. There was a cheer over the net as the Marines in First quickly followed, blue avatars making a loop at the edge of Ryck's display.

Ryck was shocked—and ashamed. How could he have been so blind? Jeff was personable, an Alpha back at camp, but it looked like he was a coward. It was the XO, the small-statured, quiet 1stLt Sandy Peltier-Aswad, who had taken over to lead the assault. And judging by the cheer that had filled the transmission, the Marines in the platoon had been well aware of it and were overjoyed to be let loose, to do what Marines do.

The XO had the assault, and Ryck had to let him take it. There were more Confeds massing in front of the rest of the company, and Ryck had to deal with that. He pulled up behind a 50 meter-wide rock and checked his display. He had about 150 effectives left in the rest of the company. Opposing him was about the same number of

---

[24] PME: Point of Main Effort

Confederation troops. He was wracking his brain for a similar scenario he'd studied of conducted in training, and nothing came up. There had to be some tactical maneuver he could do to swing the battle to his favor.

But anything he ordered, any tactical sleight of hand, could swing the attention of the enemy to the XO and First Platoon. He knew that sometimes, soldiers just had to slug it out and rely on who was the biggest mother fucker on the battlefield. This was one of those times.

He was about to order an all-out assault when he remembered, almost too late, Sgt Ling and his squad. He'd told Jeff to jettison them as they would have slowed the platoon down. He looked at his display, and there they were, some 600 meters away.

"Sergeant Ling," he passed on a P2P. "You ready to earn your pay?"

"Sure am, Skipper."

"Get your metal asses over here. Stay out of sight if you can, but get here quick," he continued, sending a position to display. "We're going over the top, and you're going to lead us."

"Ooh-rah, Skipper. We'll be there in a moment."

Six hundred meters of vacuum would take a PICS more than a moment, but that gave Ryck time to brief his commanders. He kept an eye on First as they maneuvered up and in back of the ballista team. They would have to make their way through the mass of rubble, but hopefully, Ryck and the rest of Charlie would occupy the Confeds long enough so that none of them could reinforce the ballista security.

Several more Marine's avatars grayed out while Ling brought his squad into position. He acknowledged that he was ready, and Ryck gave the simple order to all hands, "Go!"

As Ryck and Çağlar flew over the rock behind which they had taken cover, the enemy fires intensified. More avatars grayed out in those first few seconds before the fired let up. Sgt Ling and his PICS Marines were in full attack mode, their heavier weapons like scythes among the Confeds. Ryck could almost see the hesitation among the enemy soldiers as they greeted this unexpected force. A number of enemy avatars started to fall back as if realizing that they could simply outrun the PICS to safety. The rest seemed to dig in to fight back, but their momentum was gone. The Charlie Company Marines were in among them, screaming like banshees over one of the universal open circuits. Ryck hadn't ordered that, but it was a good idea.

Ryck tried to fight while at the same time monitoring First Platoon. They were in the tailings, moving slowly. Eight Marines were down, either WIA or KIA, but they kept advancing. His AI didn't have a good grasp of the Confed soldiers, but many seemed to be falling.

Ryck saw movement out in front of him while he was focusing on the display and almost blew away LCpl Pratt before he realized what he was doing. He couldn't fight and keep command, so he put his M99 on safe and pulled Çağlar in a little closer for his personal security.

Ryck wanted to tell the XO to shift to his right, but he knew the XO was on the scene and needed to concentrate. He didn't need Ryck to try and take over the fight, commanding from afar.

"We're through the line, sir," Çağlar was telling him over the P2P.

Ryck looked around, then on his screen. The big PFC was right. Charlie has assaulted right through the Confeds. Mike McAult was turning back and mopping up small pockets of the enemy.

Ryck pulled to a halt and intently watched his display. He was about to order Second to swing around to support First when the blue avatars reached the big avatar for the ballista. The platoon didn't have a weapon big enough to destroy the big gun, but they had Ryck's signature piece of gear, the frog. The XO reported putting four of them on the ballista, and ten seconds later, they were busily burning the canon into inoperability. The XO had done it.

The canon had devastated the ship, blasting huge holes into it. Large numbers of Bravo and Weapons Company Marines had poured out of the ship to meet the main line of Confed soldiers, and a fierce fight had broken out. Large numbers of Marines had fallen.

"Donte, what's your status?" Ryck asked on the battalion command circuit. There was no answer, and Ryck figured Donte had his hands full. "We're coming in," he passed on both the command and the Bravo circuit. "Watch for us."

"Gershon, leave one squad as security to watch our back. XO, angle down to meet us. Everyone else, form on the PICS and let's roll up the Confeds facing Bravo."

Ryck knew that there were Confed troops he had just faced who had not retreated and who were still technically effective, but he hoped their will to fight was gone. He couldn't wait for a 100% secure battlefield if he were going to help Donte and Bravo. He had to strike when he could and when momentum was on his side.

Because the ballista had had to be close in order to fire beyond the tailings, they were only five kilometers from the battleline in front of them. Gunny had grabbed 13 EVA Marines and put one in back of each PICS. These 13 Marines literally pushed the PICS Marines to the front of the charge as Charlie Company swept down on the Confed lines.

Those Confeds on their right flank saw the approaching Marines and opened fire. Marines started to fall, but the massed fire of four vertical ranks of Marines, over 120 in all, quickly destroyed the initial opposition.

Someone on the Bravo circuit saw that and rallied his Marines to take advantage of the confusion. Ryck didn't recognize the voice, but whoever it was knew his stuff. When the XO, with only 11 Marines hit the back of the Confed line, the Confederation assault was broken. Confed soldiers, those who could, at least, started pulling back into the tailings.

"Donte, the attack is broken, do you read me?" Ryck asked.

"I haven't been able to raise him," Preston said. "But if you could, we could use a bit of support."

"On our way," Ryck told him.

"Bravo, this is Charlie Six. Consolidate in position while we pass through your lines," he sent over the Bravo command net.

"Roger that, sir. And thanks for your help," that same voice replied.

"Charlie, we're not finished. Alpha needs us, and we're answering the call. Sgt Ling, get your push crew ready and lead us to this position," he said, locating it on the display. "First, fall in as the top rank. Everyone else, same formation."

Ryck had the company in platoon strength across and one platoon stacked on top of the other. He'd played with this formation in training, and using it here successfully validated the concept. It would never work within gravity, of course, but in space, it allowed massing of fires. It limited maneuver, but Ryck had already thrown that out the window. He wanted to hit the enemy and hit them hard while they were wavering. The century or so that faced Alpha had to know that their brethren had quit the field or were lying dead, and they should be ready to break themselves.

Ryck had wanted to call the formation a phalanx, which was ironic as he was first using it against the Confederation, which loved all things Roman and used Roman terms within its military.

As the company formed back up to take the fight on, Ryck saw that the formation had shrunk. There were only nine PICS Marines in the center of the formation, and a quick query to his AI showed 97

Marines still effective. Ninety-seven Marines, though, was still a formidable fighting force, and there was work to be done.

Alpha had run into its opposition about ten kilometers from the ship. Ryck had a clear corridor, and he started firing his weapons at eight klicks away. He wanted the enemy to know they were coming to kick ass. Returning fire reached out to them, hitting several Marines, but the massed company flew on while Alpha renewed its efforts. Charlie never even reached the enemy before they broke and fled like the others into the tailings.

Charlie linked up with a decimated Alpha. Preston, flew up to meet him, one hand bloated and blue where he'd taken a round of some sort that had destroyed his vacsuit gauntlet. Luckily, his suit had been able to isolate the arm, but the hand was lost.

"I'd shake your hand, but seems like I can't," Preston said, holding up the blue flesh.

"You OK?" Ryck asked.

"Shit, never better. I've lost 120 Marines, so great fucking day," Preston said bitterly.

Ryck knew the feeling. He'd lost Marines before, and it was horrible. But he also knew the battle was not over. Hundreds of Confeds, maybe more had fled into the tailings. They could be forming up for a counter attack as they spoke.

"Get your Marines ready to move out. I want everyone back at Blue Barrel," he said, trying to sound authoritative.

Preston looked liked he wanted to say something, but he gave the vacsuit a shrug and simply said, "Roger that."

With no CO, XO, or S3, Donte was technically in charge of the remainder of the battalion. He was three numbers higher on the lineal list than Ryck. But Ryck couldn't raise him, so he took command, essentially forcing Preston to follow orders and not be consumed by what had happened. That could occur later, but not now.

Ryck gave the order to Charlie, and within five minutes, the combined two companies were moving back to the ship.

Another five minutes, and the entire battalion—what was left of it—was consolidating into one defensive position.

SSgt Pierpont, Bravo's First Platoon sergeant, was the Marine leading the company assault. He told Ryck that Donte had been killed by the second salvo of the ballista along with most of the company staff. Lieutenant Rainer had taken over, getting Marines out of the ship only to be killed a few minutes into the attack. Within five minutes, SSgt Peirpont was the company's senior man.

The news that Donte had been killed was a blow to his stomach. He couldn't believe it. Not Donte. He pushed the knowledge to the back of his mind and encapsulated it so it would not incapacitate him. He knew he would cry later, but he was the commander now, and he had to keep the battalion operational.

When the report came in of an envoy, Ryck, still numb, went to their defensive frontage. He'd placed most of his Marines to cover a half-sphere, facing the tailings. Approaching this sphere were two Confederation soldiers, their vacsuits flashing white. Ryck, with Çağlar in tow, who Ryck knew would ignore any orders to stay back, went forward to meet them. The two Marines stopped 10 meters from the Confed soldiers, slowly rotating themselves so the four men were oriented together.

"I am Captain Hennesey," one of the Confeds said. "My commander, LtCol Brisbane, offers a truce."

While the Confederation Army was organized along Roman traditions, they used the same ranks as other militaries used.

"A truce?" Ryck asked. "Seems to me a surrender would be more like it."

"That will not happen, I assure you," the captain said. "But a truce would be mutually beneficial. Let's have no more loss of life and let the politicians play their games."

So they feel the same about their leaders? Ryck thought.

"I have an effective battalion here which just kicked your collective asses. And you don't think a surrender is warranted?"

"I, uh . . . We have suffered losses, surprising losses. But we still have over 400 soldiers ready to fight if given the order."

"More like 150 there, Captain. Don't bullshit me."

The man floated in silence for a moment before responding, "Whatever the number, we can still fight and cause you casualties. And please," he said, lowering his voice, "be absolutely convinced that if you demand a surrender, LtCol Brisbane will order an attack. There is no question in my mind about that. You might be able to prevail, but at what cost? How many more Federation Marines will die? Please, take this back to your commander, and I pray he agrees."

"I am Captain Ryck Lysander, and I am in command. It is my call. What are the terms of your truce?" Ryck asked.

"Simply this. You keep this area around the ship, and we will retreat to T-624," he said, indicating one of the larger planetoids, this one some 50 klicks into the belt. "We conduct no operations against each other and leave each other alone. That is all."

Ryck considered it. He wanted the Confeds' surrender. They'd killed Donte, they'd killed his Marines. He hadn't even gone through the list yet, but he'd seen Gershon and SSgt Grimes on the KIA list already. The grubbing bastards needed to pay.

But was that his pride speaking? Would that bring back Donte? They were pawns in a bigger game, and would any more deaths serve the Federation?

Then there was the O2 situation. The surviving Alpha, Bravo, and Weapons Company Marines had been recently charged, but with the sorting ship destroyed, there was no way to manufacture any more new oxygen. In seven hours or so, Charlie Company Marines would start to suffocate. Even if they figured out a way to transfer air from the dead, that would only postpone the inevitable.

If the two sides had a truce, though, that could work to Ryck's advantage. He might be able to arrange for O2 from the Confeds, and not have to surrender to get it. That was the deciding factor.

"Tell your commander that I agree to his proposal. What does he want from me?"

"He has it. He's been following our conversation."

"Captain Lysander, this is LtCol Brisbane. Captain Hennesey is relaying this transmission. I accept your agreement in the name of the Confederation of Free States government. We will start pulling back."

Cowardly prick, Ryck thought. *Sends a captain instead of coming himself.*

That didn't matter, Ryck knew. He'd done what he had to do.

"Uh, Captain Hennesey, there's one more thing," he said as the captain started to turn away.

"What is that? But may I add that you have already agreed to a truce."

"Well, I thought you might want to know that you've got about 20 of your men back on T-486. They were POWs, but I left them there when they gave me their parole. They won't be trying to contact anyone for another ten hours, but your might want to go retrieve them."

"I, uh, thank you, Captain. I appreciate that, and yes, we will go get them. So if you have any Marines between here and there, please let them know we will be passing through."

Ryck watched the two soldiers turn and fly back into the tailings.

He turned to Çağlar and asked, "What do you think, Hans? Was that the right decision?"

"Not for me to say, sir. But we lost a lot of good men today, friends of mine. If there was a way to make sure we didn't lose any more without having to surrender, well, I think that's a good thing. Don't you?"

"Yeah, I do think so," Ryck said.

And he realized that was the truth. He knew he'd made the right decision. Although if they ever managed to get back before they ran out of O2, he hoped the command would think so, too. If he was branded a coward, not even his Nova would help him.

Chapter 36

With a little over three hours to go and about fifteen minutes before he was going to approach the Confeds with a request, based on international treaties, for O2, the *Ark Royal* and three other ships appeared in the system.

Ryck relayed their situation, and the ship had sent shuttles to provide air and to get the Marines on board. Ryck had sent Charlie first, but he and Çağlar, after getting recharged, had waited for the last shuttle despite Captain Kurae, the *Ark Royal's* CO, requesting his immediate presence. Ryck was happy to see his old ride appear, but he was not leaving until each Marine, sailor, and the HECLA staff, were safe on board. That meant the living and the dead.

And the butcher's bill was heavy. Alpha had lost 105 Marines and sailors. Bravo had lost 133, to include all the officers and all but one SNCO. Weapons had lost 66. Ryck felt those losses. Once again, he'd been thrust into command, and while he wasn't making decisions for most of the battle, he still felt the weight of them.

But for Charlie, he felt each and every loss. Forty-eight Marines and two corpsmen had been killed. Another 18 had been wounded, with ten of them requiring regen. A land battle might have resulted in a different ratio between the wounded and dead, but in space, wounded usually meant dead.

Second Lieutenant Gershon Chomsky, Staff Sergeant Buc Grimes, Sergeant Horatio Contradari, and Doc Kitoma were among the dead. And there were so many more. Ryck hadn't had a chance to sit down and write the letters to the families.

That wasn't true. He'd had the time since reporting aboard. He was just delaying the inevitable.

Ryck had made an oath to himself that he would complete his tour as company commander without losing a Marine. He'd seen it as his job, his solemn duty. But he'd taken his men into battle when he didn't have to. Donte had even said making the long trip in a vacsuit was a non-player, and Donte had been in command at the time. Ryck could have backed off, just following orders.

He could have kept in place, and no one would have blamed him. But he would have blamed himself. He knew, without a shadow of a doubt, that if he hadn't launched into the attack, all of the Marines in the other companies would be dead or prisoners. He had given the order to sacrifice some of his men so that others could live. It was the right decision, he knew. His earlier vow had been misplaced, and it could have proven dangerous. The CO had been correct when he criticized Ryck on the *Julianna's Dream* mission. A Marine commander cannot dither. He has to make decisions and act on them.

That realization had led to his just completed talk with Jeff. It has been a difficult thing to do. Ryck had a real affection for the young man, but he'd still had to act.

Jeff had come into Ryck's stateroom, cleaned up and fed, but obviously nervous. He'd taken the seat Ryck offered, but refused to meet his eyes.

"We need to talk, Jeff," Ryck had started.

"Sir, I don't know what happened there. I just had a moment's hesitation, sure, but I was going to be OK. I just wanted to make sure the men were safe. Then Sandy, he just took over, sir, really!"

"That's not what happened, Jeff, and you know it. You froze on T-486 after the ALC was destroyed, and you froze during the assault on the ballista. You should thank your lucky stars that Sandy was with you. He saved your ass, and probably kept you from facing a court martial."

"A court-martial, sir?"

"Yes, of course. What do you think we do with officers who show cowardice in battle?"

"I wasn't a coward, sir!" Jeff protested. "I was just being cautious!"

"If you really believe that, then you are more dangerous than I thought, dangerous to your Marines."

"I can get better, sir! I promise—"

"Just stop," Ryck said, holding up one hand, palm out. "You are not fit to be an infantry officer. Period."

Jeff seemed to deflate in front of him, a balloon losing its air. "What now, sir? A court-martial? That would kill my father."

Jeff's father was a retired sergeant major. Ryck had never met the man, but he was sure Jeff was telling the truth. Ryck took out a piece plastisheet, a performance evaluation. He'd already filled it out. It wasn't good at all, with "cowardice in the face of the enemy" and "unsuitable for further service" boldly written in the text. He handed it to the young lieutenant.

If it were possible, Jeff would have deflated even further as he read it.

He took a deep breath, then handed it back, saying, "OK, sir. You're right. I have shamed you, I've shamed the Corps, and I've shamed myself. I guess I had this coming.

"Jeff, you have talen. There is no doubt about it," Ryck said as he took back the eval. "The Corps can make use of you, just not as a combat Marine."

"All Marines are combat Marines, sir."

"And we all serve in non-combat billets. I think you could do well, I think you could serve the Corps, just not in a command. I've got a friend or two that I could call, and I think I can get you a position as an adjutant to someone."

Jeff looked up, catching Ryck's eyes for the first time. There was a glimmer of hope in his eyes which quickly faded."

"Thanks, sir, but not with that eval. Not even you could pull enough strings with that."

"I'm not going to submit this one. I'll give you another. It won't be great, but it won't be a death knell. If you work hard and prove your worth, you'll be able to overcome it."

"Really, sir? Why?"

"Because I told you, I think you can serve the Corps. And if you're keeping another combat Marine from having to fill a non-combat billet, that is a plus. Not all combat Marines can fill those billets, and their careers can be shit-canned because they screwed up some piddly-ass report."

Ryck thought about his own upcoming billet, and he hoped he was not being prophetic about it with his words.

"I, I thank you, sir, from the bottom of my heart. I'll do what it takes, I'll make you proud of me."

"I don't know if I will ever be proud of you, Jeff. Just don't make me regret it. And one more thing."

"Yes, sir?"

"If you ever accept a combat billet or command of a unit, I will come down on you like you can't imagine. This report here," he said, pointing at the eval on his desk, "will be the least of your worries."

"Roger that, sir. I understand. And thank you, sir."

"Just remember my words. I am deadly serious. Dismissed."

Ryck pretended to look at some documents until Jeff got up and left the stateroom. He'd had to take action, but he hadn't liked it. He thought it was worse to give than to receive in a case like this. And he'd been on the receiving end only 45 minutes before, from the *Ark Royal's* CO, no less.

When he'd finally reported to CAPT Kurae, the man was already in a foul mood that a mere Marine captain had had the temerity to keep him waiting. But he'd swallowed that and congratulated the famous young man for once again, winning despite the odds. When Ryck told him about the Confederation forces still there, he had started putting in motion the steps to capture them.

Ryck had stepped up to remind the CO that he'd agreed to a truce, and as senior man in the system at the time, that truce was binding. The CO had disagreed, and it took the ship's SJA to convince him that Ryck was right, and breaking that truce would get him relieved. Frustrated by his own staff, he berated Ryck right there on the bridge, telling him he's screwed up big time, and if he thought his Federation Nova would protect him from a court-martial, he was sadly mistaken.

Now, 45 minutes later, he essentially threatened Jeff with the same. He'd blown of the CO's bluster, but it had hurt more to bring that up to Jeff.

He leaned back in his chair, eyes closed. His skin still itched, and he wanted a shower, but he just didn't have the energy at the moment.

He got that energy in a jolt when the first sergeant knocked and stuck his head in the door.

"They found the CO, sir."

"The CO?"

"LtCol uKhiwa. He and five Marines were trying to fly to Blue Barbell. Their shuttle went tits up when they casted, and all this time, they tried to join the fight."

"Three grubbing days? What, they had to be a couple hundred thousand klicks out, right?"

If he'd thought Charlie Company's EVA to Blue Barbell was long, this one was out of comprehension long.

"They're picking him up now in Bay 3."

"Let's go," Ryck said, his tiredness gone.

He and the first sergeant rushed to Bay 3, only to have to stand around for over an hour before a reki came in with the six Marines onboard. The Marines debarked and stiffly made their way forward, cracking open their helmets. Ryck went up to shake the CO's hand, and once again, the CO had outdone him. Ryck had thought he had been about as rank as a man could get, but the odor flowing from the Marines was overpowering.

"Captain Lysander, I trust you'll be turning the battalion back to me?" the CO said.

"Uh, sure, I mean yes, sir," Ryck said, wondering how the CO knew that Ryck had taken command.

"OK, follow me. You five," he said, turning to Major Snæbjörnsson, Virag, Drayton, Top Wojik, and Gunny Temperance, "get out of these damn suits and shit, shower, and shave. Meet me in the Officer's mess in 30, along with senior staff and commanders."

"But—" Top Wojik started.

"The officer's mess, and if anyone says anything, have them wait for me."

"Aye-aye, sir," Top said, a smile breaking out over his face.

The CO stripped off his vacsuit, and Ryck followed him as he made his way to the bridge. Ryck tried to hang back out of sight while the CO thanked CAPT Kurae for the rescue, pointing out the fellowship between the Navy and Corps. Kurae spotted Ryck and told the CO how much Ryck had screwed up, and how he was going to make sure action was taken. The CO nodded and said he was on it, then requested permission to leave the bridge. Ryck followed, a lump in his gut after he heard the CO's response.

Ah, fuck it. I'd do it just the same all over again.

The CO went to the visiting flag officer's stateroom and went inside.

"I take it you took the CO of Troops' stateroom?"

"Yes, sir," Ryck said.

I'm going to get shit on for that?

"Keep it. I'm taking this, and I'm going to be racked out for a long time when I'm done."

The rough, tough CO started stripping off his longjohns, and in his skivvies, collapsed in the overstuffed chair. He looked drawn and defeated.

"Are you, I mean, are you OK, sir" Ryck asked.

"When we casted, the shuttle went down hard. No power," the CO said, ignoring Ryck's question. "Comms was down, and we couldn't contact anyone. Thank God for Top Wojik, though. Using some spare parts that had not been powered up when we cast, he was able to rig up receivers. We couldn't broadcast, but we could hear. And since we knew where the battalion was, we could aim our receiver."

"So you heard all our transmissions?"

"All of them," the CO said.

"So that's how you knew I'd taken command," Ryck said, more to himself than the CO.

"Yes, and I wanted to talk to you about that before I get back with the Three and the rest."

Ryck waited, mentally prepared for anything. He was done trying to please this man. He'd done what he'd done and would stand by it.

"We had another talk on another ship not so long ago. I told you that you'd grown too cautious, that you were not the warrior you had been earlier. I wondered at the time if the responsibility had ruined you. Despite your record against the Trinolculars, I felt your commissioning was a mistake, and that it had gelded you.

"I didn't think it was your fault, but the fault of your godfathers, who couldn't see your strengths and weaknesses. It wasn't your fault, but in the big picture, fault doesn't matter. Finding men to lead Marines, does."

This is eerily sounding like my conversation with Jeff, Ryck thought.

"But here, I was pleased, no *proud*, of you. You took decisive action and frankly saved the day. I was mentally trying to send orders to you, and lo and behold, you were doing them as if you could hear me. Without you, many more Marines would have been killed, and the battalion, what was left of it, would have had to surrender. First Battalion, Eleventh Marines, the Tiburónes, *my* command, would have surrendered to a Confederation cohort.

"So before we meet with the rest, I wanted to personally thank you, for the men of the battalion, for the Marine Corps, for the Federation, and I admit it, for me, for being the officer that others saw in you and for leading Marines. I was wrong."

"You weren't wrong, sir. I was cautious, too cautious. I was trying to protect my Marines by becoming ineffective, and that put them in more danger."

"Hmph," the CO snorted. "You realize that?"

"Of course, sir, and you pointed it out to me. That, and a few things happened that took me down a few pegs."

"Oh, the 'Do you know who I am' thing?"

"You knew about that, sir?"

"I'd be a pretty piss-poor commanding officer if I didn't, right?"

Ryck felt his face turn red. He knew he had a long way to live that down.

"You know, sir? I thought you were calling me here to chew my ass for the truce."

"The truce? Why? It was the right thing to do," the CO said.

"Well, Captain Kurae—"

"—is a jerk, a political hack. He got command of the *Ark Royal* but has never had her fire a shot in anger. He saw the capture of the Confeds as his combat check mark."

"But he said he's going to make sure—"

"Make sure nothing. No one gives a flying fart what he thinks. You leave it to me. You did the right thing, and even more so to stand up for it in front of the worm," the CO told Ryck.

The CO looked at his watch and then stood up.

"I've got to take a quick shower. My skin is crawling, and you're pretty ripe there, too. I think you need one more than me," he said.

"Me? No disrespect intended, but wow! You need one far worse than I do," Ryck said.

"I do?" he asked, sniffing his armpit. "I can smell you, but maybe I've gotten used to my own stink."

Ryck got up, and the CO held out his hand.

"We like tradition. We like having a patron for each battalion. It gives us a sense of, of belonging to something greater, something that will be here long after we are gone. But sometimes, things seem to fit. Our patron, the Mexican Marines. They were not going to surrender, and you kept that tradition alive."

"To the *Tiburónes*, sir," Ryck said.

"*¿Mi bandera? ¡Jamás!* Captain Lysander!"

TARAWA

Epilogue

Major Ryck Lysander, United Federation Marine Corps, sat on the couch in his new condo in T-ville, just a few kilometers outside of Headquarters, Marine Corps. The condo was off-base, but it might as well have been base housing for all the Marines who lived in the complex. Most of the Marines in this complex were senior SNCOs or field grade officers, none of who were senior enough to rate base housing at the Puzzle Palace itself. The rent on the condos was higher, but with Hannah getting her promotion, they could afford it.

They had planned on staying on Sunshine while Ryck was in school on Earth and at his new posting, but with Hannah's promotion and new job opportunity at Headquarters, it made sense to make the move.

Despite Ryck's promotion ten days earlier, Hannah's bump made her technically Ryck's senior, something she enjoyed rubbing into him. Ryck took it in good stride. Promotion or not, Hannah had always been the boss in their household.

After returning from the Cygni B System, Ryck had been transferred from Charlie Company to the S-3—not for Virag, as he had feared, who had taken Donte's spot as the Bravo Company commander—but for the experience, the CO told him.

Ryck had been more than a little upset, but as he worked under Major Snæbjörnsson, he realized that the CO had just been watching out for him. During the next seven months, he'd gained a wealth of experience in battalion planning and operations. He'd even run a force on force with Second Battalion while the Three was on leave, and while the *Tiburónes* may not have been judged the winners, the experience was of incalculable value. This was going to stand him in good stead in future billets.

The CO hadn't even been pissed that Second Battalion had received a higher evaluation. Instead, he'd spent the next weekend with Ryck, dissecting and discussing the plan Ryck had developed and put into action.

The CO was responsible for all facets of the battalion, and he could change any operations planned he wanted, but usually, it was the Three who developed and ran an operation. And the CO had not let his ego get in the way, letting his inexperienced assistant operations officer get his feet wet.

Ryck had come to admire the CO. The man may not have extensive combat experience, but it was not for lack of trying. He'd taken an incredible risk to cast from the *Inchon*, and his long flight in EVAs while running on barely enough oxygen to stay alive was epic. More than once, his men had passed out from lack of O2 and had to be towed by others, but he would not let them increase the flow. If he had, they would have all suffocated before the *FS Tallyday* found them.

The CO had found out about Jeff de Madre, of course, but when he asked Ryck about it, Ryck had simply said he'd taken care of it. The CO had nodded, and let it go at that. When orders arrived for Jeff three weeks after they returned, courtesy of General Ukiah, the CO hadn't batted an eye. That small act of letting him take care of the situation impressed Ryck. He began to feel guilty for ever having disliked the man.

And the CO had been right. There had been no fallout over the operation. Far from it. The Tiburónes were heroes. Ryck had been surprised when shortly after Jeff left, the CO had called him into his office. The CO told him that certain forces in the government had wanted Ryck to be awarded another Federation Nova for the action. The top brass had resisted, thinking that two Novas when only one other living Marine, Major Timo Beekeeper, had even one, was not good politics. Other factions in the government did not want anyone to get a Nova for actions against the Confederation, fearful of the message it was sending.

First Lieutenant Albert, the recon Marine who'd driven his reki into the Confed ALC had been posthumously nominated for a Nova, but no one else would be recognized for the highest honor.

The CO's tone was almost apologetic when he said that Ryck would be put in for a Battle Citation, First Class and nothing higher despite turning the tide of the battle. Ryck laughed. He didn't need any more ribbons. But that gave him the opportunity to tell the CO what had happened with Jeff and Sandy, and how Sandy really changed the course of the battle.

The CO told the regimental commander, and both went up to the CG. The result was that an amazed and humbled First Lieutenant Sandy Peltier-Aswad was nominated for a Navy Cross. If anyone, he was the true hero of the battle, in Ryck's opinion, so he was well-pleased with that.

Ryck was promoted to major on November First with the battalion, as it should have been. The next day, he took leave to move his family to Tarawa. With Hannah immediately stepping into her new position, it was up to Ryck to play househusband and finish the move-in while getting the twins settled into school. It had been a hectic few days, and today, the Marine Corps Birthday, had been a welcome respite. He'd taken the twins to the pageant, where they oohed and awed as the Marines marched by. The flyover by the Storks got a big reaction from Noah. Ryck promised his son that if he were good, he'd take him inside one later that afternoon at the static display.

It was almost four by the time he'd gotten the twins back, and he'd barely gotten them their scrambled egg sandwiches when Tand Ariana came by with Cindi and their kids. Tand had gotten out of the Marines, but he worked for one of the many companies in T-ville that serviced the Corps. Cindi and Hannah had become close, and now that the family was back on Tarawa, they'd be spending more time together.

"How do you do, Major Lysander," Joshua Ariana said solemnly as Tand pushed him forward. "Happy birthday, sir."

The seven-year-old named for Hannah's brother—has Joshua been gone from us for that long now, Ryck could help but to wonder—was a serious boy, as if he felt the burden of being named for the man who had saved his father's life. He was nothing like Joshua Hope of Life, but Ryck knew the little boy was precious to his wife.

"Thank you," Ryck told Joshua. "Did you enjoy the pageant?"

"Oh, yes, sir," the boy said, his eyes lighting up. "I loved it. I'm going to be in the pageant some day, sir."

Ryck noticed the slight clouding of Tand's eyes. Ryck knew he didn't want his son to become a Marine, but it was as if things were in motion that were too big to be stopped.

"Noah and Esther, finish up your sandwiches and take Joshua and Greta down to the playground, OK?"

"Congratulations on your promotion, Major," Tand said as the kids filed out.

Ryck and Tand had never formed much of a bond, either in the Corps or now with Tand out of the Corps. Ryck knew that Tand would never completely get over the fact that he had initially wanted to send Tand on that suicide mission, not Joshua. If Joshua had not interceded, then Tand would not be alive today.

That was OK with Ryck. He understood it. Let the wives become fast friends, but the two of them merely tolerated each other.

When Hannah came home, Ryck made his leave, going into the master bedroom. For the pageant, he'd had on his ribbons, but that wouldn't do for what was next. He wanted full hangers. He took off his blouse and put it on a homemade tree, took off his ribbons, and carefully put on his medal bar. Once they were aligned to his satisfaction, he put the blouse back on and took his Nova from the case on his dresser. He put the black ribbon around his neck, letting the multi-pointed nova hang at his throat. He stared at his reflection, wondering how he had gotten to where he was today. He'd made great friends and lost great friends. Why he was still alive was a question he couldn't answer.

Ryck looked at his watch. He still had some time, so he went back out to the living room and sat on the couch. The Ariana's were with Hannah and the kids in the kitchen, so Ryck had the room to himself, which was just as well. He wanted to be alone.

As if she had daddy-radar running, Esther came walking out into the room and stood staring at him, spoiling his solitude. She didn't say a word but crawled up beside him, then forced her head under his arm. He relaxed and enfolded the little girl. Maybe he didn't want to be alone after all.

"Don't be sad, Daddy," she said with her high little voice.

Tears came to his eyes at her words. So many of his friends, so many of the men trusting him to get them through a fight, had died. He had learned not to blame himself so much anymore, but that didn't make the loss any less intense.

His tears dripped on his medals as he sat there, arm around his little girl, drawing comfort from her warm body. Esther was life—she was potential. She was why he fought, for all the little Esthers, Noahs, Joshuas, and Gretas. For new life, he thought as he pregnant wife came out, surprised to see him.

"I thought you had left already. Esther, come here and let Daddy go. He has someplace to be.

"Give me a kiss, snugglebunny," he said, offering his chin.

She gave him a sloppy one, and Ryck got up, straightening up his blues blouse.

Hannah came up and adjusted the hang of his medals and gave him a kiss on the cheek, too. "You'll be back by eight, right? The ball starts at eight-thirty, but I don't want to stand around too much."

"Yes, eight o'clock sharp," he said, reaching to cup his wife's belly.

She was huge, having gotten pregnant just before he'd taken off for the Cygni B System, and the baby was due in another three weeks. He'd offered to skip the ball, but she said no. He thought she enjoyed it more than he did.

He gave her one more kiss and left, carefully getting into the new Lancer they'd just bought. It wasn't a sexy car, and it screamed "family," and that was fine with him. He pulled out and made the short drive to the Globe and Laurel.

Several others were present when he arrived, and he exchanged quiet greetings with them. He hadn't seen some of them since commissioning. More trickled in over the next 20 minutes until 51 of them were there. Others coming to pay their respects were in the pub, outside in the main room, but when Jorge Simone nodded at Mr. Stuart, the pub manager, he cleared the club, sending general and lance corporal alike outside to wait.

The gathered Marines were in the back room, where the class time boxes hung silently on the wall, some empty, some with one or two bottles, and only three boxes with all three bottles in them. One was for the latest class that had only graduated a few months ago. Another was from the class previous to that, and as soon as this ceremony was done, that box would be down to two bottles as well. The third was Ryck's class' time box. Over the years, while other classes had removed the bottle of port, Class 59-2's box had stood proud, all three bottles present. The class began to earn a reputation of being lucky. Ryck getting the Nova and no less than five classmates earning Navy Crosses added to the class' mystique.

That mystique was broken, as they all knew it would be someday. They gathered around the time box, looking and remembering.

They'd been so young back then, so full of idealistic fervor. They were all going to be heroes; they were all going to become generals. Well, for one of the 67, that dream ended back in the Cygni B System a little over seven months earlier.

Ryck stood with his old friend, Prince Jellico. He hadn't seen Prince since they graduated, but they'd kept in touch. Prince reached out and squeezed Ryck's shoulder.

Jorge stepped in front of the time box and addressed the gathering.

"We are gathered here in remembrance for our fallen brother, Major Donte Williamson Ward, the first of us to fall in service of the Federation. Let us not mourn Donte but celebrate his life. As long as we remember him, he is with us forever."

"Forever," the gathered Marines intoned in unison.

"On this solemn occasion, I would like to ask Ryck Lysander to come forward and say a few words about our brother."

Jorge was still the senior Marine in the class based on his lineal number, but Ryck knew Donte the best, having served with him three times and having been with him when he was killed. Jorge had already told Ryck he would speak, so Ryck was ready with a speech he'd prepared.

Ryck walked forward and turned to face his classmates. Sixty-seven had graduated, and 66 were alive today. Fifty-nine were still in the Corps. Fifty-one of them had made it back to the Globe and Laurel for the ceremony.

The bottle ceremony was not official, yet the Corps bent over backwards to ensure Marines made it back to Tarawa for it. The Corps could be a son-of-a-bitch at times, but not for things like this. The Corps cared.

"Fourteen years ago, 67 midshipmen about to be commissioned gathered here to place their bottles in the time box. The port to remember the first of us to fall. The champagne to celebrate the first of us to earn a star. The sherry to be shared by our last two surviving classmates," Ryck started, before stopping to look at his classmates.

Most had been in combat. All had unique experiences. Suddenly, he knew they didn't need a lecture on the Corps and tradition. This was for Donte, nothing more. He folded up his notes and dropped them on the floor.

"Donte Ward was a fine Marine, a great leader. More than that, he was my friend. We were not close while midshipmen, but later, in 2/3, we became true brothers. I was overjoyed when I was assigned to 1/11 and found out he was to be a fellow company commander.

"Donte was irreverent, funny, and had a heart the size of the galaxy. There was nothing he wouldn't do for me, or for any Marine, for that matter.

"Donte died while commanding his company in battle against great odds. Abandoned by our task force, he took command of the battalion and with unwavering determination, he did his duty. He fell as a Marine, a commander leading Marines. I can think of no better way to leave this mortal plane.

"Classmates, I give you Donte Ward, my friend, and a great Marine."

"Here, here!" several voices called out.

Jorge turned and reached into the box and took out the bottle of 298 Quinta do Vesúvio off the cradle that had been holding it for 14 years.

Mr. Stuart, the only person in the pub other than the class, came forward, and while Jorge held the bottle, pulled the cork. Jorge, as the senior surviving classmate—Donte had been posthumously promoted to major, backdated to the day he was killed—poured a tiny amount of the port into 52 glasses, one for each Marine present, and one for Donte.

When he was done, each Marine filed past and took a glass. Ryck retreated back to stand with Prince, glass in hand.

When everyone had a glass, Jorge stood facing the rest of them and raised his glass. "For Major Donte Ward, United Federation Marine Corps, in remembrance!"

"In remembrance!" the rest shouted, lifting their glasses and draining the small swallow of port.

Ryck felt the tears welling in his eyes again. But he was content. Donte was his friend, and he would miss him deeply. But death was a part of a Marine's life. For some it came sooner, for some, many years later in the old Marine's home. Sooner or later, it came for them all. But as long as they retained these traditions, as long as they remembered, the dead were still alive. Donte was still among them, his glass filled with port. He would be there, reunited with the rest, when that final bottle of sherry was drunk by the last two of them, two men waiting to join their brothers in the hereafter.

Individuals passed into dust, but the Marine Corps carried on. And all of them *were* the Corps. They helped create it, they were part of it. Through the Corps, each of them was immortal.

Thank you for reading *Captain*. I hope you enjoyed it.

If you would like updates on new books releases, news, or special offers, please consider signing up for my mailing list. Your email will not be sold, rented, or in any other way disseminated. If you are interested, please sign up at the link below:

http://eepurl.com/bnFSHH

Other Books by Jonathan Brazee

The Return of the Marines Trilogy
The Few
The Proud
The Marines

The Al Anbar Chronicles: First Marine Expeditionary Force--Iraq
Prisoner of Fallujah
Combat Corpsman
Sniper

The United Federation Marine Corps
Recruit
Sergeant
Lieutenant
Captain
Major
Colonel (Coming soon)

Rebel (set in the same UFMC universe)

Werewolf of Marines
Werewolf of Marines: Semper Lycanus
Werewolf of Marines: Patria Lycanus

To The Shores of Tripoli

Wererat

Darwin's Quest: The Search for the Ultimate Survivor

Venus: A Paleolithic Short Story

Non-Fiction
Exercise for a Longer Life

Author Website
http://www.returnofthemarines.com

Made in the USA
San Bernardino, CA
13 September 2015